Loving Mozart

LOVING MOZART

A Past Life Memory
of the Composer's Final Years

by Mary Montaño

Foreword by Gary Zukav

Cantus Verus Books
1995

LOVING MOZART
A Past Life Memory of the Composer's Final Years
Cantus Verus Books, 1995
All Rights Reserved.
Copyright 1995 by Mary Montaño

Cover design: Carolyn Kinsman
Portrait: Wolfgang Amadeus Mozart (1756-1791), pastel portrait about 1800; signature bottom right: W M 1786.   Private possession, Switzerland.

Cantus Verus Books
P.O. Box 30853
Albuquerque, New Mexico 87190-0853
Printed in the United States of America
ISBN 0-9642577-0-X

Foreword

Loving Mozart is a story of relationships that extend beyond the domain of the five senses. It is an example of the relationships that bind each of us to others in this place and elsewhere, and in this time and other times.

Histories compiled from events that the five senses detect are incomplete. They do not reveal the intimate connections and causations that lie beneath all experience. The experiences of a lifetime are a small part of the history of the soul that lives it. The lines of force that converge in each moment of physical existence extend far beyond that physical moment.

Our species has entered a new phase in its evolution. It is no longer limited to the perceptions of the five senses. Its awareness is expanding. It is taking its place consciously in a larger landscape of experience.

This changes everything.

From the point of view of the five senses, nothing survives death. From the point of view of the growing awareness of humankind, death is the end of a learning episode which serves the evolution of an immortal soul. That lesson is part of a larger curriculum.

The people whom we encounter, and the aptitudes and interests that motivate us, are not accidental. They are the products of actions taken, or begun, in pasts that precede our births, and which serve the evolution of souls that will remain after our deaths.

Our experiences are part of an immense and intricate fabric that our species is only beginning to glimpse. *Loving Mozart* is such a glimpse. The love and richness that underlie the lives of its heroes and heroines is no less than the love and richness that underlie the lives of each of us.

We are all participants in a voluntary enactment of Love—the incarnation of immortal souls in order to learn, contribute, and mutually assist. *Loving Mozart* is a heartgiven example of this dimension of relationship, a dimension that is now becoming integral to human awareness.

Gary Zukav

An Introduction

These memories are a gift, given to me by my guides to heal my soul and dissolve long entrenched feelings of guilt and abandonment. It began one night in 1984 when the extraordinary music of forgiveness and compassion from the finale of *The Marriage of Figaro* began spontaneously sounding in my head as I reeled from the heartsickness and confusion stirred by the funeral scene in the film, *Amadeus*. Five years of revelation, struggle and gradual self-forgiveness followed.

I learned I was not alone, and never have been.

I learned the dead never abandon those left behind.

I learned we are as alone as we choose to feel—that we can look inward and find we are most definitely not alone. I say this not in a rhetorical or even mystical sense, but as a fact. We are guided every moment, and cheered on. We are admired for our courage and determination in engaging in the most difficult and challenging level of all existences, an Earth life. And, of course, we are loved.

Loving Mozart is a blend of past life inquiry and conventional historical research. Much of its content was seen or sensed in past life regression, dreams or meditation. The only variance between what I experienced and what you find here is the weather in Vienna at the time of Mozart's death. While I saw rain, I depicted snow because numbness and cold dominated my perceptions of those scenes and of Sussmayr's sensibilities. Situations and dialogue came in meditation as pure Thought. I chose to present these events in reader-friendly narrative form rather than as a dry research report of each experience. To assist the reader unfamiliar with the traditional biography of Mozart, and for the sake of comparison with this biography, I have provided in the Appendix a brief recounting of his life as accepted by scholars. It is my hope and expectation that someday past life regression will become an accepted tool of the historian.

I have been encouraged throughout the years of this book's preparation by my family and friends. Unaware of the content of this project, a sibling often would play a little Mozart at the piano during a visit, or a friend would speak of Mozart's genius. One friend sent a postcard of Dufy's *The Blue Mozart* with a note urging me to start a book on my life, while another cornered me into discussions of the errors of *Amadeus*. A friend and musicologist made an unexpected gift of software and computer paper, unaware that I needed them precisely then. Another loaned me her computer for months, as mine is a virtual antique.

I have always taken these events and generosities as superconscious encouragement.

I give heartfelt thanks to all for graciously holding their questions until I could answer them, and to:

Marie Smith, Reeve Love and Frances Rico, all genuine patronesses of the arts, for their generous spirits;

The owner of the portrait appearing on the cover of this book, for his openmindedness and generosity. This is the most true likeness of Mozart I have seen yet.

Gary Zukav, Dr. Edith Fiore and Pat Rodegast, for their gracious support;

Ray and Kay Lewis, my true godparents, for showing me a whole new reality through the works of Edgar Cayce, and for demonstrating through example the responsibilities of such knowledge;

Linda Ulibarri and Elaine Shannon, for providing the final push;

Elda McMann and her entities, the Lo Tsi Group, for bringing me Kapell;

My former husband, Nick, who brought me the entities known as:

The Lady in White, who confirmed the concept of the oversoul and my connection with Mozart, verified information and supplied additional information;

My Spirit Guides, with Robin, my Teacher, and Nathaniel, for all the dreams, the subtle inklings and the breathtaking astral flights;

Dian Buehler, a gifted psychic who patiently and carefully accompanied me through the veils of time.

My deepest gratitude goes to Mozart/Kapell for his remarkable patience and unending good humor, grace and support. Even when I rejected him out of fear, his extraordinary, ennobling love never wavered. For this I am eternally and joyfully grateful.

M.M.

To those who grieve

I.

One truth stands firm.
All that happens
in world history
rests on something spiritual.
If the spiritual is strong,
it creates world history.
If it is weak,
it suffers world history.

—Albert Schweitzer
January 9, 1955
New York Times Magazine

SALZBURG, Summer, 1760.

Faint laughter filtered into the kitchen from the front of the house. Herr Bullinger's house was always filled with laughter. But here, alone in the clean, warm kitchen, little Wolferl stood as still as he knew how, listening to the music that sang in his head.

The boy wore a pale blue suit, with white leggings and a white shirt. His face was aglow as he listened. Suddenly, he stood up and walked, then ran, out the back door and into the sunny, green yard that surrounded the house. It was quiet here, with an almost mystical peacefulness that warmed the sensitive child's heart. He looked up and reached up with one arm to catch the sparkle of light hovering above. He giggled with delight as it dropped within reach; he tried again to catch it.

The light made him happy, like when Mama lifted him onto her lap and hugged him.

Suddenly Wolferl was in the air. His Papa had picked him up. Through the garden gate they went, down some stone steps and into the waiting carriage. It's time to go home, Wolferl, they said, laughing. The horses jolted the carriage forward, down the lane. He sat next to Theresa; Nannerl sat on her other side. He bounced inside the open-topped conveyance for a moment before looking up. He squealed in delight and reached out. The tiny ball of light danced and floated merrily alongside the speeding carriage. After several minutes, Wolferl stole a glance at the others to see their reactions to the light, but they didn't see it. They weren't paying any attention. Puzzled, he looked back at the light, then sat still.

The light had disappeared.

ANTONITO, Colorado, Summer, 1951.

The warm summer sun felt good, so little Lina didn't protest when her mother lowered her into a wooden walker next to her cousin, Tommy, who also was propped in a walker on the sun-drenched porch. Her father knelt in front of them, holding the camera, chatting, smiling and waiting patiently for a good shot of his infant daughter. Then Lina looked up into the brilliant blue southwestern sky. Her little hand reached up, toward the small light flickering beyond the lilac bush.

SALZBURG, Spring, 1762.

Seven-year-old Wolferl stood very still, holding his small violin under his thin little neck. His father sat in front of him for his lessons, at once stern and abiding. Nannerl sat solemnly at the piano. Wolferl was an astute, serious student and anxious to please his father. He concentrated hard for a small boy, watching his father's eyes and movements, listening intently to every sound.

"Leopold," called Mama from the doorway. "Someone here to see you."

"Here, Wolferl, play the adagio through with Nannerl until I return." And Papa was gone.

Both children sat quietly for a moment. Wolferl studied the opening bars of the adagio, then grimaced. His eyes rose to the ceiling. The sparkle of light appeared above their heads, close to the low ceiling near the middle of the room.

"Look, Nannerl!" he called out as he danced up and down. Nannerl looked up to where his finger pointed but saw nothing. She turned to her practicing. He beamed back at the light with excitement. Impulsively, he pulled his violin up to his chin and began a little melody for the light. It responded by bouncing and swaying in rhythm with his ditty. He laughed as his sister turned to throw a suspicious glance at him.

Then the light faded and disappeared. Wolferl was still searching the ceiling when Papa returned to continue the lesson. Wolferl smiled wanly at his father before contemplating the notes of the adagio once again.

NEW YORK CITY, 1931.

Willy was bored, bored, bored, as it snowed, snowed, snowed.

Winters were very long and often severe in New York, and he'd been indoors far too long today. It was almost dinnertime, and he sat at the window of the Kapells' apartment, waiting. Waiting, waiting, waiting.

The young boy heaved a sigh. The chattering noises of

Mama and the others followed the aromas from the kitchen where they busily prepared the evening meal. His eyes surveyed the lonely, white, sunless scene outside. Then they caught a luminescence in the white air not far from the window. He straightened up, eyes widening as he watched a sparkling light growing as it floated gently to the ground with the real snowflakes. He scrambled to his feet to peer down to where it landed below.

He smiled, fascinated.

After touching the ground, the tiny light rose up again until it was level with his nose. It hovered there briefly, then floated down again, this time in wide, gentle spirals. After touching the ground, it shot up again to fall in graceful loops, again and again, delighting and fascinating young Willy.

He turned and looked casually around the room, then, satisfied that no one was about, he turned back to the light again, happy and content, eyes aglow. The light was swaying, back and forth, down to the ground. He laughed and pushed his face against the window to see the light touch the ground. It's so pretty, this light, he said to himself. Suddenly, he was startled by the sound of Mama's voice behind him.

"Willy, come to dinner." She was standing at the door, smiling, glad that he had found something quiet to do. Then she disappeared.

Several minutes later, Papa came to the door and repeated the announcement. Willy turned away from the window guiltily. "Yes, Papa," he said. Papa disappeared into the other room. Willy turned to the window to see the light hovering. Small beams of light pulsated as they widened the circle of luminosity before fading to nothing. The show was over. Willy sighed his reluctance and climbed down from the window and left the room.

SCHWANENSTADT, Austria, 1772.

It was early spring when they buried Franz's mother. She had struggled through the winter with the lung disease to be known later as tuberculosis. Six-year-old Franz had been told she was dying, but it wasn't known truly in his heart until he peered into the deep hole into which they were to place her as soon as the priest stopped talking. The hole frightened him.

4

The day was unseasonably pleasant, aside from the bracing breeze blowing occasionally out of the north. It did not escape Franz's notice that his father stood apart from his four children, and that he was completely devastated. As he stood listening to the Latin intonations of the old priest swaying at the graveside beside the church, the slight, tow-headed boy wondered how much his life would change now that his beloved mother was gone.

A light caught his eye and he glanced upward, above the crowd surrounding the deep hole. A pinpoint of light hovered near a tree. Franz blinked. His eyes widened as the light flickered rapidly, then vanished. He looked around to see if anyone else had seen it.

No one had.

VIENNA, 1788.

Franz Xaver Sussmayr appeared in the doorway and scanned the room. Viennese of all stations were crammed shoulder to shoulder on the theatre's wooden benches, noisily waiting for the concert to begin. He absorbed the excited anticipation of the multitude and smiled. His was an unimpressive presence: a slight young man, with warm brown eyes in an oval face and a large forehead under sandy hair. His natural expression was a smiling one. At five feet, five inches, he was of average height for his time, though he still often was mistaken for a boy.

At age twenty-two, he was excited to be alive and, most especially, in Vienna, where living could be done with style. After ten years of intense and seemingly endless schooling at the Kremsmunster monastery, he had refused the life of a liturgical composer in a country church. He didn't care to trudge into old age by his father's side in tired, tedious old Schwanenstadt. He left, instead, to pursue a career in Vienna as a composer of opera. He had not done it alone. Father Pasterwicz, his teacher and mentor at the monastery, was a Dominican priest who had become a successful composer for stage and church, dividing his time between Kremsmunster and Vienna. He had been instrumental in Franz's transition to Vienna, helping him sell some of his works there and making some useful connections.

As soon as he was able, Franz began accompanying Pasterwicz to concerts, for he was anxious to absorb all the music he could in this frenetically musical city. Today was one such occasion. It had been an overcast day, but the weather was mild and the huge ceramic stoves in the theatre proper were not yet needed. The large, airy windows brightened the room with natural light. Filled with anticipation of another concert—for he loved music—Franz had barely noticed the absence of the aristocracy in the audience. He sat on the aisle side of one long bench with Pasterwicz, who had insisted he come with him to hear the great Mozart. His improvisatory feats, he had whispered dramatically, were astounding. A miracle! Like most rural Austrian musicians, Franz already knew of Mozart, but had neither met him nor heard him perform. He quietly studied the crowd as he waited for Pasterwicz to finish an animated conversation with a nearby student.

In his observations, Franz noticed a strong showing at these concerts by the lower classes of Vienna, who attended dressed in their best—brightly colored muslin dresses and fichus on the women, and somberly colored waistcoats and breeches, with homespun woolen stockings, on the men. Their best clothes, but still shabby next to those of the middle class. Yet he noticed early on these humble folk were Vienna's real lovers of music in an immediate, sensuous way. It puzzled and amused him that in this famous city of music, the poor were the most enchanted by the muses. One could see the transformation on their faces during a concert. Franz watched a young family take their places on a bench near the door. The children were pointing to the handful of violinists tuning up onstage. Franz followed their gazes. The clarinetist ran through scales while other instrumentalists were gathering onstage, chatting and readying themselves for the concert. The fortepiano stood in the middle of the small circle of about twenty chairs. Franz turned his attention back to the audience.

The middle-class women were dressed elaborately in comparison with their poorer sisters. Their elaborate hats caught the eye before anything else. What possessed women to exhibit such preposterous headwear? wondered Franz as his gaze settled on one particularly silly example of feathers and flowers. Some women wore silk or cotton mantuas, in prints or stripes, and fichus of silk. The men wore warm, subtle colors, yet they were as aware of themselves as they were of others. How ironic and curious, observed Franz, these richer folk are so full of themselves and their clothing.

Experience showed him that, as a rule, the better dressed members of the audience were less fascinated by music. Was it that they had become bored with life, or maybe simply more interested in themselves? Or was it part of a city dweller's sophistication to be so indifferent to music? Did the aristocracy care the least of all for music?

There were, thankfully, the inevitable exceptions, he reminded himself as he watched the women closely. Like everyone else, Franz ignored the heavy smell of pomades and perfume used to cloak the typically strong odor of bodies. He noticed with delight how the crowd's chatter sounded like a bubbling mountain brook. People were still meandering in to take their seats as he turned to scan the back of the room. He spotted there a small man sitting with his back toward the stage as he leaned forward, legs crossed, elbow on one knee, engaged in lively discussion. That's Mozart, Franz told himself. I'd know him anywhere. Franz was surprised at his own certainty.

Perhaps because of his short height, Mozart gave the appearance of a child—a boy in his teens, maybe—probably because he was also somewhat thin. His rather big head was not wigged. He showed off his own full, fine auburn hair pulled back into a short queue. He was finely dressed in a dark blue coat and breeches with gold braid and white stockings.

Franz studied him for some time, finding the figure, so far back in the huge hall, somehow eclipsing everything else, demanding his complete attention. So this is the musical genius of all Europe, Franz mused. He studied the way Mozart used his small, graceful hands to emphasize a point. How he threw back his head in a hearty laugh as the others laughed with him. The sound of his laugh made Franz smile. It, too, sounded like a brook.

At length, the musicians began tuning their instruments as one large instrument, and the master composer and musician glanced toward the stage. Franz watched intently as Mozart stood up, pulled at his silk waistcoat and strode purposefully down the center aisle of the room toward the fortepiano and the orchestra.

Franz was unaware that he was staring. As Mozart approached, their eyes met. Franz held his breath. The man's stride slowed imperceptibly as a spark of recognition passed between them.

I know that man, thought Franz. But how? I've never met him. Yet his face is so familiar. So familiar. He is obviously a man of integrity. I can see it in his face, and in his eyes. An inner wisdom lies there, too...and more. Longing, and a kind of quiet sadness. He gives it all away in one glance. In one look. What must I be showing him with mine?

They smiled simultaneously, Mozart in formal congeniality, Franz in awe and deference. Then the master was gone, headed toward the stage, and the next of hundreds of concerts.

Franz turned to Pasterwicz impulsively. "Will you introduce me to him?"

Pasterwicz, who finally had taken his seat, whispered, "Certainly, why not? I would hope you might arrange with him for composition lessons. The man has a lot to teach, if you can talk him into it. He doesn't like to take pupils, I'm told. He considers them a nuisance. He'd rather compose."

The room was suddenly silent. And as suddenly filled with the brilliant sounds of an extraordinary concerto for fortepiano and orchestra. Its wondrous sound enveloped the room like a diffused rainbow of colors, touching Franz's soul, transfixing him. He was inspired with the utter beauty, the fire, the lyric sweetness of the music. There was a bittersweet melancholy in the bold, colorful harmonies. Franz closed his eyes and he was in another world, so affected that he didn't look up until the music stopped.

He leaned over slowly and hung his head as the rush of applause sounded in his ears, shattering the color images of sound he had built around himself. As quickly as it came, the applause died away. The Viennese did not believe in long ovations. Franz was shaken. He had never heard such music. The man was not a composer, nor was he a musician—he was a magician. He created his magic with music, with tones. Franz's eyes were moist with effort, and he was breathless as he sat up and stared at his hands, half in despair and half in ecstasy. There was no one he knew of who could match or even approach the music of this man. Most especially himself. Mozart, he thought, must be the despair of every other composer in Europe.

"I must meet him," Franz heard himself say to Pasterwicz.

The marble floor shone like faceted glass. Room after room, it spread out before them as they marched through. Their heeled shoes clicked against it, echoing off the brocaded walls and high casements swathed in velvets of brilliant colors.

As he struggled to keep up with Pasterwicz, Franz wondered if this kind of opulence was a sin or a crime, or both. Since moving to Vienna, he'd been in only one or two minor mansions of the nobility. Each time, he was utterly startled that people lived in such opulence. He didn't even know the name of the nobleman who called this place home.

Stringed instruments sang briefly in a distant room, then stopped. Rehearsals, he guessed, looking at Pasterwicz, who strode without looking to either side.

"We'll probably have to wait for a break," he said. "As usual, rehearsals are few and frantic." They turned a corner and stopped in the doorway of a large music room. Franz blinked.

The white room dwarfed the small ensemble of five near the fortepiano as they again began to play. It was a quintet with Mozart at the keyboard. Each player was deep in concentrated thought as they stepped gracefully through an adagio, articulating each note and infusing it with luminescent beauty that itself overpowered the gilded, sunlit room. Franz and Pasterwicz stepped quietly to a group of chairs under a large, gilded mirror.

Franz focused on Mozart. For all the shimmering beauty and depth of feeling of his works, he showed only the slightest physical involvement at the keyboard. His was an unaffected, straightforward style that revealed the complete professional at work. Mozart watched the others as he played, occasionally shaking his head when he heard a dropped note, or simply arching his brow at a better moment. The adagio came to an end and he initiated several comments to each of the players, not moving from the keyboard, where he stayed to play certain passages. He was polite but firm, for he knew what he wanted.

Suddenly everyone was standing and leaving the room. He had called a break before working through the final movement. Pasterwicz whispered, "Come, Franz," and stood up. Franz felt hesitant, but obeyed. Across the marble floor they approached the fortepiano and the little man as he stood marking scores in silence. He looked up, one eyebrow arched, then smiled warmly on seeing Pasterwicz.

9

"Georg! Where have you been hiding? Are you angry with your old friend? Why do I never see you anymore?" He slapped Pasterwicz on the back. Pasterwicz laughed and embraced him.

"You're a rather difficult man to keep up with, I'll have you know. Maybe it would be better if you came to see me, eh?" he said.

"You're right, I'm afraid, quite right," Mozart replied, still holding Pasterwicz's arm as if he regretted letting go. His eyes wandered toward Franz, waiting quietly. Their smiles warmed one another.

"Apropos of nothing, Wolfgang," ventured Pasterwicz, "I'd like you to meet a former student of mine. This is Franz Xaver Sussmayr, a fine pianist and singer, and an even better composer. For no other reason than that, I think you should know one another."

Pasterwicz stepped aside as Franz stepped forward to clasp with both hands Mozart's outstretched hand. His hand was cold, but in his eyes Franz saw sudden recognition and puzzlement.

But I already know you. How curious!

"I know you," said Mozart to the young man with the strong, warm grasp. Smiling, he added, "You were at the concert the other day, were you not? I saw you there, didn't I?"

I know you from before the concert....

"Yes, I was there," said Franz intensely as they let go their grasps.

"How did you like it?" he asked quickly.

"It was...," Franz started, "I was...." Franz strained for words.

"Speechless," interjected Pasterwicz. "I thought he would faint after it was over, but he soon recovered. I think your music has a magical effect on the boy...don't you, Franz?"

Franz smiled, still remembering the concert. He was not embarrassed.

"Well, I'm flattered. And I'm glad you enjoyed it. Not too many people do, these days," said Mozart archly. Franz observed him carefully as he spoke in an even, tenor voice. His manner revealed the personal integrity and inner wisdom that Franz had read in his glance at the concert, and in the music of the concert. Now, to his surprise, he saw in his quick movements and penetrating gaze an intense, almost desperate en-

10

ergy that seemed to drive him. He was, up close, larger than life.

"Herr Mozart," Franz found his tongue again, "I would like to discuss the possibility...of studying composition with you. That is, if I am good enough, and if...you are willing."

"Oh? At least two ifs to consider, have we?" Mozart's eyebrow shot up as he looked at Pasterwicz briefly. He sat down and continued to study Franz intently. Franz shifted once from one foot to the other, wondering why he'd set himself up for rejection like this. Certainly a master of his stature had better things to do than teach country church composers how to write operas. Why, this man has been everywhere, and heard everything.

"Are you any good?" Mozart interrupted his thoughts. His eyes were twinkling now.

"*I* think so," ventured Franz. "But I want to be better. I want to write for the stage." Suddenly calmer, Franz leveled his gaze on Mozart.

I know you.

"Franz has written much church music, and he shows promise in other areas of composition. He's a hard worker and won't disappoint you," said the old man. "You'll see."

"I'd like to see some of your work first," said Mozart to Franz. "When can you show it to me?"

"As soon as you can look at it," replied Franz, gaining confidence.

"Tomorrow afternoon?"

"I'm at your service, sir," answered Franz, smiling broadly.

"Tomorrow, then. Meet me at one," said Mozart, "and we'll lunch together. Our friend the priest here can tell you where I live, despite the fact that he's rarely been to visit lately."

"Thank you, sir," replied Franz.

"Pray don't be late," Mozart smiled. "I get critical when I'm too hungry." He continued to study Franz as the two men bid their farewells and left the room. Then he turned to his score and continued exactly where he had left off.

NEW YORK'S UPPER EAST SIDE, 1934.

At age twelve, Willy Kapell knew no one survived the

11

Upper East Side without a certain tough facade. It was a kind of prelude, he guessed, to the world. So he played at being tough. He even had a kind of reputation for being unmanageable, which was good for garnering respect from the other kids. But, even better, most adults left him alone whenever they could. Then he had time to think. There was a part of him that was entirely foreign to the street-wise kid: behind the smart-mouthed exterior lay a compassionate nature and a sensitivity to beauty in all its forms. His poetic soul was a side few others saw or suspected.

His mother saw it.

She remembered that her infant son was fascinated with flowers—and colors. She remembered that he began to sing when only three months old. He would hum and sing to the birds. At two, he was singing little melodies. She would say he always had a song in his heart. It was a song he would strive for the rest of his life to express to others.

Willy's first good piano teacher, Miss LaFollette, saw his keen sensibility whenever he poured out his heart at the piano. Then, it was like a personality change. His big city élan gave way to a grave seriousness and depth of feeling she had never seen in a student before. So she was later to say he was her most extraordinary student. And she would say it remembering not only his incredible technique, but remembering those unusual, and private, transformations at the piano.

While she puzzled over his two-sided nature, Willy himself wondered whether it was all that normal. Surely no one who knew him suspected that under the tough boy attitude beat a heart that was always in love—with movie stars, mostly. With visions of loveliness to which he assigned certain human qualities that he was sure had to be a part of that face, that body. Whether or not it was true was neither here nor there, because part of his lovelorn agenda was the hopelessness of never seeing the girl, ever. Somehow, he suspected it was safer that way. In such fantasies, Willy spent a good deal of time at the movies.

His energies burned pink around him as he played his heart out at the piano—lonely serenades to absent objects of love. For these lonely dedications, he had discovered early on the works of Schubert and Chopin, and Mendelssohn. They added fuel to his fire, and together, Chopin and Willy, or Schubert and Willy, sang songs of love at the piano. And he wrote poetry.

He was a beautiful boy. He resembled in childhood the cherubic children of European cathedral choirs who spent their Sundays singing to God. He was a small child and would grow up to be a man of relatively small physical stature, but possessing an extraordinary intellect and such intense psychic energy that his presence was larger than life. His energy endowed him with an air of intense purposefulness rare in humans, but typical in the highly driven. When excited, his eyes were all anyone could focus on, for they demanded one's full attention. They were also the real barometer of what he felt, despite an occasional, and peculiar, appearance of aristocratic ennui.

ANTONITO, Colorado, 1951.

Three little fingers curled onto the ivory keys from below the piano. Up and down, up and down, sounding high tinkling notes.

With one chubby hand clutching the piano leg, Lina steadied herself while the other hand again reached up to the piano keys and pushed down. Three fingers on two keys at a time. Up and down, over and over. She couldn't see them. They were high, out of sight.

I remember this! Just then, she lost her balance and thumped down on her bottom. Easily distracted, the child crawled away.

Years later, Lina would remember vividly the piano in her uncle's living room. Its sounds were the fascination of her childhood years. The single sounds, the combined ones. The blue ones, the yellow ones. The happy ones, the sad ones. Above the instrument hung a mirror with etched flamingos framed in shades of blue. Flamingos merged with the memories of these tones, like the brilliant sunlight of a Colorado summer. Bright aural lights and flamingos on the wing made up her first remembrances of a new life.

One clear morning, Lina's mother let her out to play after an overnight snowfall. Then five years old, she gasped in delight as she stepped out onto the sunsplashed porch. Before her, a vast crystalline field lay like a glittering cloud under a deep blue sky. She stared as though in another world. Enveloped by the music that often played in her head, she walked out into the cloud of snow with arms outstretched, lifted her face up into the sky, and closed her eyes to listen.

Even at seven, Lina couldn't remember when she first had heard music. Even more curious, it seemed no one else in her immediate universe, outside of her father, had a record player. Nor did the people of Antonito seem to need one.

The record player sat in the middle of a corner bookcase in the huge, cool living room of the house her father and grandfather had built. She spent many hours here in her white wicker rocking chair, turning the pages of picture books and listening to Katchaturian, Tchaikovsky, Grieg and Mozart. Or she would simply rock to hear the faint chimes of the chair's music box. Or she might hide on the wide window ledge behind billowy lace curtains as she plinked the keys of her toy piano—her most favored toy.

Winters were long and bitterly cold in Antonito, and often as not filled with the music of the record player, her chair, or her toy piano. Often, too, they were filled with the melodic voices of family and friends chatting at the kitchen table.

In the summer, she sat in the crab apple tree, humming along with the music in her head as her cousins laughed and cavorted below her, calling her to play. A locomotive roared by, spewing its black clouds of smoke across the blue expanse. Dramatic crescendos would sound in Lina's inner ear, fitting the action she saw.

Thus it was, many years later, that she could not remember a time when she did not know music.

Several years later, her father would buy a piano; but there would be no money for lessons, so she and her sister would teach themselves to play. For Lina, it was a natural progression from the passive hours in front of the record player to active hours at the keyboard. In time, she would make the piano sing the way her music did in the snow and in the apple tree.

Learning was a remembering.

VIENNA, 1788.

When Franz reached the street on which Mozart lived, it was deserted. It was not the best part of town, by a good measure, and Franz was surprised at that. The narrow passageway that led from the cobblestone street into the inner courtyard of the apartment building was cool and dark on this warm August afternoon.

He lingered in the passageway. He needed time to gather himself. Ten years in the monastery had not exactly prepared him for life in the big city, and he often suffered from a mild case of social insecurity despite his enthusiasm for being there. He fidgeted with his portfolio as he tried to remind himself how generous in spirit Mozart had seemed at their last meeting.

The young man's uncertainties were swiftly forgotten as Mozart bounded around the corner to shatter his musings.

"Franz Xaver Sussmayr! What are you doing here? I live in a house, not a hallway! Come, I'm starving." Franz smiled in spite of himself.

Without stopping, Wolfgang took him by the arm and guided him out into the open air, turning right to walk briskly down the narrow sidewalk. He was dressed smartly in dark brown, and he carried himself with an air of worldly distinction, yet he was approachable. Overawed in spite of this, Franz thrashed around for something intelligent to say.

"Beautiful day, don't you think?" asked Mozart, breathing in the freshness of the recent rain.

"If you like rain," said Franz shyly, and immediately decided it was a stupid reply to a friendly enough question. The wet cobblestone glistened in the sun.

Are you here to help me? wondered Wolfgang. *I've prayed for help.*

Yes, I'm here for you, and the soul we share.

"We can lunch at the Hungarian Crown," said Wolfgang. "It's not far from here and the Hungarian is fair."

Franz remained quiet as they strolled briskly through a crowded street, sidestepping massive woodcarts, and skirting around shoppers and vendors laden with everything from bread and chickens to cloth and ironware. Wolfgang stole a look at Franz's face as they reached the church square. He looked uneasy. The young man must be intimidated, he concluded.

"Have you lived long in Vienna?" he inquired casually. He'd been in the presence of awestruck admirers before, albeit not so many recently, and he hoped he knew by now how to put them at ease when he cared to.

"Since last fall," replied Franz, glancing briefly at him.

15

"Where are you from, then?" continued Wolfgang. They crossed the narrow street and turned another corner. The noise of horses' hooves on cobblestone, of shouting children and loud bargaining in doorways made it nearly impossible for Franz to hear. He was determined to get used to the clatter of Vienna.

"I was born at Schwanenstadt," he shouted. "Then I lived and studied at the monastery school at Kremsmunster from the time I was thirteen. And then at the Ritterakademie when I turned eighteen. It was time to leave Kremsmunster after all those years and Vienna seemed like the best place to begin a career."

"What did you study in school?"

"Violin, voice, organ...and composition," said Franz. "And philosophy and law at the academy."

"Well, you must be very learned, *n'est-ce pas?* After all those years of books and professors."

"Actually, I'd like to see how far it gets me before I answer that," said Franz. Wolfgang laughed out loud as they passed in front of the church. Franz looked up to catch a glimpse of the clover-leaf shaped windows high above them.

"How old are you, anyway?" continued Wolfgang as his eyes followed a fetching female cheese vendor holding a basket on her head.

"Twenty-two," answered Franz, smiling. "And you?" Shocked at his own audacity, Franz winced.

"Thirty-two," Wolfgang beamed back. "Not old enough to be your father, but enough to be your brother with seven sisters in between." They entered the crowded tavern, rich with the smell of beer and smoke and sausage. A few men played cards at a corner table while others engaged in small talk at another. The familiar room was cozy and inviting, with its dark paneled walls and thick windowpanes, its candles set in heavy pewter holders and big, accommodating tables and chairs. A barmaid ran about trying to tend to everyone at once, while in a corner another barmaid sat quietly nursing an infant.

Franz laid his portfolio on the table and folded his hands over it, looking Wolfgang squarely in the eyes. He admired the man, but he also was growing fond of him, which had the effect of making him more accessible at the moment. Wolfgang returned his gaze. He sensed a basic honesty and integrity in the young man, which was a relief. He already had decided that even if the boy had no talent for music, he would take him on as a student anyway, just to have someone around he could trust. Besides, his open, innocent demeanor reminded him of a maturing Cherubino, which amused him.

At length the barmaid approached and took Wolfgang's order for a beer followed by soup.

"And you?" she asked, looking at Franz as she pulled back loose hairs from her moist neck.

"Nothing for me, thank you."

"What? Nothing?" demanded Wolfgang. "I won't have it. I refuse to drink alone. Bring him a beer, Madeline." She left with the order. Franz sighed.

"So, what have you got to show me?" Wolfgang eyed the portfolio as he spoke.

Suddenly insecure again, smile gone, Franz blinked as he slowly began pulling on the strings of the portfolio and spoke gravely, "I've written only a few singspiels. The rest of my work is mostly cantatas and religious pieces. This—" he tugged on its contents "is my most recent singspiel. *A Father's Revenge.* It was performed at Kremsmunster before I left."

He handed it over to Wolfgang, who opened it to the overture. "*A Father's Revenge.* Nothing worse than that," he mused. "Except, maybe, a woman's...."

Wolfgang studied the score for several minutes, turning pages slowly as he heard the music in his head. Franz noticed his head as he bent over the music. Fine yet full hair, almost unmanageably so. Franz looked around nervously, his anxiety having come to visit him again now that his life's work was in the hands of a master for review. No, he had to know. He leaned over to read Wolfgang's face. He was smiling as if in response to something familiar—a scene or tune maybe. Franz finally looked away again. He couldn't stand to watch, and Wolfgang gave no indication of the score's worth, one way or another. The wait was tearing him to pieces. Was the room getting stuffy, or was it all in his head?

"You have some original ideas." Wolfgang's voice startled Franz to attention. "Your strength seems to lie in melodic invention, which is good if you want to write opera. Your orchestration needs work, however, and so does your sense of musical drama." *Much* work, thought Wolfgang, he has not been taught well. "Yes, I will make you a fine composer, if you're willing to work."

"You like it, then? You'll teach me?" Franz could hardly

17

believe what he had just heard. "Oh, thank you sir! You're too kind! Surely, too kind!"

"Too kind? No, I will make you work!" Wolfgang smiled at him as they shook hands on it. The barmaid arrived with the tray and they took up their mugs.

"To your health and your music!" declared Wolfgang.

The candles flickered and light and shadow danced on the walls of Wolfgang's apartment. Franz sat at a worktable, surrounded by manuscript paper. Wolfgang stood next to him, his hand resting on his shoulder. They had been working quietly, each on his own music. Occasionally, Wolfgang would stop his own work to look at Franz's.

Wolfgang had been reading over Franz's music for *Drunken Hans,* his latest theatre project. Wolfgang frowned, pointed to a passage and said, "What's the reason for this? What purpose does it serve in the music? In the scene?" He reached behind him and pulled up a chair to sit. "Everything has to have a reason for being," he said as he sat down, looking urgently at his student. "I may be wrong, but as far as I can tell, this passage serves no apparent dramatic purpose."

He continued, "The music must be solid. Compact. And everything must count for something. If it doesn't, then out it goes."

He spoke with equal portions of conviction, passion and courtesy. Even so, Franz felt as close to stupid as one could feel in the presence of such a master. He allowed that the fragment in question didn't seem to have any observable purpose, dramatic or otherwise, and secretly blamed the librettist. Then, together, they looked over the rest of that section. Wolfgang suddenly picked up a page and took it to the fortepiano. He sat down and played another passage, speaking as he played.

"I like it. It will move well after you clean up that one portion. You're making good progress, Franz." Franz watched his fingers move over the keys with effortless grace. He was a considerate, encouraging and enthusiastic teacher. Franz noticed that he never changed what he, Franz, had written, no matter how clumsy or stupid it was. Past teachers so often had felt free to pick up their pens and simply mark up his score. Wolfgang only made suggestions and left it up to Franz to follow through, if he wanted to. Unless they were exercises, Franz noticed, the score changes were always in his own hand. On

18

exercises, Wolfgang freely marked the music himself.

They had been working all afternoon. The late afternoon sunlight was slanting through the small window. Franz's stomach growled above the sound of the music. He glanced at the clock. Seven-thirty. "Are you hungry?" he asked when Wolfgang had reached a cadence. "I can go get us some dinner if you like."

Wolfgang let a long sigh and stood up, glancing briefly at the waning light of the window. "If you would, I would be grateful. I must finish this piece. I can do that while you're gone. Do you need money?"

"No, I have some." Franz took a cloth sack from the wall hook and was out the door and down the stairs before Wolfgang could protest. He made his way to the market, where he found bread, sausage, fruit and wine. He was unabashedly elated. To be a student of the great Mozart! It seemed unbelievable. And, what was better, Wolfgang had not thrown him out, laughing, after seeing more of his work. That was the best part.

Of course, Wolfgang's music was not in as much demand now as it had been several years ago. But that was beside the point. The fact remained, and was acknowledged by anyone with any musical sensibility, that he was the best. Other composers acknowledged this, grudgingly, to be sure, but with the surest sense of knowing that Mozart was the best musician and composer among them. And *he*, Franz Sussmayr, was one of his students! He would never have been so lucky in Schwanenstadt.

When he returned to the apartment, he found that Wolfgang had already cleared the worktable. As Franz emptied the sack onto the table, Wolfgang emerged from the bedroom, where he had been resting. They sat down.

Wolfgang's cramped, cluttered, second floor apartment surprised Franz. He had expected a much larger, more organized arrangement. The fortepiano and several tables took up the largest of three rooms. Papers, candles, wine bottles, ink wells, quills, books, dishes and a viola covered every available surface. A glass-fronted cabinet held more papers and books, and a large round table near the stove held the remnants of a previous meal. On either side of the stove were two doorways leading to a bedroom on the right and a spare room on the left, which Wolfgang called the music room. It was here that manu-

19

scripts were stacked on the floor or in chests until he could find more cabinets. Tall windows let in the sunshine in summer, and bitter cold drafts in the winter. There was no kitchen.

Nor did the neighborhood prove to be the best or most quiet, except in winter when no one roamed about and snow covered the dingy walkways.

Wolfgang slouched in the chair, exhaustion lining his face. "Ha, apples! What a treat," he said softly as he reached for one. His eyes weren't smiling. It occurred then, to Franz, that Wolfgang was in pain.

"Do you have a headache, Herr Mozart?" he asked tentatively.

"Only a mild one. Tell me, Franz, why are you so formal with me? Are we not friends yet?"

"Oh...yes, I hope so...."

"Then call me Wolfgang, and I will continue to call you Franz, unless you have another name you'd rather I used," Wolfgang added, reaching for the wine. He poured two glasses and began a mock toast as Franz slipped into a chair with a knife and the sausage.

"To *Drunken Hans*—and maybe a drunken Franz as well!"

"On both accounts, I'll do my best!" returned Franz before drinking half the glass in one swallow.

For the next half-hour they dined and chatted. Franz spoke of life at Kremsmunster as Wolfgang listened, occasionally prompting him with a brief question. He held his hand to his forehead as he leaned on the table, casually watching Franz speak, occasionally smiling or laughing at what he said. Franz noticed in himself a natural ease in speaking to him—was it the wine or was he finally at ease in his presence? Their friendship now seemed so natural—almost as if they were merely resuming what might previously have been interrupted, as with school chums who meet again years later.

The light through the window gradually waned into darkness. Franz lit a candle.

In the dim light, Wolfgang's face looked even more drawn as he spoke of all the work he'd still to do. His biggest expense, he explained, was paying a copyist to write out separate orchestral parts, and, in the case of operas, parts for cast members as well. And then managing to keep the music out of the hands of plagiarists and thieves, who often worked hand in hand with certain unprincipled copyists, made such matters even more difficult. Still, for the good copyist, it was even more work having to read his handwriting, Wolfgang jested.

Franz was listening quietly when the idea came to him, as smoothly and silently as the morning's first light. He twisted the stem of his wine glass, frowning as he analyzed the ramifications and probabilities of the idea. Sensing something unusual was going through Franz's mind, Wolfgang frowned slightly and inquired, "You're suddenly quiet. What is going on in that head?"

Franz looked up slowly, solemnly. Wolfgang noted his serious mien and sat up, waiting.

"I will be your copyist," Franz announced gently. "I want to help you."

Wolfgang set his wine glass on the table, waiting for more. Franz could hear his own breathing. The candle flickered. He leaned forward across the table and spoke urgently.

"If you will let me...if you think, that is, that I can. I see you need more than just a copyist—you need a discreet and honest assistant. And an accurate one."

"How curious," Wolfgang uttered. "I sensed from the moment I first saw you...that you would help me somehow. I know you would make a fine assistant. My God, we even have identical handwriting. But what of your own work?"

"It will do me no harm if I lay my work aside for the time being. And anyway, I expect to learn much simply from copying your work—it stands to reason, doesn't it? I ask for nothing but your friendship and loyalty in return. What do you say?"

Silence enveloped the room as Wolfgang carefully studied Franz, whose gaze radiated an earnest confidence. It was unheard of that one composer would suspend his own work to help another.

It's uncanny good luck, thought Wolfgang. Maybe it's common knowledge that I need help. And what of it? What composer wouldn't jump at a free copyist for even a week? This boy is guileless. As guileless as I myself was at that age. There is no doubt about it. Franz Sussmayr is the answer to my prayers. Here is much needed help, and friendship, in one childlike stranger. But is he such a stranger?

"What do I say? I say...you are about to learn quite a lot! But you shouldn't work for free. Where do you live now?"

"I have a small place near the Prater...."

"If you're going to be my copyist, I'll need you here. I'll take you in as I have with some of my other students. If you live here, we will manage better with expenses. Two can live cheaper than one, I've come to discover. It's much better than starving at home alone, isn't it? Can you live here, then?"

"Yes, of course. I...I would be honored!"

Wolfgang stood up smiling broadly and declared, "As would I! I needed a copyist two months ago—what kept you?" Franz grinned broadly and stood up as Wolfgang did. He surprised him with a wordless embrace as if to seal the agreement. Franz caught his breath as a subtle yet powerful energy passed between them, like a fine vibration surrounding and permeating his head, chest and arms. It was a feeling he'd never felt before. The embrace ended too soon for Franz as they stood clasping a handshake, still basking in the fine lightness of that hold.

"Thank you," beamed Wolfgang. He sat down, wordless and pale. Franz also sat, gazing at his hands, lost in thought.

What have I done? he pondered. I surprise myself sometimes—I've just more or less impetuously written off, or at least postponed, my own work for an undetermined length of time...but, strangely, it doesn't seem to matter. Still, where do we go from here? We? Yes, we.

"You will tell me when you no longer wish to stay," Wolfgang murmured sagely. It was almost a question. Franz looked up.

I'm here to help you. It's part of the plan.

"I want to do it," Franz answered at last. His voice echoed in his ears.

They worked late that night on Franz's opera, at Wolfgang's insistence. In the dim light of two candles, they studied a passage of long, ascending scale runs. Wolfgang queried, "What's happening onstage here?"

Exhausted, Franz squinted and concentrated, "Flight, running." Again the score was carried to the fortepiano. Wolfgang played it as written. Then he varied it, playing the runs broken up into shorter, repeated sections that changed harmony at each repetition. Franz could hear immediately that it was better. Then Wolfgang asked why he had chosen that time signature and that key. Franz remembered that everything had to have a purpose.

They worked diligently, stopping only as Franz lit a new candle, and another one. At one in the morning, he groggily suggested that it was time to stop. Wolfgang looked at the clock, and agreed without an argument. He disappeared into the bedroom and emerged with a quilt and pillow for Franz, who gratefully slipped onto the sofa. He was asleep within minutes.

That night Wolfgang dreamed he met Franz on a familiar hill overlooking the city. Franz was at ease and direct with him, though he communicated, Wolfgang noticed, without speaking. As they casually surveyed the distant landscape, Franz asked, *What do you hope to accomplish with your music?*

Wolfgang smiled as he swept his arm in a wide arc to include the sleeping city and the world beyond. He answered rather as a child would. *I hope to bring beauty to the world. And joy.*

Their auras blossomed into a light, clear yellow, and Franz replied, *Yes, the world is assuredly better for your presence.*

Will you stay long? Wolfgang asked.

As long as you need me. And if you turn me out, I'll remain close by. I came to help.

Why?

The brilliant yellow light around them pulsated and swirled. Wolfgang lost sight of the city and Franz, whose voice echoed through the light. *You and I are threads of the same fabric, fragments of the same oversoul. Remember this. In your darkest hour, you prayed for help. Help is here.*

Shining bands of glistening blue light unfurled around Wolfgang, energizing him with love and new courage. Then it faded and disappeared.

He awoke.

For the first time in many months, he felt completely rested. It had been a deep sleep and now, relaxed, he remained still as he savored the warmth of the bed. He glanced lazily toward the window and knew from the angle of the shaft of light that he had overslept. His hands slid over the extra quilt on the bed. Easing out of bed, he slipped the quilt over his shoulders and wandered into the next room. Franz was bent over a sheet of music paper, scratching away. He looked up from his work and his face broke into a smile.

"Good morning. Did you sleep well? I've started hot water for tea, and there's still some bread and sausage from last night." He got up to fetch a cup as Wolfgang sat at the table.

"You're still here," observed Wolfgang, clutching the quilt and studying him in amusement.

Franz smiled back. "I've been waiting for you to wake up and tell me what needs to be done," he said as he poured hot water into a cup. "Of yours, that is."

Over the months and seasons that followed, Wolfgang grew to admire and appreciate Franz's kind heart and quiet disposition. He was devoted, ready and heartbreakingly self-effacing. He was easily moved. And moved, also, to laughter by Wolfgang's own wry wit and under-the-breath comments and observations. Wolfgang amazed Franz with his uncanny ability to read his mind, or his face, or both. In fact, he was as readable to Wolfgang as keyboard exercises. Franz had quickly recognized the genius and utter beauty in the music of his master. It was, to him, an elixir for which he lived in another otherwise quiet world of copying and studying of scores.

He came to love and admire Wolfgang not only for his winning, humorous disposition, but for his day-to-day courage in the face of ever-increasing odds. For his part, the worse things got, the harder Franz clung to his convictions, whispering to Wolfgang that there was no one better, no one more deserving of a decent salary, of a wife who loved him, or public recognition, than he—Wolfgang. Privately, Franz glumly pondered life's seeming inequities. How, in this world, could someone of Wolfgang's genius and talent be treated so carelessly by those who should know better? But things would get better. They had to.

While they lived, they shared. Much of whatever money Wolfgang made from composition usually went to his wife, Constanze; consequently, they were forced to rely heavily on whatever Franz earned playing the organ at church services and teaching music. Privation was not new to either of them, but it was wearisome, nonetheless. There were days when Franz would find Wolfgang in the bedroom sitting quietly in a chair, as if waiting. Inquiries brought only a weak smile or an impatient wave of the hand. Franz withdrew, knowing it was his time to be alone—to find himself, within himself. On those occasions, it didn't matter as much if there was no food or firewood, for Wolfgang didn't seem to miss either. In fact, he hardly knew where he was, it seemed. Then, as quickly as he had withdrawn, he returned.

VIENNA, 1790.

Twilight was the most desolate time of the day for two very concrete reasons. Candles and food. Twilight heralded the darkness of night, broken only by the pale light of one candle in one room. Candles were too dear to burn more than one at a time. Also, Franz and Wolfgang often skipped the evening meal for lack of money, and their stomachs began their nightly grumbling at twilight. The combined hardships of hunger and darkness stirred in them an elemental anxiety that was often too pervasive to ignore. Unless a distraction caught their attention.

Franz stood at the window of the darkened music room watching the last streaks of a pale orange sunset fade into turquoise and dark blue. Nearby lay chests of manuscripts around two sides of the room. Here Wolfgang often played the viola alone for his own pleasure, and, less often, Franz played his violin. With no furniture here, or curtains on the windows, the sound reverberated more consistently. But, most important, it was a place to be alone.

Franz stared longingly out the open window, smelling the cooking dinners of other households, and gazing at the dwindling light of the now faded sunset. He turned around and glanced toward the main room where the weak light of the candle reflected from Wolfgang's face as he worked at his desk. At times like these, Franz envied his ability to leave the world behind and lose himself in his work. True, he wasn't always as lost in his work as he looked. Often, it was merely mechanical copy work—from his memory to paper. More often, Franz realized, the "losing" of Wolfgang's self was in those times when he sat still as a statue and stared at nothing in particular, mentally scanning the music of his mind, arranging it, writing it in his head.

As Franz mused on the day's work, the door flew open.

He startled and blinked as Constanze swept in. Wolfgang turned as if awakened from a dream. He smiled calmly.

"I can't stay long, Johann is waiting downstairs," she started curtly as she deposited a large cloth-wrapped bundle on the table nearest the door. Darkness hid Franz from her sight. He didn't move, and he remained quiet except for an almost inaudible sigh at the sound of Johann's name. As Constanze's live-in lover, he at least had the decency to stay away from this household.

"Stanzerl, so good to see you again!" Wolfgang approached her with open arms. She turned her face at the last moment and his kiss landed on her cheek as she grimaced. Constanze long ago had decided she disliked visiting her husband. He was no longer important to her and he looked terrible, besides. Worse, he still asked for her wifely attentions. It was simply too much to expect. It's best to simply make this short and be gone immediately, she decided, before he brings it up again. After all, I'm not really his any more, anyway, even if everyone in Vienna thinks we're still together.

"Wolfgang, I'll need another payment as soon as you can manage it. I'll be leaving for Baden in a week and you know how expenses are there," she said hastily as she scanned the room. It's looking particularly shabby and unkempt today, she thought. She stared uncomfortably at her husband. "Johann would like to come round for it tomorrow."

He stared at her with the shadow of a smile. How she wanted the good things in life, he mused. And he had failed her. He had failed to turn fame into fortune, and so she had found someone who would give her what she wanted. He could hardly blame her. After all, she was only a woman, and women are weak. They tend naturally toward infidelity. It's in their nature. It's up to the men to simply accept them for what they are—weaknesses and all. Love, and patience, would win out in the end. It was already a good sign that she did not seek a permanent separation, or a divorce. Yes, soon, she would return to him and he would again find love in her beautiful eyes. Love as strong as that which he still had for her, and always would, no matter what.

"The ten ducats I gave you this week. Is that all gone?" he asked patiently.

She had expected resistance. "I don't remember, I must have spent it at the market. But this is different. I'll be traveling. You don't want Karl to suffer because you refuse to give us travel money, do you? How can you treat your son so callously, even if you don't care what happens to me?" she snapped. The comment visibly stung him.

"Did I say I would not give it to you?" he asked reprovingly. "If I had it, believe me, dearest, I would. And you know I would no more let Karl suffer than you." Why could she not love me as I love her? At least a little!

"Well, if I don't go to Baden, I will suffer," she announced hotly. "I'm not entirely cured, and the doctor says if I get worse, it will be for lack of the baths. I can't understand why you refuse to take care of me, it's not fa—"

"It's not that I refuse, Constanze," he interrupted. "I have no money. None! Trying to keep two households is breaking me. It's impossible!"

Franz closed his eyes and leaned against the window ledge as he witnessed the scene with increasing dismay and anger. His hands clutched on the wooden casement.

"So where am I to turn then?" she demanded. "Mama has no money, Johann says...."

"*Don't* talk to me of that man!" Wolfgang raised his voice. He had reached his limit. He swept past her toward the dark music room. She turned and followed him, but as he approached the doorway, Franz silently and deliberately moved into the corridor of light cast by the candle. Constanze gasped as she saw Franz's still, straight figure in the light. She stopped at once, obviously embarrassed that this "stranger," as she often called him, should be witness to their argument. Not that it really mattered much, she told herself, they were both cut from the same cloth as far as she was concerned. And they were obviously lovers. Why else would this young nobody have refused her advances? She still couldn't believe it. This insolent bumpkin had refused *her,* the wife of an important and very famous man. No, she would never forgive him for that. And now, here he was—again. In the way—again! Wolfgang would be much easier to deal with if he were rid of this impudent young lover and heaven knows what else they are....

Wolfgang had spun around and was pointing to the bundle. "And what is that?"

Constanze struggled to maintain her composure in front of Franz, who no doubt remembered her admittedly awkward sexual overtures. Her voice was quiet and reserved. She wanted to leave, but Wolfgang had her by the arm.

"Letters. I have no room for them. They're yours. You keep them," she replied stiffly.

"What letters?"

"Your father's, and your sister's," she said indifferently as she jerked her arm away and rearranged her shawl. "They're in the way. If I keep them any longer, I may be tempted to dispose of them." She reached for the door.

"Goodbye, Wolfgang. Thank you for nothing." The door slammed and silence reclaimed the room.

Wolfgang sighed wearily as he sank onto a chest on the music room floor. Resting his elbows on his knees, he dropped his head and slowly ran his fingers through his hair as he stared at the floor. Franz took another chest from the corner, placed it nearby, and sat down. They were silent for several minutes. Then Wolfgang sighed deeply. He looked up.

"I don't know what to do," he said at last. "She hates me. I never thought it would be like this. She truly hates me. I can't get used to it. Oh, God, it hurts."

"I'm sorry."

"It's not her fault. They've poisoned her against me. You know, Franz, she's not the kind of person to decide for herself to hate someone. They did this to her. To us. To our marriage."

"Come, let's go into the other room. It's depressing in here." Franz helped him into an overstuffed chair nearer to the candlelight. Wolfgang's arms fell limply across the chair's arms. Franz placed the bundle of letters in the music room. He'd put them away later. He pulled up a chair and straddled it.

"What's it all for?" Wolfgang asked disconsolately. "What's the use?"

Franz fixed his eyes on him. "What are you saying, Wolfgang? What's the use of what?" Then he remembered to put out the candle, as neither of them were working now. He jumped up, put it out, and returned to his chair. The moonlight helped, a little.

"Of working so hard," Wolfgang began. "So hard. Look at that." He waved his arm toward the music room. "A room full of music that no one hears but once, if at all. And for a pittance. Worse, my operas are performed all over Europe now and I still go hungry. I don't care if it is 'the way things are done,' I don't like it. It's unfair. It's wrong."

Franz sighed relief. Constanze was not only gone, but forgotten for the moment.

"Why do I bother?" asked Wolfgang out of the darkness. "Maybe I *should* take a position with the goverment. I'd be able to support my family that way. Then Stanzerl would love me again. Maybe they're right. Why should I let being a musician ruin my life? Why do I do this?"

"What are you saying? A government position? You? You're an artist! It's what you were meant to be, don't you see?" Franz paused to collect his thoughts before continuing. "Who are we to say when it will all be appreciated? Whether it is now or in a hundred years. Isn't that up to God? Isn't ours merely to create and then give it over? The less our reward here, the greater our reward in heaven."

"Do you really believe that?" asked Wolfgang in mild disbelief.

"Yes, and I must be completely honest, I don't think I could endure doing anything but writing and playing music."

"Neither could I, but we're *starving*, Franz!"

"I know."

"Is that also part of God's plan? That we pay with every fiber of our beings? It doesn't make sense, Franz!"

"It doesn't make sense from our point of view. But maybe on a larger scale, one that, one day, we may understand. Maybe there it all falls clearly into focus with beautiful logic and sense. When you were a child, did your father tell you what he had planned for you and your family? I daresay he didn't. He knew what to do and didn't need a child's limited viewpoint."

Franz studied the moonlight streaming through the window. "I'm sorry, I'm an impossible optimist."

"You certainly are." Wolfgang's voice sounded brighter. "Is this another example of what those addled monks taught you?" Things were looking up, thought Franz. Wolfgang was feeling well enough to taunt him.

"Indirectly," he replied sagely. "My notions arose from my disappointment at being there. From my having nothing to do or say about being in a monastery school. At having no alternative. It's how I explained it to myself."

"Why *were* you there? Refresh my memory."

"I told you Mama died when I was six. My father married again when I was about nine. She couldn't cope with all four of us children, so as soon as I was old enough, they sent me away to school. I rarely went home after that. Except when I left the school for good. Then I only lasted eight months at home."

"Why? Was your father not happy to have you back?"

"My father and I don't agree on many things, so we avoid each other as much as possible. I am a disappointment to him because I'm not at his side teaching and playing the organ." Franz sighed heavily. "Worse, he thinks I'm dull-witted and can never come to anything worthwhile here in Vienna." Franz usually avoided the subject of his family because it hurt, but he noted that he felt little pain in talking about them now. Maybe it was the new distance.

"Franz, you're an orphan, aren't you?" Wolfgang's voice was soft now. "I mean, not in truth of course, but in essence, you are alone in the world."

"I suppose so," Franz conceded. "Except for you. You are my brother."

He clasped his hands in the dark. He hadn't thought of it that way, but he was right. He had only Wolfgang. His siblings were far away and wrapped up in their own lives. He could not expect support or help from his father. His mother was dead....

"And I have only you now," sighed Wolfgang. "To be sure I started out with many, as did you. Is this also part of God's plan? To be abandoned by our families?"

"It must be," replied Franz evenly. "It must be...."

Wolfgang fumbled in the dark for a bottle of wine that he knew was on a nearby table. He found it. As they talked, he took a drink straight from the bottle and then handed it to Franz. "But you had a girlfriend, once, no? Didn't you tell me that?"

"Yes, once," Franz answered. He weighed the bottle—almost full. Then he tipped it up and took a long drink and handed it back. "If you don't count the girls I knew before I went to school. There were plenty of those. Some were more fun than others." They laughed. "But for real love, I knew only one. Briefly."

"She broke your heart?"

"I think she broke many hearts. Mine was just one more. She was not beautiful, but she was exciting. We were very close. She's gone now. Her family married her off to a wealthy Italian."

30

"Damn! The Italians are taking everything!" Wolfgang was feeling lightheaded and the hunger pains had stopped. "Did you have a chance to ask for her hand first?"

"Yes, but her family had no intentions of marrying her off to a poor church composer with poorer prospects." Franz tried to laugh. He took another swallow. He was beginning to feel warm inside.

"Was she passionate? Did you make love?" Wolfgang asked candidly. Franz suddenly blushed and was glad for the darkness.

"No. Ah, yes and no...I suppose," he stammered.

"Snai! Why not? Didn't she want to?"

Franz had to stop and remember. "I think she would have, if I hadn't stopped her...us."

"Why did you stop, for God's sake?" prompted Wolfgang in astonishment.

"Well, what else could I do? She was a good girl, from a good family! Imagine the scandal if she had gotten...if there had been a...," Franz sputtered. This conversation was beginning to unnerve him. He had never spoken frankly about such things to anyone. He took another drink before Wolfgang took the bottle.

"But if she wanted to...oh, well. I don't suppose it makes any difference now. But I wonder, Snai...have you ever?" Wolfgang leaned forward over the bottle, peering intently at the shadow in front of him.

"Not yet," came the small voice out of the dark. "Some day."

"How about tonight?" proposed Wolfgang. Franz smiled involuntarily at his impulsiveness.

"I know one or two lovelies from the chorus at the court theatre," Wolfgang continued. "They admire me. They've so much as said I might have whatever I ask for. We can visit them and maybe one will take a liking to you, eh?"

Franz wanted to. He longed to. But his strict Catholic shadow said no. Wolfgang seemed to read his mind.

"Snai, you're letting your strict training get in the way of good fun. Sex is only a diversion! It doesn't mean your spiritual life has ended in flames of desire! Would God give us women and then damn us for admiring them? Don't let those monks follow you around all of your life. Let them go. It's time to be yourself. Wait! Let me see!" He grabbed Franz around the middle. Franz jumped. "No, I don't think you're wearing a cassock, or a robe. I suppose that means you're human—like me, God forbid!"

"This is nonsense...," Franz protested.

"No, it isn't! Come with me and let's find some willing young sopranos who can sing out at the right moment." Wolfgang stood up and pulled Franz up by the sleeve. Franz grabbed the bottle and together they found the door in the dark.

Wolfgang slapped Franz on the back as they descended the stairs. "So God watches over musicians...," he repeated jauntily.

"Um-hum."

"I'll take your word for it," he laughed. Franz chuckled. They proceeded, hand on shoulder, down the long cobblestone street, the brilliant moon lighting their way, shining off the half-empty bottle.

VIENNA, Summer, 1790.

Wolfgang looked up from his work briefly to watch Elisabeth. Ironically, the lusty Baroness Waldstatten was more like a mother in so many ways, he mused. On seeing Wolfgang after the many months she was away, she had been shocked and dismayed that he looked even more pale than when she last had seen him. "Like a little ghost!" she had exclaimed. On recovering from what Wolfgang perceived as another attack of overacting, she insisted in mock horror that he must spend more time out-of-doors in the fresh air, and she would see to that herself.

He knew, of course, that she enjoyed his company and that the garden visits for "fresh air" were a pleasant if transparent ruse to have him around. So here they were, the three of them—the Baroness, Wolfgang and Franz—languidly sitting around a wide, sun-dappled table built near an ancient tree in her spacious, fragrant garden. Around the table was a long circular bench. Beyond this green Eden rose high stone walls, and beyond that, the rest of Vienna.

Wolfgang sat at the table and worked on a composition. Franz also sat and copied while the Baroness stretched her legs along one side of the bench and worked her needlepoint. Covering the table were sheaves of paper lying under many of the Baroness's fanciful glass weights, brought out to guard against the occasional breeze.

The crickets sang their afternoon song as the trio sat in as little clothing as was considered appropriate in mixed company—shirts and breeches on the men, a loose-fitting country dirndl on Madame. All three were barefoot and bareheaded in the shade.

Occasionally, Franz stood up to walk around and work the kinks out of his shoulders and arms from so many hours of writing in his typically hunched position. Wolfgang stretched out more often.

It really wasn't such a bad idea being here, he thought. The shade, the greenery and the clear sky rested and refreshed his eyes. The solitude was so different from the colorless, still-born solitude one found indoors.

He looked at the Baroness again. He had finally figured out that she loved him as the son she never had, but with a bit of incestuous attraction, nevertheless. She hummed lightly as she worked, occasionally glancing up to smile at him. Franz, as usual, was the Eternal Monk, slaving fastidiously over his work. Still, even for a monk, Franz never looked better than out here in the open air. In fact, the shade of the tree seemed to turn everyone's face a pleasant, healthy-looking color. It was nearly idyllic.

Wolfgang threw his quill down. Franz looked up. He knew the signal well. It meant Wolfgang was ready to let the work go in favor of visiting, laughing or music-making. Wolfgang stretched one more time, looked around, winking at the Baroness, knowing it would elicit a blush or laugh, or both.

"Elisabeth, what a gloriously fine idea this was. I think I'll join the crickets and sing to you," he announced cheerfully.

"Wolfgang," said Franz as he continued to write swiftly, scarcely looking up from where he was bent over his work. "Are you done with the solo part?"

"Who was that?" Wolfgang asked in mock attention. "Did I hear a voice?"

Elisabeth giggled and looked across the table at Franz. He was such a serious fellow sometimes, she thought, until you got him drunk. Then he was as wild as Wolfgang. He was a most unusual young man.

Franz looked up at Wolfgang. A faint smile played around his mouth, but he refused to let it bloom.

He was always so intense when he was working, thought Wolfgang, and he never knew when to quit. You had to snatch his pen away from him. But I suppose I'm the same way.

Franz waited patiently for a reply, but Wolfgang smiled and nodded at him, no longer in the mood to talk scores. No matter, Franz shrugged, and returned to his work.

"I had the most curious dream last night. Would you like to hear about it?" asked Wolfgang, lazily reaching up to the low-hanging branches.

"Oh, do tell us, Wolferl," said the Baroness, "and I'll tell you what it meant. I can interpret dreams quite well, you know."

"Oh, really? Well, it's only a short dream, but it was extraordinarily vivid and real," he began, suddenly thoughtful as he watched the dappled shade shifting on the papers. "I was a gardener of hundreds of pink flowers of all kinds. Each flower was special, and different from all the others. I saw myself standing among them. There were others, my assistants, working in this glorious garden with me. I knew I could count on each one of my assistants for help and support, and there were so many. We worked hard. All in all, it was a striking sight, and a good feeling. But do you know what?"

"What?" echoed the Baroness. Franz had stopped his work to brush a bug off his paper. He looked blandly at the pair.

"I was growing the flowers to *give them away!* They were not for me, they were for strangers! All that work...just to give them away! Is that a good joke?" He answered his own question by laughing again.

The fresh air was good for his spirits, thought Franz. We should do this more often.

"That's incredible," said the Baroness, pronouncing it as the French would. "And extraordinary, too. Do you know what that means?"

"No, but I'm sure you do. Now tell me before I burst with obscene curiosity," he replied, settling down for the explanation. He fidgeted with a sparrow's feather he'd found on the ground.

"Pink!...is the color of love, *mon ami.* Your flowers are the fruits of your labor. Your hundreds of flowers are your hundreds of works of love. Oh, yes, it's all so perfect." She placed her needlepoint on the table to free her hands to hold an imaginary flower, wrists together, fingers fanned out. "Your

34

music is the expression of love. And these you tend carefully, each one being special in its own way. The presence of assistants means you are not alone, although you alone are responsible for the flowers. And in the end, you give them away...to the world! How poetic this dream is. And how true, don't you think so, Franz?" She hoped he would join their genial conversation.

Franz had stopped to stare at her.

What a silly woman, he thought, deciding not to say anything for fear his words would betray his feelings. Instead, he looked at Wolfgang for aid, making sure to keep his openmouthed incredulity looking, hopefully, like fascination. As lunatic as she sometimes seemed, he liked her and didn't want to hurt her feelings.

Wolfgang had stopped fidgeting to stare at the Baroness, transfixed. Oh, my! thought Franz, he liked it! Or so it seemed. One couldn't always read his face with certainty.

"That's most interesting, Elizabeth, most interesting," allowed Wolfgang slowly, weighing his words carefully. "But how do you know what it all means? Why, for example, does pink necessarily signify love?"

This should be good, thought Franz, looking back at his work but listening intently.

"It's simple. Our minds gather the stuff of dreams from our lives. If in our waking lives, pink begets thoughts of love, as it often does for many, then so it does in our dreams as well. Other notions come from common sense, from which our sleeping selves are also quite capable of drawing. A flower blossoms forth to give pleasure and beauty to those with eyes, *n'est-ce pas?* Your music, Wolfgang, blossoms forth with each performance to provide pleasure and beauty, does it not? And you too, Franz! Are flowers not a fine and accurate metaphor for your work?" she asked. "Go on, Wolferl, admit it! Your works are each a new measure of love from yourself to the world!"

Wolfgang sat hugging one knee to his chest as he twirled his feather thoughtfully between his fingers. "Possibly," he ventured. He wasn't sure what to make of it. Better to tease her with hesitance.

"'Possibly'?? Don't you mean 'probably'?" She thumped her fist lightly on the table. "You don't get nearly as much for your music as you should. To me, that means you must virtually give your art away, no? You could stop at any time and make the Webers happy by getting a paying position doing something else, but you don't! Why? Because you were born to deliver your flowers of love. Do you not think that your own inner being knows what it's doing? That somehow there are more blessings in what you do now than if you were rich and well settled as a mute government official?"

"You argue convincingly, my dear," observed Wolfgang, who had taken on his enigmatic mien, Franz noticed. He wondered how much of what she said really impressed him. He would have to ask him later.

"That's because I'm right," she beamed, surprisingly self-assured. "Dreams never lie."

"Umm," Wolfgang replied. "Indeed."

The golden late-summer sunlight was beginning to creep across the table, and beyond, across the lawn. A light breeze rustled the paperweighted manuscripts on the table. The horn part here, the cello part there, drying, over here the violas, and in the middle, the conductor's score. And Wolfgang sitting with his chin resting on his knee, like a child, watching Elisabeth's mouth as she spoke.

Franz gazed thoughtfully at the many papers with the hundreds of notes scrawled across the lines. Lines and lines, and notes and more notes. Maybe what she said was right. Maybe many more minds and hands than were immediately evident were involved in this, the greatest project of their lives— a gift of love to humanity through these thousands of lines and notes. But where were these so-called assistants now? On a separate level of existence, maybe? Certainly not here. But...what if....

Franz looked at Wolfgang and Elisabeth, who also stared at the papers. "I think I see it. That must be it," Franz cut in at last. "It explains where your ideas may come from."

"What are you talking about?" asked Wolfgang, resting his head sideways on his knee to direct his amused gaze at Franz. He was curious to hear what the sober Snai was thinking.

"At Kremsmunster, I knew an old Russian scholar who would tell us often—so often, as a matter of fact, that it's almost the only thing I remember from so far back—that angels come and sit on our shoulders when we think or pray. I remember wondering how such big beings found any room to sit on our thin little shoulders. You know, where do the wings go?

36

And was that the fluttering I so often heard in my ears? But I was only thirteen. Anyway, he said all creative thinking was a cooperative effort with God, through his messengers, the angels. These assistants in your dream, Wolfgang, did they have wings?"

Wolfgang burst out laughing. "No! But I think your head does!" Franz frowned.

"No, Wolfgang," interjected the Baroness. "He's right. If anyone here has wings in his head, it's got to be you. You fly quite high when you write, even if your body stays on the ground. I don't know where you go, but it must be a wonderful place, don't you think, Franz?"

"Maybe. Maybe not," said Franz archly. "What do I know? I'm only a country-bred fool." Wolfgang looked up. Damn! he thought, I've hurt his feelings. Me and my big mouth!

"Snai," he said casually, getting up to move around the table toward him. "I'm such a twit sometimes. Elisabeth is right, I'm not all here, you know. Sometimes I'm sitting here in front of you, sometimes I'm standing here...behind you, like this." He had dashed around behind Franz where he reached out to pull his ear. Franz had anticipated it and turned to defend himself.

"What? No wings?" laughed Franz. "Only hands?"

"The better to box you with!" shouted Wolfgang. The Baroness laughed in delight as they exchanged mock punches while Franz laughed so hard he began slipping to the ground under a barrage of playful fists. Wolfgang shouted fiercely, jumping on the bench to finish him off. Franz was laughing too hard to fight him off.

"Wherever you go for inspiration," cried Franz from under the table, "try to remember to bring back more wine, will you?"

Ripples of laughter echoed through the trees.

VIENNA, 1970.

Lina and Kathy dropped their bags on the floor and collapsed onto the two beds of the hotel room.

"Damn! I thought we were going to have to *walk* all the way from Salzburg!" sighed Lina wearily from her side of the little room.

37

"I don't understand it," said Kathy in her soft Pennsylvania accent. "Why wouldn't anyone pick us up? We never had this much trouble getting a ride before."

"Maybe we look dangerous." Lina pulled up her legs and began rubbing her feet. "So far I'm not very impressed with these weird Austrians. I still get the shivers thinking about the hungry leer on that revolting old Salzburger who showed us our room. Ugh!"

Kathy giggled. "He *wanted* you, Lina."

"Oh, he did, did he? How about that repressed Frenchman who wanted *you*? The one who kept slipping love notes under the door?" Kathy made a sound of disgust as Lina continued. "Remember him? I don't know, maybe we shouldn't try hitchhiking through the entire continent, even if it is cheaper. Even if we are poor college students."

Lina was all of five feet tall, with long, dark hair framing a pale complexion. Her penetrating brown eyes and aquiline nose reminded Kathy of a classic Greek face, or even a madonna by Raphael. Then that sparkling laugh would gaily shatter whatever revered aura of antiquity the face had inspired. It was a laugh that once had prompted another friend to express a wish to bottle and sell it. Her pet parrot, Ulysses, had already perfected its lilting patter.

The Spaniards and Italians generally fell for Lina. The French, Germans and Austrians generally fell for Kathy, with her sandy blonde hair, soft-spoken voice and mysterious wide-set blue eyes.

"Yeah, even if it's the only way we can afford to travel."

"No, really, I mean it. We've been lucky so far. But barely. I can still see the look on your face when those two teenaged truck drivers pulled off the highway and into a clearing in the woods. I saw it all over your face, 'This is *it*. We're going to be raped and killed right *here*.'" Lina laughed as she got up to check out the view from the window. Sure enough. It was still there. Still Vienna. She looked around for the backpack of food. As traveling partners, Lina and Kathy were a matched set. Kathy was a patient, almost submissive follower. Lina read the maps and found the roads. She was high-strung, impatient and capable of a good amount of bilingual backtalk when and if needed.

"Yeah, I know," replied Kathy. "I'll never forget that. Ever. And how about the semi truck ride through the Alps in a blizzard, eh? You caught that cold? Lost your voice? Girl, was that a relief!"

"Very funny," Lina called back as she spread peanut butter on a stale piece of bread. The peanut butter from home had been waiting for them at the American Express office in Nice. For weeks since, as they wended their way through southern France, Switzerland and western Austria, they hoarded and savored it. It was almost gone now.

"So what do we do first? I mean, here, in Vienna?" asked Kathy.

"Learn German, I suppose."

"Besides that."

"I mean it," insisted Lina. "Think about it. If we could say more than 'ja' and 'nein' and 'bitte,' we might have gotten that nice old farmer who finally did pick us up today to change the radio back to the Beethoven concert instead of that post-nuclear mutant rock music he switched it to as soon as we got in the car."

"What a nice old guy. He did it for us, you know."

"Yeah, yeah, okay, he was nice. You can die of frustration from such niceness."

Lina noticed that Kathy was falling asleep. She frowned. Kathy used to do this at school—fall asleep before supper. Then Lina, the obliging roomie, would bring her a tray.

Lina said casually, "I wonder if Vienna is safe at night, for two sweet young things, I mean. Looking for dinner at ten p.m. because one of them fell asleep at five p.m. and didn't wake up until nine p.m."

"Why don't you just go find a grocery store and bring something back for when I wake up?" Kathy mumbled as she pulled a blanket up. Lina studied the floor.

"Maybe I will...." She felt like being alone anyway. Vienna was having a strange effect on her. It was a depressing city, somehow, and she could feel it rubbing off on her. She put on her coat, grabbed a net sack for the food she would find, and slipped out, wondering how she would ask, in German, for a grocery store. Hand signals, maybe? she wondered. Or I could point to my open mouth. She smiled at her own joke as she descended the stairs.

Vienna was gray and cold. The walls, the sky, the sullen faces on the drivers and pedestrians. The acrid smell of diesel fuel was familiar. Lina made her way, unhurried, through

39

the rush hour crowds. On a wide sidewalk near a restaurant, she stopped to watch an old gentleman bend over at the waist and kiss the hand of a matronly woman, who obviously savored it.

How quaint, Lina thought. I hope they know each other. How utterly old world. But does he really mean it? How serious is this show of studied gentility if they can as easily let you walk from Salzburg to Vienna? Polite neglect, that's what it is. Look what they did to Schubert and Mozart.

Suddenly, the square buildings, the narrow streets, the gray hollowness of Vienna, all fell like a smothering shroud on her spirit. Her heart was heavy. Just as suddenly, she noticed how tired and weak she had become.

I must have overdone it today, she thought, turning a corner onto a narrow cobblestone walkway to lean against the wall and catch her breath. Got to get back. I'll find food later. This is too much work. God, this place is sad! I wonder what the altitude is. It couldn't be very high. Certainly not higher than Colorado.

She turned back, mustered her energy to make her way to the hotel. Climbing the hotel stairs took longer than she anticipated, with all the pauses for air. When she got to the room, she fell on the bed and stared at the ceiling anxiously.

"Kathy?" she called gently. No answer.

Lina turned to the wall and closed her eyes. Her heat beat faster as the anxiety triggered adrenalin. "I'll be all right. I'll be fine," she murmured quietly, careful not to awaken Kathy. "Someone is missing here. That's all. I'm missing something, someone, here. I'm here too late. But that's all right. It's all right. *Stop it!*"

She was gasping, on the verge of panic, when she remembered that deep breathing relieved fear. She closed her eyes and began the long, sustained breaths as her thoughts continued.

I can see it on their faces: the people are cold and uncaring. *Still indifferent!*

Gradually the anxiety subsided. Soon she was able to stand again at the open window and continue to breathe deeply as she watched the city below.

People went to and fro, having destinations, business to attend to, people to see, consult, visit.

What an empty city! she cried to herself.

The long trolley ride from the city center to St. Marx Cemetery was monotonous. The dreary industrial road was unusually wide for a European street, with trolley tracks fanning out in wide arcs at the endless succession of intersections south of Vienna. Just when Lina had decided the trolley had probably reached Hungary's outer provinces, a long cemetery wall came into sight on the right. The wide avenue no doubt continued into infinity, but Lina and Kathy left the noisy conveyance there.

For a hazy weekday, not too many people were about, even at the much larger cemetery adjacent to the older St. Marx. A woman stood near the gate of the larger cemetery, selling flowers. Lina bought two carnations from her—a white and a red. Kathy chose one white carnation.

They visited first the larger cemetery, with its massive and inventively designed marble headstones and monuments of a sort. They strolled around, pointing out to each other the sometimes maudlin, sometimes marvelous and striking marble works. In that garden of heavy, sweeping yet bizarre forget-me-not sculpture, they eventually came across the grave of Beethoven, whose monument was a respectable size, though the leaves and debris of winter had not been swept out. The grave was autumnal in spirit, even in spring, and sunlight shone through the high, old trees that surrounded it. Lina left her red carnation there in silent tribute to the composer's passion and fire.

She was still vaguely depressed, though no longer anxious. Together, she and Kathy had already been through France, Spain and Switzerland, and nowhere had she been plagued with such a profound sense of desolation. The city seemed to her a large, gray marble and concrete monument to what once was. She repeatedly thought to herself—and once even mentioned to Kathy—that it felt here like all the lively, witty people had left, never to return. The city was now only a tomb.

Why are we at a cemetery, for God's sake? We've been in Europe for two months and this is the first time I've felt the urge to visit a cemetery!

Lina and Kathy meandered into St. Marx. Its smaller area held many fewer outsized monuments. The bushes, trees and undergrowth there were more out of control. It looked vaguely like the untended back lot of a commercial nursery—peaceful but unkempt, and slightly tacky. Curiously, the trees were not as old as those of the other, more recent cemetery.

41

They noticed many graves were marked only with metal tags in which yellowing, waterstained slips of paper were encased in plastic.

Mozart is buried here somewhere. Here, amid the young trees, the metal tags and the undergrowth. Why did it seem so incongruous? An elegant artist in a decidedly inelegant place. No one she asked could point out his grave. The two travelers wandered up one lane and down another.

"Don't these Viennese know where they put their most famous son?" asked Kathy.

"Maybe they don't care," replied Lina.

Bewilderment had turned to annoyance when they trudged past a little grotto-like area encircling a modest marker surrounded—isolated—by bushes and unpruned trees. The name "Mozart" was etched on white stone. Lina stopped and stared as if taken by surprise. She gazed mutely at the spot as Kathy stepped gingerly toward the headstone. The soft breezes rustled the new leaves of spring. The "nursery" was coming alive again in shades of pale green overhead and pastels of the flowering brush below. It had been a winter too long and too cold, and the buds had begun to fly open, seemingly unbidden.

Lina approached the marker, there in the church-like grotto. "This isn't his grave," she said to Kathy.

"What do you mean? How do you know?"

"I don't know. I don't know why I said that, but this isn't his grave," she said, hesitating. "But it's close enough, I suppose." Kathy shrugged and waited quietly while Lina kneeled to place the white flower on the mound of earth. Her thoughts were as in meditation—solemn and unaware of her surroundings except for the name, "Mozart," and the snowy whiteness of the flower that was so long in coming.

To match the white of this snow, and his soul....

II.

Come, take a sweet embrace,
My faithful friend,
And likewise may heaven
Forever keep you as a friend to me.

—*La Clemenza di Tito*
Opera by W. A. Mozart, 1791

VIENNA, Winter, 1790-91.

The embers were almost out now, but the shell of the stove was faintly warm. Franz closed its door slowly, contemplating the cold that would envelop the room now that they were completely out of wood. Without thinking, he stretched his arms around the short, round porcelain stove and clung to it, attempting to capture some of the warmth. He shut his eyes and his head swam. He opened them again. The warmth felt good against his cheek. He turned the other cheek to the fading warmth. His head still throbbed from the headache he'd awakened with that morning.

Ah, yes, this isn't so bad. But it won't get better. When the last of the embers die away, then what?

He squinted against the bright glare of light shed by the light, overcast sky. Outside, the cold winter wind whistled around the window panes. Franz tried to shut out the lonely, sad sound. It reminded him of the nights at Kremsmunster— endless, lonely nights lying awake in bed, wanting the warm touch and kind word of another person, be it mother or sibling. But that was long ago, and far away.

"Franz, where is the staff paper? And the new quills. I can't seem to find anything." Wolfgang came out of the music room and stopped short at the sight of Franz hugging the stove. "What are you doing?" he said. Without waiting for an answer, he strode across the room to rummage through the cabinets.

"Trying to get warm," Franz muttered, staring at the floor.

"I saw them yesterday, so I know we have some." Wolfgang slammed the cabinet doors shut, creating a loud booming sound in Franz's already besieged head. "Damn!"

"I think I might be sick," Franz offered morosely.

More slamming. "Aha! I found them. Did you know you'd put them in the desk?" asked Wolfgang. Then, "What do you mean 'sick'? You never get sick, Snai, don't be so dramatic."

Silence. Wolfgang seated himself again at the desk and proceeded to write swiftly. For several minutes, the only sound in the room was the methodical scratching of quill point on paper. At length, he said, "Come here, will you? I want to show you something now that I've got it on paper."

Franz groaned and tried to speak. Instead, he began to

cough. Wolfgang looked up quizzically. He disappeared into the bedroom again. When he re-emerged, he was carrying a large quilt, which he placed around Franz's shoulders, tucking it in where his arms met the stove. He knelt down and squinted at Franz, who stared back groggily. His eyes were swollen. Wolfgang held his hand to Franz's face and frowned. Feverish.

"You have a fever, Snai. It won't do for you to be cold. We'll need heat if you're to get better," he concluded. Funny that Snai is ill, he observed. He hasn't been ill in all the time I've known him. This must be serious.

"I'm going for firewood," he announced, going for his greatcoat.

"No! Don't!" exclaimed Franz anxiously. "I'll be better, really. I don't want you to be ill, too. Stay here, please." If Wolfgang goes out into that cold, hard wind, he will be ill much more quickly and with worse consequence than whatever I could catch, he thought. Franz saw that his words were having no effect on Wolfgang, who was busy taking the last of the money out of the little leather box.

Dammit, he's stubborn. "Wolfgang, please, don't go out there." Franz was pleading now as he stood up and lurched toward the door, just managing to intercept Wolfgang as he reached for the latch. Franz suddenly felt the room sway and Wolfgang found himself holding up his friend, still wrapped in the quilt.

"Snai, Snai," he said softly, holding his head steady. "Come here, get in bed." Wolfgang half carried Franz to the bedroom and helped him onto the bed.

"Please don't go out in the cold," Franz murmured weakly. "I'll be fine. Stay here. Don't leave. You'll catch your death." He began to shiver while Wolfgang scanned the closet for more quilts. Suddenly fear gripped Franz as he realized he could be fatally ill. One never knew where a fever might end.

"Wolfgang...don't let me die," he grasped Wolfgang's arm and whispered fearfully, "...I need you and you need me...if I die, what will you do? If you die, what will I do?" His voice faded as he spoke. Then he fell asleep.

He must be exhausted, thought Wolfgang, placing Franz's arm under the quilts. He took a chair and sat down by the bed to think out the situation. He looked again at Franz's weary face. He was deep in sleep. So suddenly. How strange. He's afraid of dying on me. What if he does? What *would* I do?

His gaze shifted to the bedroom window, where the wind whipped around the corner room and whistled in through both window casings. Another long, hard winter had gripped the city. He sighed. Winters were hard on everybody. But how would he keep Franz warm? *Basta!* No one else could be paid to go out in this storm. He stood up and leaned over the bed.

"Forgive me, my friend," he said to his sleeping assistant. "But I'm going for wood. I promise not to get sick. A Mozart, like a Sussmayr, keeps his promise. Remember that."

Minutes later, the door closed behind him.

VIENNA, Winter, 1790-91.

The last chunk of glowing wood collapsed in the stove, breaking the stillness of the dark room.

"Are you still awake?" Franz's voice broke the silence. He was too cold to sleep.

"Yes," Wolfgang answered from beneath the quilt. It was almost pitch black where they lay on cots near the stove, wrapped and huddled under all the quilts they had been able to gather up before this first winter storm arrived. Now it was here, and they were still unprepared for it.

"Are you very cold?"

"I may as well be lying on the road outside," Wolfgang answered stiffly, "...I wonder." A few seconds passed.

"Wonder?"

Wolfgang sighed loudly. "Will we survive the winter?"

Franz shifted uneasily under his quilts, trying to get comfortable. This had not been their best idea—these low cots were not comfortable, they discovered. They should have simply moved the bed into the main room and closed off the bedroom and music room for the winter. Of course, there would have been no room for anything else. Franz resolved to do it anyway, in the morning. For now, however...at two a.m., or whatever time it must be now...what was there to do but shiver?

"Will we?" Wolfgang was thinking out loud again. "I wonder how much longer we can manage like this." Winters in Vienna could be bitterly cold, long and relentless.

"Were you never this cold, even as a child?" asked Franz in an effort to shift the emphasis, if only a little.

"Not like this. I'm not sure why. Children are smaller,

46

so shouldn't they chill faster?" He stopped to chuckle. "Maybe I didn't notice it as much. Maybe I was too overwhelmed by the incredible boredom of life in Salzburg, or the terrible filth of so many inns we visited when we traveled that I never noticed the cold. Then, I imagine cold was the last of our discomforts."

He began humming a clock tune he'd just sold. Humming turned to guttural intoning, which in turn became full-throated singing. Franz soon joined him and together they harmonized for several minutes, ending after two cadences instead of one, just for the fun of it.

Franz shifted in his cot.

"When you write," he asked, "Where does it come from?"

"You mean the music?" Wolfgang was staring at the ceiling, remembering the fields of summer. Trying to remember the warmth.

"Yes. Where does it come from...its essence?"

"Where does my music come from...," Wolfgang repeated to himself. "Not many people ask me that any more. I suppose they still assume I pull it out somewhere between my head and my hand. My heart, maybe."

"And? Is that true?"

"Not likely!" he chuckled. "Maybe somewhere between my head and the sky...." Franz waited patiently. "...Sometimes I wake up...and it's singing in my head. Most often, though, I just hear it. It occurs to me, Snai. That's all. It just occurs to me."

"But...."

"But I must also be aware. I listen for it, sometimes. But...not in the way of a concert. It's more like...this is difficult to explain. I hear the whole thing at once. I am aware of the entire structure at once."

The silence was broken momentarily by the sound of a lone carriage rattling along the cobblestones below.

"It's a part of *me*," he continued. "Sometimes what I hear later, in performance, I realize is embarrassingly personal and I wonder why I have bared my soul so. But as far as its essence, I assume you mean where it ultimately comes from?"

"Yes."

"I don't know. It's just there. It comes, it sings, I write it down. Or if someone plays a tune for me, I immediately hear variations, or a better tune if it's a bad one. It's very complicated and simple at once, you see? People shouldn't carry on

47

so much about it. It makes me too self-conscious. This whole genius business is a nuisance."

"Is it like a thought that comes unbidden, then?" Franz persisted.

"What a nag you are! Yes, rather like that. But much more insistent than any idle thought. I write the music down almost to clear my head of it. But then more comes. And I write more. But after so many hours, the headaches come. And then it's a struggle...."

"Has it always been like that? Since you were a child?"

"More so now than when I was younger." Wolfgang's voice was tinged with melancholy.

"Do you miss being a child?"

"In some ways. I miss the special sense of anticipation, and the feeling of well-being. But not the loneliness, or the boredom."

"Do you sometimes wish it were all over?" The way I do, Franz thought.

"Not often," replied Wolfgang, taken aback at the question.

"I do...sometimes," Franz said glumly. "Except when...your music. It makes me grateful to be alive to hear it."

"Thank you, Snai. Would that all of Vienna felt that way."

Several moments of silence passed as they contemplated. The muffled sound of the dying stove fire grew fainter.

"I love you," said Franz.

"I know." Moments passed as Franz decided how to explain his feelings.

"I love you first...and your music second, you see, although it is difficult to separate the two...you are so much like your music...I don't know quite how to put it."

Wolfgang smiled. "You mean if I were a farmer, you'd still love me?"

"Of course," replied Franz seriously. Realizing Wolfgang's mood, he added, "Then I'd be a field hand, wouldn't I? And we'd be very bored, I think."

"Yes, but maybe we wouldn't be so cold. They say hay is better than a hundred quilts."

"Well, what are we waiting for? Is it too late in the winter to grow hay?" Chuckles soon gave way again to silence.

"I love you, Snai. You're the most loyal, generous, goodhearted friend I've ever had." The wind began to whistle mournfully around the window panes. "Even my own father turned against me in the end. So did Nannerl. My mother, God bless her, didn't live to see that. And Constanze thinks she doesn't love me any more. And maybe she doesn't. When she left me, I gave myself up as unlovable and unwanted. That's when I prayed for help."

Franz turned on his side and peered in the darkness toward Wolfgang's cot.

"Life had become impossible, you see," he continued, hesitantly. "I don't care to...live when there is no one to love. And no one to love me back. And I had always had that. At least I thought I did. So I had nearly decided to...give up and die, when I met you at that rehearsal, so intense and completely guileless, like the brother I never had. I don't know where you really came from, Snai, although I know where you're from, but I'm grateful you're here...."

Franz was grateful for the darkness that hid his welling eyes.

"May we always be brothers," Wolfgang continued, his voice wavering. "Promise me that."

"I promise. If you promise me...never take your own life...Promise me that...."

Silence.

"*Promise!*" Franz insisted hoarsely.

"I promise."

Through the night, the storm had wrapped itself around the city like a shroud. By morning, it left its chill covering of white to bedazzle the rich and curse the poor. Several very young and very old had died in the night.

LOS ANGELES, 1950.

With a brisk and purposeful walk, Willy led the way through the orchestra to the concert grand piano that stood gleaming under the bright stage lights. The conductor followed him as he approached the front of the stage. They acknowledged the low rumble of applause with a brief bow.

He cast a strikingly handsome silhouette. His brown eyes were at once bright and penetrating. He had a sharp profile, a look of cool intelligence and a shock of dark hair that

49

often fell over his forehead during performances. At five feet, seven inches, he was slight, but his was an enormous presence onstage.

The son of a Russian/Spanish father and a Polish mother, both immigrants, he had grown up on Manhattan's Upper East Side where his father owned a bookstore. Harry Kapell always listened to the classical music station on the radio, so it was no surprise to the family when Willy asked for piano lessons. He exhausted a series of mediocre piano teachers, none of whom were successful with him, because none of them had thought to teach technique, or to hand him a book of unabridged classics. Dorothea LaFollette finally did. Six weeks later he had won his first competition—a dinner with pianist José Iturbi. Willy was ten years old. By age nineteen, he had appeared twice with the Philadelphia Orchestra and in New York as a winner of the prestigious Naumburg Award. As the winner of the Town Hall Endowment Series Award in 1942, he was the youngest person ever to have received that award.

And now, eight years later, his performance career was in high orbit. In more ways than one. He had performed before audiences in South America, Europe, Australia, Israel, and the United States. People were comparing him to Horowitz and Rubenstein. He was very, very good. And he knew it.

Applause sounds like a huge waterfall, Willy decided as his eyes scanned the crowd. The overhead lights shone unusually bright on the stage. He sat at the piano and adjusted the bench as the conductor mounted the podium and turned to the orchestra. Moments later, the conductor's baton cut through the air in a wide flourish. The concerto began.

Willy sat, tense and motionless, concentrating, listening, waiting for his entrance. He felt it curious that he could simultaneously ignore and acknowledge the presence of so many others out beyond the lights. This performance was for them as much as it was for himself. More so, in fact. If everything went right, they would soar with him tonight—and he would make it go right! After a full summer sabbatical absorbing Mozart's music and letters, Willy was ready to play Mozart. Ready to infuse into the music all that it demanded, and possibly more.

He closed his eyes. The light, graceful music of Mozart's piano concerto in A, K. 414, poured out of the strings like liquid silver. The woodwinds' notes flew like doves in a sunlit field.

Willy's hands at last lighted on the keys with a touch at once commanding, gracefully expressive and exquisitely articulated. His tone was like spun gold. Orchestra members watched him out of the corners of their eyes as they had so often in rehearsal. Here was a consummate master of the piano.

At times, Willy sat almost rigid at the instrument, the only evidence of involvement being his occasional glance at the conductor for a cue. His eyes were fixed on the keyboard, or were closed in intense concentration. Then his body swayed to and fro, or side to side, following his fingers as they moved swiftly up and down the keyboard.

It's going well, he thought. Quite well.

As before, he began to feel the familiar tingling in his head and arms as he played, and his solar plexus again seemed to reverberate with the music. His chest, too, filled with a pleasant urgency, not unlike the feeling of being in love. The warm energy gradually radiated throughout his body and upward to his head, exciting, uplifting his spirits as the music pressed for expression.

ALBUQUERQUE, Summer, 1984.

Lina opened her eyes to the limitless sky above New Mexico, her fingers slowly curling around the sides of the hammock. A gentle breeze rustled the leaves of the cottonwood trees. But she was unaware of the cool summer evening. A cord snaked from the portable cassette player in her pocket to the earphones on her head. Since the appearance of the portable players, she had worn one like another piece of clothing, with the headphones hanging forever around her neck or on her head, and the player hanging on a belt or tucked into a skirt pocket.

Though she was rarely without music throughout the day, she always waited for the solitude of evening to listen to her latest acquisitions. Tonight it was an old performance recording of the Mozart Piano Concerto K. 414, with the Los Angeles Philharmonic and William Kapell—she'd received a copy from a friend in Santa Fe whose passion for the piano was unmatched among her friends. The unusual beauty and sensitivity of this performance had caught her by surprise, and

51

now she listened carefully, shutting out everything else.

Perfect balance of technique and expressiveness, she mused. This Kapell played like a god. Too bad he's dead. Wonder how he might have developed after a few more decades if he played like this at...what age? She reached for the cassette case and read the performer's dates on the label. Mentally calculating, she concluded he died at age thirty-one.

She flipped the case back on the hammock and closed her eyes again. The second movement filled her head and chest with a sound like light from the heavens. The sensation of warmth it created in her head and chest radiated to the rest of her body. It was especially strong in her arms and hands. She tried to analyze what was happening.

It's like an aura, she realized. I can feel every nuance of the melody, rhythm and harmony...exactly...like an actress might know every subtlety of emotion, movement and interplay. The trills and mordents seemed to spin off into brighter, higher concentrations of energy. The tones of the piano sparkled like sunlight in moving water—blending, fading, flashing, swirling, splashing. Phantom fingers lightly touched her forehead, as had often happened in meditation. She wanted to sing along, but knew it wouldn't be enough.

Better to merge with the music, to *become* the music, the light, the color, the rhythm.

When the music ended, she felt balanced, caressed. Loved. Her eyelids felt heavy. Already the sunlight slanted as the sun lowered in the west. She put the tape player down and closed her eyes, giving in to her drowsiness. Moments later, she was asleep.

Pink flowers. Carnations, roses, field lilies, tulips, chrysanthemums....

There must be hundreds of flowers here! Lina slowed her pace as she sped airily through the brilliant, sunlit meadow. Music rang in her ears as she slowed to light on a patch of grass near a field of pansies. As she sat, a shadow fell across the flowers near her. She turned, looking up to meet the eyes of a tall, white-robed figure. She recognized her Teacher.

Lina, he said without speaking. His smiling eyes were the color of the sky. *Come with me.*

She looked to see two hands, palms up, held out to her. She took them and, again feeling a fine lightness of body, felt herself rising swiftly into a clear, blue sky. Connected by one grasp of outstretched arms, they passed together over vivid, brightly colored terrain. Lina gasped in delight. From her unique vantage point, she saw crystal clear lakes glistening in the morning sun, and boldly colored sunsets above rolling green hills. Her eyes widened—she could see the bottom of the lake! She saw the molecules of light, the hues of the sun's rays. They went higher still, where she saw the earth's broad curve on the clear horizon.

Look there, below, said her companion.

She saw cities and villages, jets cutting through the air, cars like ants coursing the highways, ships at sea. She saw life on earth. The joys, dreads, accomplishments, failures and the ever-present hope and endeavor that drove mankind and womankind forever forward.

In years past, you were part of a great experiment to bring beauty and balance to the people of the world. And you succeeded. Never forget this. Seek peace in yourself.

Her Teacher was gone. A loud buzzing and feeling of immobility overtook Lina's senses as her astral body returned to her sleeping figure in the hammock. At last, after regaining herself and awakening, she lay motionless, staring blankly at the dark sky.

It never failed to amaze Lina that night lights in New Mexico, those on the ground and those in the sky, twinkled in the rarified atmosphere. But what would ever hope to match the colors of her dream? The brilliance of light she had just experienced? If those lights were a hint of the real existence, then surely this earth existed only in shadows.

And if that were so, then artists who worked with light and color could only be attempting to recapture those colors. Could they have experienced similar dreams? And what of composers? Did they not also try to recapture what they heard in the other dimensions? To bring those sounds "down to earth"? Is this what art is all about? Remembering a far-off existence that is, in fact, as close as an early evening nap? And dancers! Aren't they attempting to be as light and effortless as she had just felt, flying around the world on the palm of a cosmic guide?

She pulled the earphones up and absentmindedly wound the cord around the player. And wasn't Mozart similarly reaching for the cosmos?

A warmth filled her heart at the thought of the name. *My friend. My dearest and best of friends. I'm sorry. I'm so very sorry.*

Tears stung her eyes. She blinked, puzzled as she observed her reaction. What is *this*? She moved her arm up to rest across her forehead. Her mouth tightened, a little at first and then more. She broke into sobs.

"I'm sorry," she cried softly in the darkness. "There was so much more to do, wasn't there? It's all my fault. All my fault...."

The dull, far-off roar of a night flight gradually filled the air as it approached and then faded. Somewhere in the distant neighborhood a dog barked at unseen danger. Out of open doors and windows, the sounds of a television comedy spilled into the still night air.

The stars shone like so many spirits in the night.

ONE WEEK LATER.

Dear —,

Agh! Spare me another visit to my hometown! It's so deadly depressing. The people there are goodhearted and generous enough, but so *morbid*! Oh, yes!—and the invariable result is that I get so anxious and desperate to leave!

Have I ever told you about my aunts' interminable *mitotera* (gossiper) sessions in my grandmother's kitchen? They inevitably wind around to the obituary call. You see, everyone in Antonito is dead or dying—it stands to reason, after all, since all the young people moved away thirty years ago. I predict in ten years, no one will be left except dogs and priests.

Well, I finally noticed their pattern of conversation during the obits. It's always the same phrase, and the upward lilt of the last syllable leaves a peculiar aura of fatalism in the air: "*Se murió*"—meaning he or she died. One aunt will say this about some poor neighbor or friend or relation, and she will speak quite matter-of-factly, while her inflection adds, "and nothing we do or say will change that." Then, as if on cue, they all look at the floor. It's a ritual.

"Se murió."

I realize death has a special hold on the Hispanic people—it's a kind of perverse fascination with death—its inevitability, its terror, its capriciousness. The grief it brings. But you know, I think for them grief is a luxury of a sort. It's easier (and somewhat self-indulgent) to remain idle and grieving than it is to move forward and continue with the business of living. Even to dwell in memory once in a while, as in the ramblings of these conversations on dead friends. I don't know, it seems to me a waste of time and thought.

When I saw them all staring at the floor, I wanted to jump up and say, "Hey! We're all alive! Let's go for a walk! Let's sing! Let's get out of this kitchen and *do* something!" Or I'll do something desperate.

On the way home, my sisters were having a lot of fun mimicking them—"se murió" and its curious cadence. I don't suppose it's very gracious to laugh at the ways of our elders, especially since we aren't really part of that culture anymore. Not entirely. Liz calls us "cultural *coyotes*" (coyote is "half-breed" in New Mexico slang). We moved to Albuquerque when I was six—so Dad could find a living wage. So we could move into the 20th century. So I wouldn't die young, of the overwhelming boredom that only living in The Sticks can bring.

Now that I think of it, it would be confining to be entirely Hispanic, or Anglo for that matter, with a certain inevitable narrowness of view. I have a good view here, on the cultural fence. I see the best and the worst moments and characteristics of both groups. I also see what keeps the two sides forever apart, and what occasionally brings them together.

Unfortunately, it's also quite lonely on the fence. I don't belong to either side, really. Who cares.... You know, if I didn't have you to write to, so far away at school, I'd go crazy. So it sounds like solitude is a career with me, maybe. Hum?

I found a wonderful t-shirt. It says, "If I'd known I was going to live this long, I would have taken better care of myself!" It's black with little white lettering. I'll wear it next time I take Mom back *there*.

From the fence,
Lina

VIENNA, 1791.

Die Zauberflote was not Wolfgang's most challenging libretto to set to music, but it had been a challenging libretto to write. He and Franz, who first outlined a plot, worked diligently and carefully. Emmanuel Schikaneder, the commissioner of the work, frequently read the libretto in progress and felt free to alter plot lines or verses. While Schikaneder was quite pleased with his own writing, such as it was, Wolfgang proceeded tentatively and with many second thoughts. Franz suspected Wolfgang had little faith in his own ability to write verse, and was therefore inclined not only to fret, but to joke about it. Hadn't he already labeled it a "grand opera"? As if this story of animals, half-humans, fairies and magic were in the grand Italian tradition to which he was accustomed?

Wolfgang wasn't entirely sure why he'd agreed to write an opera after so long away from the genre. He was frankly weary. The pull of money was the main motivating factor now, although he couldn't rule out Franz's fervor for the project. There was a curious passion in his manner whenever he held forth about Austria's "desperate need" for an indigenous operatic tradition.

"Real Austrian opera," Franz would say, envisioning the best of his dreams. "Our own stories written by our own poets in our own language, sung to our music. Written by our own composers." This last comment made as he looked pointedly at Wolfgang.

"How shall we do it, then?" asked Wolfgang. "What will your Austrians want to see?"

Franz considered for a moment, then spoke slowly. "Didn't you tell me once that in France, where they have no taste in music or theatre, they go wild over magic and legends? Wouldn't that capture the simple minds and hearts of our fellow countrymen, while at the same time singing to them of things that mattered, like Fraternity and Loyalty?"

Wolfgang studied the candle flame. He said, "German legend, yes. Fantasy is innocent, though I wouldn't care to do it all the time. You know, as a child I often wondered how much more memorable the church's teaching would have been to us all had it been presented onstage with music, bright costumes and well-acted stories."

"This will be even better. I've been reading a fascinating book on Egyptian legend. It would allow for more exotic scenery and costumes than anything Biblical or...."

"But you just said you wanted Austrian opera for Austrian people!" Wolfgang interjected.

"I only meant that Austrians should be employed to

perform anything they want. Even Italian opera, if it comes to that."

"Well, I suppose...."

"Does it matter how an opera champions Fraternity and Loyalty as long as it does so in a language most people will understand completely? And so long as it doesn't offend the Emperor?"

"To hell with the Emperor!"

"Please! Keep your voice down," cautioned Franz. "Don't forget, you *are* still a Freemason. One impulsive remark is all he needs to destroy your standing in Vienna for good."

"What standing?!" Wolfgang muttered angrily. "And what terrible notions to threaten the royal ass: brotherhood, universal love and beneficence. Why, I can't think of anything more disastrous for the crown than these!"

Franz frowned and said nothing. He heard only second-hand of the lively Masonic meetings with their revolutionary ideas of equality, wisdom and, above all, brotherhood. Not that Wolfgang was so avid a member these days. Not since the argument. Now he minded his own store, and visited with friendly brothers only in casual gatherings.

One such Masonic acquaintance, Schikaneder—theatrical manager of a grimy little theatre on the outskirts of town— had approached Wolfgang with a commission for a singspiel. At first Wolfgang had avoided him, but it soon became clear that he could scarcely afford to turn down any commission, no matter how demeaning.

"Franz, I really don't care how far you go in tweaking the Emperor's nose with this libretto," said Wolfgang wearily. "Nor do I much care how much Austrian or Masonic fraternity goes into this opera—love is the best operatic element I know of—but if you can possibly keep the pretentious Herr Schikaneder off my back, I would...."

"I'll take care of him."

"Yes, well. I suppose you will. How can you not?" Wolfgang smiled resignedly. Franz had already had several disagreements with Schikaneder over the story line, which the latter had seen fit to rearrange. At first Franz was annoyed, but realizing that he was dealing with an actor, he decided the best reaction was no reaction. It was discouraging enough that this work was not destined for the court theatre, but instead a third-rate theatre, and that he must deal with a hard-headed, calculating traveling minstrel such as this.

Furthermore, Franz knew Wolfgang could write verse well, despite any criticism Schikaneder put forth. He remembered the poem Wolfgang had shown him, written for his sister Nannerl on the occasion of her wedding. He also had shown Franz, with more than a little pride, a poem he had written when a pet starling had died. In preparing the libretto, Franz immediately had laid out a simple plot, with characters drawn from books and tales, found here and there. He even drew some of his story from vivid dreams he continued to experience at the time.

When his turn came, Wolfgang found that writing verse wasn't as difficult, or time-consuming, as he'd thought it might be. He actually took great joy in it, and looked forward to his collaborative meetings with Franz and, later, their friend Karl Gieseke, a poet of some repute to whom they referred as "the expert." Together, they hammered out a fantasy-laden allegory of life in which the quest of a young prince is aided by three spirit guides and a magic flute, all of which serve to teach and assist the prince in his encounters with evil and misfortune. The final tests of his worthiness come in three trials—silence, fire and water. Only after proving himself in these trials does he emerge a true Brother in the Light. His fair princess proves herself as well, and joins the prince in ruling over the enlightened Temple of Wisdom.

"It reads well, and it looks like a great vehicle for fun and mechanical stage tricks," Schikaneder had told them. "And with your music, Wolfgang, it will be irresistable."

Schikaneder had shrewdly given them an advance payment. It was shrewd, Franz later realized, because now they were locked in. If he needed to, Schikaneder would add further conditions to the work's performance. It occurred to him almost immediately to make his first demand.

"The libretto," he told them, "unfortunately, will have to have my name on it. It's only a formality, to be sure, but it's a necessity in light of the fact that the theatre is mine, and without my name somewhere in the production—other than performer, I mean—the production will be impossible, I'm afraid. Damn these lawyers, you know how it is. They insist if this isn't possible, that we must cancel the agreement and I must collect my advance."

"Damn *him!*" said Franz later. "We should have known

better than to get involved with a snake like that. What were we thinking? That we could trust that bastard?"

What to do? Agree to put his name on the libretto. It would never harm the work—or its message—but it was an annoyance nonetheless. To be used so easily by an obviously unprincipled traveling performer.

"It's no wonder he travels," said Wolfgang. "He probably has enemies all over Europe." Wolfgang pretended not to care much, but he was as outraged as Franz. When was he going to learn to be more shrewd himself? This was precisely the kind of situation his father so often had warned him about. Trust no one, he had said. Get everything in writing, he had said. Wolfgang shrugged. It would always be like this, it seemed. Someone always taking advantage. He might have dropped the opera right then and there, except Franz was so devoted to the project. It was the right thing to do, somehow. So he continued, diligently setting to music a libretto that now would have someone else's name on it. Never mind that it was not that good a text anyway. If Schikaneder wants his name on it, let it be. I was never meant to be a librettist anyway, nor was Franz for that matter—apparently.

BADEN, July, 1791.

Dear Wolfgang,

I haven't heard from you in two days. Are you all right? You really must remember to write more often—for my sake. I'm enclosing the last of the finale to Act I. I'm sure I'll get more from you soon. Accompanied by a letter perhaps?

How are you really? Are you getting enough sleep? Are you eating? Don't forget, the mind works when the body is fed. If you haven't eaten today yet, do so now if you will. A fair exchange, I think: I'll follow Constanze to tonight's party, if you eat a meal today.

"Madame" is fine, but she doesn't like it when I follow her anywhere, so it's not often pleasant between us, but rather tense. I hope this doesn't distress you, but you should know I am doing my best under the circumstances—those circumstances being that she doesn't want me here. But we've gone over this before, so I won't bother going over it yet again.

I have not been well, which is quite a joke considering

I'm at a health resort. It might be this high mountain air. Or the boredom. I've taken, in moments between copywork, to writing a few little airs. When I get back to Vienna, I would like for you to look at them, since you say my melodies are the best element in my work. Don't make me sing them, though, as this supposedly healthful water has given me a sore throat as well.

Yes, I know we shouldn't drink the water, but they told us it would clear out whatever needs clearing out. Who told us, you ask (demand, I daresay)? Why, Monsieur LeBec, the greedy bastard who runs the baths. He has Constanze talked into drinking the water. What's good for the outside is good for the inside, he says. So now I'm sick. I don't suppose I had to follow her order, but she does get rather harsh when she's crossed.

Do you suppose that in the near future, after Constanze's baby comes, we might never have to come to Baden again? I get so terribly lonely for Vienna here. Yes, the work helps. It gives me headaches to think about, and it keeps me out of the sun, but it's the long evenings at these damned parties that are wearing me out. Constanze has everyone convinced I'm no better than a stableboy, and so they treat me as such. I might as well be standing against a wall holding a torch, for all the serious consideration I get after she's done talking me down to her friends. Do you see what I mean?

If I may slip into Latin for a moment, *I only want to say that I don't think this is working out quite the way we expected it would. I mean to say that she resents both of us for what she considers my intrusion into her life. I can't say for sure that she is having an affair, because whoever he is, together they are rather good at hiding themselves. And I regret having to report that I have strong suspicions that she is, indeed, involved with someone. Now I don't want to upset you, but I don't know that my presence here will help alleviate the situation, any more than it's helped it disappear. I want to come home, Wolfgang. Living here is hell. There, I've said it. Now I won't bother you with any more bad news, but you did insist that I tell you everything, good or bad. Just chew on this news a little and let me know in your next letter what you want to do.* [Italics signify Latin throughout this letter.]

Stoll the Kroll has asked for another piece of music. Apparently the *Ave Verum* was just the beginning. "Anything," he says, " as long as Wolfgang writes it." So. There you are.

Hop to it. And, mind you, make it quick. Quicker, I daresay, than it took him to return the last piece of music you sent him. (Shall I suggest he wait until hell freezes over?)

Today's coach brought no letter from you. Now I'm really worried. This is another reason *for my wanting to come home. I know you aren't taking good care of yourself. I know you aren't eating at all because you are, instead, paying for all this at Baden. Not that life here is much better. Constanze found it necessary yesterday to take me to task for asking her where she was going. But we both know how easily ruffled she is.*

Do try to come here next week. I have so many more things to tell you. Give my regards to both Josefs. *Tell Schikaneder to eat shit,* but, oh, I think he may already have done that, since it's all he spits. *He should be grateful that you're doing this for his stupid theatre. It's the best thing that ever happened to him, or it. If he tries to change* Zauberflote *again, I would tell him to cancel the whole arrangement!* I hear a bird outside. Now I hear two. I can't manage this excitement. When will it end?

Good day, *buon amico.* Pretend I am there, a fly on the wall, and take care of yourself for the fly's sake. A thousand warm embraces from your humble servant and maligned torch-bearer,

F: X: Sussmayr
Buon Amico II

VIENNA, July, 1791.

Dearest Snai von Baden,

Baron von Snai? How shall one address the torchbearer of all the best gatherings of Baden? I hope you received my letter. I would hate for you to think I've abandoned you now that you have moved up in the world from composer to keeper of the flame.

Seriously, I have asked Constanze to behave herself regarding her disgraceful attitude toward you. If she continues, and I fear she will, I am counting on you to tell me, as this will not do. Please accept my apologies on her behalf. I have also written to her about the water. Don't be foolish, either of you. You should be drinking wine.

Well, dearest Franz, how are you? And your throat? Do take care of yourself. Heaven knows I don't know how I would manage if you, too, became ill and required the baths and God knows what else there. An affair, too, maybe? Now that might be something you would benefit from. Go ahead, then—as your dearest brother and truest friend, I dispatch you to the den of womankind with my best wishes and strongest urges. After all, you still must find your Papagena. Only take care not to fall too much in love. That would be disastrous.

I am firmly convinced that you should stay in Baden and continue to keep Constanze and her mysterious friend in check. Imagine if you were not there now, what outrageous and shocking behavior they might be flaunting in front of our friends at those same parties where you now suffer. No, Franz, you must stay there for now. Until it is over. That is, I mean to say, the pregnancy. When that comes to a finish, so will Baden. At least until her next "illness."

You are right. I have not been eating. I don't have time. There is too much to do with the singspiel. Schikaneder hounds me with messages every day, which I, of course, toss. And, then, as you know, there are those days when I just don't feel like working. It's strange, but those days seem to come more often now. Have you ever had spells like that? I've had whole months where I didn't want to write, but never days where I couldn't even if I wanted to. I wonder how much longer I can keep up appearances. And why I should bother. Who would hurt more than me if the world knew Constanze was untrue and behaved as she does? Who would care? Why do I care? I wrote Pamina's second act aria last week in precisely this mood.

At any rate, please don't worry about my health. I promise to make greater efforts to keep the body healthy and moving. No, really. And you, my friend, must promise me again to keep after her. Don't let her out of your sight. It will gain her nothing to complain to me about you, and what could Frau Weber or Thorwart say if she complained to them? I tell them you are there for her safety. Please continue to do this for me.

Tell Stoll I haven't the time to write him anything. You know I don't have the inclination either, but there's no need to tell him that. Nor do we want to lend him anything. Tell him *Zauberflote* is taking all of my time. Incidentally, when you get the next set, see that you use the white paper with the markings instead of that paper you used on the last set. I find it's easier to write on, don't you?

Well, I must tell you today I had a queer visitor. He came by quite unexpectedly and now I'm wondering why. Or maybe I know. I don't even know why I'm mentioning this, except that possibly it unnerved me a little. First of all, the fool wouldn't give me his name, or even the name of the person who sent him. Secondly, he came to commission a requiem, of all things. Thirdly, he swore me to secrecy. And finally, he looked rather startlingly sinister. It's strange, but I can't help but guess that this was no mortal. That maybe it was an omen. What do you think? He wanted a requiem. No one has ever asked me for a requiem. Now I wish he never had come. I don't want to do this, and then again I do, because I rarely have the chance any more to write in the old church style. I took his money and now I am having second thoughts. I don't know where to find him to return it, either. Ah, well, even if I did know, I couldn't return it because I've already sent most of it to the Webers. There, you see? I'm already committed. *Basta!*

I saw Pasterwicz today at the tavern. He asked for you, of course. I told him you were chasing skirts in Baden. He sends you his warmest but most bewildered greetings. I have seen neither Deiner nor Eybler. I have spent most of my time at home composing, and composing more again, which is just how I want it if I'm ever to finish. I expect another letter from you today, as that is the best part of my day—receiving letters from you and my Constanze. If I don't write back immediately, or as often, it is because of this cursed opera.

Did I say cursed? Did I? Quickly, someone throw water on my Papageno before he catches fire. Yes, yes, I know what *Zauberflöte* means to you. I completely understand what it means to you, but—yes, you might be right in wondering if we should offer it to another theatre. But then again, what other theatre? We wrote it to appeal to a certain kind of audience—one we're not likely to find at the court theatre. "Real Austrian opera for real Austrian folk," remember? Besides, Schikaneder has us tied in. Still, we might yet get out of that. Give it some thought and let me know.

Do you know I cannot keep that nameless visitor out of my thoughts? I can't help it. Why am I to write a requiem for someone I don't know and who won't tell me his name? Write and tell me to stop thinking about it.

Here, I'm eating some delicious bread—for you! Do you

see the crumbs? They're falling on the paper even as my pen scratches lazily across it. Are you happy now that I am making a tablefool of myself? *Lacci Bacci!*

It is later now, as I had to put the letter aside. We're living past our time, Franz. We no longer belong here. What else can I say? It is the truth. But—also the truth—we're still here. So what to do? You take that end of the paper and shake it, and I'll take this end and hold it fast. See what happens? Our music and words fall here and there and no one hears it, no one reads it. So why continue?

Do I frighten you or make you laugh? I frighten myself tonight. Snai! Love me always, as I love you! Never leave me, as I will never leave you!

Ever your,
Truest Friend & Most Loving Brother,
W: A: Mozart

VIENNA, August, 1791.

"Look, Snai, what a Mozart we have here!" declared Wolfgang, holding the infant at arm's length. Franz thought he detected a note of sarcasm as he stepped forward hesitantly, hands clasped behind his back, smiling cautiously in spite of the tense atmosphere. Constanze's newborn baby boy, barely two weeks old, began to squeak and fuss.

Constanze stood by, typically quiet and dour in Franz's presence. They stood in old Frau Weber's parlor, overfurnished with bright rugs, old portraits and gaudy cushioned couches. Young Karl played quietly at the large oak table by the open, lace-curtained windows.

Wolfgang quite suddenly had decided it was time Franz saw the child, and so they came, unannounced. Wolfgang ignored his wife's rudeness toward Franz, though it always puzzled him that she should reject him so completely.

"Here, you hold him, Franz. Go ahead," said Wolfgang, still beaming. Out of habit from so many weeks at Baden responding to her every beck and call, Franz looked to Constanze for permission. Wolfgang caught the glance and shot his own stern look at his wife, then back to Franz.

"Well, of course you can hold him. You don't need her

permission. He's my child, too...." He turned again to Constanze. "Isn't he?"

A chill ran through Franz. Wolfgang's gaze fixed on Constanze as the color slowly drained from her face. She returned his comment with cold silence and a neutral glare. Wolfgang met her stare with a level, self-righteous gaze before turning away and calmly handing the baby to Franz.

The air was still for what seemed an eternity to Franz. He knew how Constanze's unfaithfulness was Wolfgang's greatest heartbreak. He lived in the constant hope that she would come home for good, rather than for the occasional night's stay, which he always welcomed. He missed her. He needed her. And so he never had openly accused her—until now. For Constanze's part, Franz could see she was horrified that he had to bring it up in front of Franz—the "stranger."

Franz turned, sat down and pretended to ignore the cold exchange and quiet outrage between the parents as he centered his attentions on the child. No one had noticed how the baby had quieted down in his arms almost instantly. The child's eyes widened as he gazed up at Franz, who was immediately charmed.

Noticing Franz's reaction, Wolfgang softened and said, "There, you see? He likes you, Snai, so you must be his godfather. His name will be Franz Xaver Wolfgang, in honor of his godfather and his near-father."

"Wolfgang! We haven't even discussed this!" Constanze hissed, as if Franz would not hear.

Wolfgang regarded her briefly and turned to Franz. "Do you accept?"

Franz smiled with pride at the sudden offer, despite the tension surrounding its delivery. "I would be honored!" Franz found that he rather enjoyed annoying Constanze.

"It's settled, then."

"I'll be in the bedroom if you need me," Constanze said in a voice that was at once barely audible and decidedly outraged. "Karl! Come with me."

"Karl, too?" Wolfgang asked as Karl obediently slid off his chair.

"Yes, Karl too. Come, Karl." In a moment, she and the boy were gone.

Wolfgang's won this round, thought Franz as he played with the baby's fingers. But Wolfgang's flippancy was gone and he was now trembling.

"Did you see her face? It's true. This isn't my child!" Wolfgang whispered. Beaten, he sank down next to Franz and the child, and let his eyes wander to the infant. The baby was watching him.

What a serious little man! thought Wolfgang, and he reached over to touch the child's hand.

"No, I'm sure this is your child," said Franz studiously. "See how he resembles you...those blue eyes, that forehead. He *must* be yours. It's undeniable!" Please be happy, he thought, this is your son. This is an event that should make you happy, not suspicious.

Franz glanced at Wolfgang and noticed that he was showing every sign of sinking into another one of his long, introspective moods. Still, a faint, far-away smile crossed Wolfgang's face as he regarded Franz. "Do you really think so?" he asked hesitantly.

"Look at how he looks at you. He is your son. Why, he doesn't even look like a Weber, let alone anyone else. He's all Mozart!"

He really is, Franz thought. He's a little replica of Wolfgang. How can he not see that?

"I can't see that because I'm too upset to concentrate on it now," said Wolfgang. "Constanze is all I can think of."

Franz was startled. "What did you say?"

"I said Constanze is all...."

"No! I mean, how did you know what I was thinking just then? I was thinking 'How can he not see that?' and you answered my thought!" Franz stared incredulously at him.

"Oh, yes...," he replied distractedly. "Franz, I'm afraid...what if this child dies, too? We've lost four others. I can't seem to raise a family, or even keep one together."

The baby cooed and kicked energetically. It was the only sound in the room for several minutes as they watched the infant with growing enchantment. Why, mused Franz, was Wolfgang so unimpressed with his own seemingly magical ability to read his mind? Had he been reading his mind all these years? Was he some kind of a wizard? What a fascinating idea. He would have to ask him again later when he was not quite so preoccupied.

Wolfgang began speaking, slowly, measuring each word. "If he lives...and if I die...will you watch over him for me? As well as you have watched over me? Will you do that?" The child was studying Franz.

"Come now, do you think she would let me near him?" asked Franz at last, still watching the child's lucid eyes. Immediately he regretted it. Reminding Wolfgang of the hopeless situation he was in with regard to the Weber family and their hard hold on his life would serve only to depress him more. Wolfgang was silent. He took the baby from Franz and held him close. Franz wondered if this was the first time he had done that. The baby's hand reached up to touch his face. Wolfgang turned and kissed the little fist thoughtfully.

"You're right," he said glumly. "Franz Xaver Wolfgang is no more my son now than he ever will be. My children are trapped in the same web as their sad father. How often have I really been with Karl since he was born? Maybe it was a blessing that the others died. Maybe this one will want to join them. I don't seem to have anything to offer him...not even you."

Franz protested. "What of your name? Is your name worth nothing? He'll grow up with that, and with your example as a great artist. Look at him. Look at his face, and then tell me he isn't yours, or that you have nothing to offer him!" It seemed impossible, but the child's penetrating gaze was unnervingly wise.

Franz wondered again, could little Franz Xaver Wolfgang know what we are saying? If the father could easily read my thoughts, could not the child understand his words or emotions? The child was watching Wolfgang, cooing again, and reaching his little hand up to him.

Wolfgang watched the child for several silent minutes and then quietly announced, "You know, I think he *is* mine."

The Webers had seen to it that little Franz Xaver Wolfgang had another, "more suitable" godfather. The name was not changed.

"With any luck, and with our names, he'll have my musical abilities and your kind heart," Wolfgang had told Franz later. Then they had cried together, for Wolfgang knew little Franz Xaver Wolfgang would never feel his direct influence, musical or otherwise. He was a dispossessed father.

PRAGUE, September, 1791.

Ah! Food! What a wonderful surprise, thought Franz as he beheld the tables of Bohemian delicacies gloriously laid out before him. What heaven! Who could have imagined this? His eyes stopped at a mountain of exotic fruit arranged in colorful layers. Guests casually milled around the long tables, delicately choosing, here and there, from their generous offerings. White and gold liveried waiters slipped gracefully through the elegant crowd with trays for those too indolent to approach the tables, while still other waiters restocked the tables at a steady pace.

Franz approached an impressive mountain of fruit and was about to reach for a banana—he had always wanted to taste one—when something else caught his eye and his hand stopped in mid-air.

What delightful indecision! What excitement!

No wonder Wolfgang calls me a tablefool, he thought, just look at how I'm behaving!

He took the banana and some sliced pheasant...and then he saw the plates. Ah, yes, plates. For the civilized. Trying to move unnoticed, for he still couldn't believe it was all free, he casually took possession of a white and gold plate and proceeded to let his stomach be his guide.

Finding a secluded alcove near the orchestra, he sat down to savor his plate's contents, wondering briefly how grateful his stomach would be to receive these exceptional entries. If he got sick from stuffing himself, it would have been worth it.

With an appreciation born of prolonged bouts of hunger, Franz savored every bite. The late afternoon sun shone brilliantly through the many large French doors of the ballroom, casting the revelers in bronzed light as they milled about chatting. A small orchestra played an endless string of divertimenti in accompaniment to the chatter.

What a wonderful idea, coming to Prague, Franz mused. Well, maybe it *was* a lot of work, and Wolfgang was not well...and they were working frantically to finish the opera. But one had to have a break now and then or fall apart.

Extricating himself at last from a small group of admirers, Wolfgang moved purposefully through the crowd in search of Franz, at last finding him in an alcove busily stuffing himself with food, oblivious to all around him. Wolfgang quickly claimed the chair next to Franz and rested a tired hand on his arm.

"Let's go," he whispered.

"Go? Now? Wolfgang, look at this! Food! Lots of it, isn't it beautiful? How can you turn your back on this?"

"I must. It will make me ill again if I touch it," he replied, smiling faintly at Franz's delight. "I want to get back to work. We haven't much more to do." He squeezed Franz's arm, sat back in the chair, and closed his eyes. Let him finish, he thought, at least let him finish.

Seeing Wolfgang's anxious exhaustion, Franz took one or two more mouthfuls and set the plate aside. He tucked the banana in his waistcoat pocket and said, "All right, I'm ready." Wolfgang opened his eyes and got to his feet reluctantly. The room swayed briefly. He reached out to steady himself on the chair while Franz took his arm.

"You stood up too quickly...."

"I know, I know. Come." They walked slowly toward the big, open double doors leading to the gilded, mirrored foyer.

Franz was incredulous. "Have you ever seen such a wealth of food in one place?" he gushed. He knew he would never forget the sight for as long as he would live and starve at home.

"You should see how the French eat," Wolfgang said quietly. He winced. Arrows of swift pain shot through his stomach now and then as they descended the wide marble stairs of the palace.

"Really? More than this?"

"Much more."

Their carriage came forward quickly and the two men boarded it. As it lurched down the brick road leading to the city, Wolfgang suddenly slumped over, clutching his stomach and moaning.

"Wolfgang!" murmured Franz, slipping off the seat. He helped Wolfgang lower himself to one side, eyes closed in pain. Franz quickly tore off his own coat, rolled it up, and placed it under his head. Then he crouched on the floor of the small carriage and hugged his knees. He noticed Wolfgang's natural pallor turning even whiter. Had he not already seen him like this on several other occasions, he might have been alarmed. Today, he simply touched Wolfgang's arm in quiet support as the carriage rumbled down the road to the city.

Wolfgang began feeling nauseous. He calculated mentally how long it would take to get "home" to their lodgings, as he preferred to be sick there than in the road. By sheer force of will, he withheld his stomach's urgings. At last the carriage stopped in front of their inn.

"Can you walk?" Franz asked softly.

"I think so."

Together they stepped gingerly out of the carriage. Franz gently slipped his arm around his friend's waist as they entered the building. As they slowly ascended the stairs one step at a time, Wolfgang groaned, clutching the railing with one white-knuckled hand and holding Franz's shoulder with the other. At last they reached their rooms.

"To the closet, quickly," whispered Wolfgang. Franz helped him to the water closet and discreetly shut the door as the vomiting commenced. He turned, somewhat shaken, to ready the bed and look for bedclothes. When it seemed over, Franz opened the door and handed him a glass of wine. This was getting to be a familiar ritual and Franz performed it with sober resignation, if not still a bit of shock that it was happening at all.

As Wolfgang emerged from the closet, he nearly collapsed before reaching the bed. Franz assisted him, then stood at the foot of the bed and heaved a sigh.

With his hands holding his aching head, Wolfgang said at last, "Get the chorus. We'll start with that." Frowning, Franz obediently turned to find the music in the stack on the table. He knew better than to argue. Still, while there was no questioning that Wolfgang would not rest fully, it was worth the try to compromise....

"Don't you want to get in your nightclothes before we start?" he said from the table.

"No, it's not necessary. Bring that table here by the bed. I'll dictate and you write. This way we'll need only one candle."

Franz sighed. Thus arranged, thus resigned, he set to work with rolled-up sleeves, writing swiftly as Wolfgang dictated—sometimes speaking his intentions, sometimes singing them. The minutes melted into hours. The late afternoon sunlight faded away unnoticed. Franz lit a candle. Occasionally he obliged Wolfgang to stop in order to catch up with a passage, or to shake and stretch his arm and hand. At these times, Wolfgang would close his eyes and seem to drift away on some

70

private current of thought. Franz watched him as he lay motionless, eyes closed.

It just wasn't like him to be so still, even lying down, he thought. It was somewhat disturbing. Why was he so listless at times? It wasn't like him. Of course, he still insisted on pushing himself further than most would consider normal. Wolfgang had always been like that. He wouldn't retreat to his sickbed until near collapse. And then he would continue to work in bed until he couldn't lift the pen any more. But he always had spirit, or hope, or whatever one might call it. Stubbornness, maybe?

Later, as Franz rapidly filled in accompaniment passages, Wolfgang suddenly said, "Where are my bedclothes?"

Franz looked up and smiled through his own exhaustion. Wolfgang seemed a bit better as he smiled back weakly. Then he remembered, where was Constanze?

"Is Constanze staying at the Dusheks tonight?" Franz asked.

"No, but she wasn't sure how long she'd stay." Wolfgang's voice trailed off.

Franz looked at the clock. It was eleven p.m.

"Will you sleep now?" he asked. "I can finish this in my room. It will be done by morning, I promise. But only if you sleep now."

Wolfgang closed his eyes. He still had a headache. "All right. I'll sleep, then, and you finish the section. Then in the morning we'll start on the finale." The door opened and Constanze appeared, smiling from several rounds of wine.

"Oh, you're still up," she said lightly, removing her cape with a flourish and draping it over a nearby chair. Wolfgang's eyes opened to follow her around the room. A smile came to his face. "Stanzerl," he said softly. Franz glanced at her briefly as he gathered papers and prepared to leave.

Where the hell has she been? he thought. What will people say?

Constanze approached the bed and looked at her husband. She didn't touch him. "You're not well, Wolfgang, did you take your medicine?"

"I forgot," he lied. He hated Constanze's medicine. It was like drinking iron shavings in gutter water.

Franz continued gathering his material. He replaced the table by the wall and headed toward the door. Constanze shot a glance at him. "Why didn't you remind him, then?" she asked. She hadn't wanted to come on this trip, and especially not with *him* along. But she had to come. It was her wifely duty. Her only consolation was that she didn't have to pretend in front of Franz that she was even mildly enjoying the visit to Prague, or his quiet, disapproving looks.

Franz stopped and gazed evenly back at her. "I forgot, too." The stuff was garbage. It always seemed to make Wolfgang feel worse than before he took it. He didn't trust it, or the doctor who gave it to her, whoever he was. Constanze hadn't bothered to tell either of them.

"Where is it?" she asked, looking for the medicine. Her dress rustled as she moved around the bed to the dresser.

"Stanzerl, stop fussing over that, I feel fine," Wolfgang said. "Really." What an irritation this was becoming. And she was so adamant about it.

Franz watched her snap up the little bottle from the dresser and pour some of the vile brown liquid into a glass to mix with wine. He slipped out the door and returned to his room to work into the night on several sections of the recitative. He would probably finish at dawn.

ALBUQUERQUE, 1985.

"No!" Lina's spirit rose above the massive curved shadow of the earth, shooting high into the heavens in rigid revolt as the poison infected his body. Her soul echoed revolt with all the power of its essence.

Her scream cut through the darkness of the night. But it was too late. The horrid brown poison was spreading through his body. She shuddered violently in a fog of dread and fear. She was wet with sweat.

What an awful dream! Oh, God, never again!

She shuddered again, and again.

It was too late. Too late.

III.

You have no idea how often the exchange
between your world and mine takes place.
It is a constant thing.
The separation of our worlds
is a thin screen of learned illusion.

—Emmanuel, 1985

ALBUQUERQUE, 1985.

Dear —,

You know, because I told you, that I have been meditating for years in the late evening. It has become an essential part of my mental life. I'll tell you how it goes: first I sit very still and calm down as much as I can. I envision being surrounded and permeated with a luminescent golden white light—I imagine every cell infused with this light. Nice, yes? Then I say a short prayer for protection. Sometimes the inner voice that "says" the prayer isn't my own. Sometimes there's an accent, or it's a male voice. The struggle then begins to clear the mind of remnant thoughts and feelings and sights of the day. It's no easy trick. When my mind is occasionally "empty," even for a moment, the next moment becomes full of self-congratulatory thoughts, thus filling the emptiness!

But then...then! My psyche dives off its rooted consciousness and into the Great Otherness that meditation is. In minutes I feel a rush of energy through my whole body. In the early days, this rush startled me, and out of nervous uncertainty, I would put a stop to my meditation. Then I realized it wasn't overwhelming or uncontrollable, so I let it happen. Once, I even had the sensation of moving in a semi-circle up and down simultaneously. It felt like a ferris wheel ride, only the down and the up of it occurred at once. It was an achievement in that I didn't panic, but went with it.

The reason for this preamble is to tell you of one particular meditation I recently experienced. It is so extraordinary, please understand I can't explain it—I've never "traveled" in meditation before this—I will simply relate it as I remember it.

Moving effortlessly from where I sat deep in meditation in the blue darkness of my room, I found myself hovering near the ceiling of an unfamiliar, darkened room. It was late at night in early winter. A double bed dominated the rather small room. Someone lay in the bed. He was sick beyond any hope of recovery—I just *knew* this. Further, this very sick person was someone I knew. Almost from that moment, a tightness in my chest and throat began to grow. Spontaneous grief is a mysterious thing.

I wanted to be closer to this person. In a snap, I was there, to the right of the bed, standing and staring. A lone candle burned, giving off long shadows against the walls of the room. It was an unearthly atmosphere they evoked.

The little man in the bed seemed to be breathing with difficulty even as he slept. It was the only sound in the room, a breathing as if gasping for air. It filled the room, and my head. I must tell you now that never have I felt such compassion as I did for this person, who was at once unknown and known to me. I began to cry softly, for this man and for—myself? Maybe. I touched the quilt that covered him. I could feel the silent tears running down my cheek, and the tightness pulling in my chest.

He was terribly thin and pale. The quilts seemed to smother his slight body. The only lavish or vigorous feature about him was his fine auburn hair. His mouth was closed tightly. I wondered if he was in very much pain. The tightness in my chest turned to aching, and my legs grew weak. I found it necessary to sit down in a chair by the bed. The room was warm. A round furnace blazed in one corner. The furnishings were of the old 18th century style—rococo lines, whitened wood, floral motifs and decorated ceilings.

As I glanced around, the room blurred. I thought I was coming out of this vision until I realized I was blinding myself with tears. I looked back at the bed and reached haltingly for his hand. It was cold. I wrapped my hands around it. From that point, an unusual sensation began. My vital energies, which seemed concentrated in my arms and hands, seemed to flow from me to him. It was so intense a sensation that I soon lost touch with my surroundings.

Presently, the dying man stirred. His eyes opened and he looked at me. I knew immediately how ill he really was. I also felt like an intruder. Yet he didn't seem puzzled to see me; in fact he seemed pleased that I was there.

By now, I began to perceive that I was not myself but someone else. I saw my hands and arms were those of a young man—a friend of the dying one, who by now was peering intensely through his weary, exhausted eyes. They reflected pain and resignation. He looked old beyond his years and terribly tired. Even so, behind those blue eyes I saw a brilliant lucidity.

He was dying and he knew it. I knew it. He touched me deeply. His lips began to move and I moved forward to hear him whisper.

"Wasser," he gasped quietly. It was almost a question.

He was asking for water.

I looked around again and saw a pitcher and a cup on a nightstand. I poured water into the cup. Or rather, we did— the young man whose hands I shared. I saw his gray-stock-inged legs as we moved between the bed and the table. He, too, was rather frail in appearance. His shoulders were slightly hunched forward. He was exhausted, too. We put our right hand at the back of the dying man's neck and lifted his head to drink. He barely tasted the water before wincing and pushing his head back. I knew at once he could hold nothing down, even water. This drink was only to wet his lips. I put the cup down.

I felt a hollowness in my throat and midsection. The young man's body was aching for food. The pain was intense and could not be ignored much longer. It seemed I was becom-ing, slowly, and in stages, more and more involved in this man's very person. I looked at his hands again—they were long and slender and stained with ink. He wore a wilted white shirt with long, baggy rolled-up sleeves. His breeches were the color of moss, and he was shoeless in his stockings. I peered in the dark corner as he did, to where he had made himself a bed of quilts on the floor. He slept there when he wasn't tending to his friend. He longed, now, to retreat to those quilts.

I again looked toward the bed. He was looking at me. As our eyes met, his mouth frowned imperceptibly in silent anguish and he closed his eyes once again. Tears ran from the corners of his eyes and, one by one, rolled down into his hair, leaving a glistening trail on his sallow skin. The young man's heart skipped a beat.

Oh, my God, I thought, don't let this be the end. He can't die. Not now, there's so much still to do. We've been through so much together. No! He mustn't die!

I sensed that between these men there was an unac-knowledged but mutually nurtured courage that emerged peri-odically to keep them from crying out in fear. The man in the bed spoke, again in German. I knew what he said, though I can't explain how. He asked to be held.

I wiped my tears on my sleeve and leaned forward to-ward him. He looked at me intently with a curious combina-tion of love and melancholy, tenderness and pain, as I slipped my right hand around his small shoulders and my left hand behind his head. I pulled him up and toward me carefully. I could sense he was in the most excruciating pain in his muscles and joints. I sat on the edge of the bed, then, holding him close to me, his head against my chest, my chin touching the top of his head as I closed my eyes to battle grief and tears privately.

In that bittersweet moment I absorbed the extraordinary love, the exquisite tenderness and concern between them. Their sensibilities strained beyond grief into despair. The dying man was so weak he was unable to lift his arms to hold the young man. He lay helplessly, hopelessly, in his embrace as they rocked gently.

I love you, he murmured. It was so softly spoken that I nearly missed it. I wanted to hold him tighter—out of death's reach?—but it would have hurt him. Already he was slipping away from us.

I love you, I heard the young man gasp. He was trying to steady his voice. His chest began to convulse with sobs. It seemed, at that moment, that his world was caving in.

As I sat there frantically considering the future, the sick man's body suddenly went limp. The strain of being upright after being so long on his back had been too much. The young man laid him down gently, replacing the quilts on his still labored chest. He knelt by the bed. With his friend's hand protectively wrapped in his own, the young man began to pray in Latin.

I couldn't take it any more. I cried out for help and in a heartbeat I was out of that room and back in my meditative pose in the darkness of my own room, exhausted and tearstained.

It took me several hours to pull myself together. I couldn't even bring myself to write it down—this letter is the first effort I've made to record it. Its vividness—the heat, the intense pain, the overwhelming grief and sadness—it's all still with me. I doubt I'll ever forget it, even if I can't explain it. You should probably assure me I'm not going bonkers in a big way. Write and tell me everyone, sometimes, has dreams like this. But this wasn't a dream....

It's given me some insight. I've never experienced that intense a love. It's good to know it exists—that kind of love. *Agape*, I think it's called. So, if only to know that, the experience was worth the pain and being quite startled out of my senses. Call me, will you? I don't much like being alone lately.
Lina

Lina's car rounded the curve leading at last to the home of Dorothy Metzgar. The shadows grew long as she parked the car before a suburban home partly hidden by piñon and sage. Dorothy had come highly recommended by several persons, most of whom reported having gone to her as skeptics and left feeling there was more to sixth and seventh senses than they had previously, or half-heartedly, admitted. While their admiration for Dorothy was obviously now whole-hearted, Lina wasn't entirely convinced that regression through hypnosis was such a workable idea. Nor was she sure what it involved.

She wondered, gathering up her purse and tape recorder, was it like someone slipping something into your drink? And then ending up somehow permanently regressed? Is that what would happen? That's just peachy, she thought as she walked up the driveway—to be regressed to some far-off century and never come back.

And what if I uncover something I can't handle?

But I can't go on like this either—not knowing what it's all about...the feelings, the dreams, the sudden waves of melancholia.

A slight, vivacious woman with warm brown eyes met her at the door. She introduced herself, and Lina was relieved to find the psychic so normal in appearance and manner. Dorothy spoke with animation and sensitivity as she led Lina into her kitchen for a chat. She had been psychic for as long as she could remember. Her father had been a psychic, so her own experiences had never been cause for anxiety or reprisal in her formative years. The family was devoutly Catholic, as she still was, but that posed no conflict for them either.

It wasn't so unusual, Lina mused as she sat listening to Dorothy at her kitchen table, that one could justify psychic studies with Christianity. In fact, she often wondered which of the two was more mysterious or complex. At any rate, Dorothy also found time to be a member of the Association for Research and Enlightenment, also known as the Edgar Cayce Foundation, a group dedicated to psychic research, healing and spiritual growth. This was encouraging. The Foundation had a long tenure and respectable reputation in the promotion of legitimate psychic application.

Ten minutes later, they were preparing for the session.

Lina was confident. She lay back and began the relaxation exercises led by Dorothy, whose ultimate goal would be to lead her into a hypnogogic state. In minutes, she was completely relaxed, strangely detached, yet fully aware, and on instructions, moving to the past. Her limbs felt curiously absent, but she was not uncomfortable. Her mind was alert and listening to Dorothy's words.

"Where are you, Lina?" asked Dorothy.

Amazing. I see something! "Stone steps. Children playing and laughing in a small, shadowy courtyard. Steps lead up to a second floor apartment. Moving up the stairs without touching them. A cluster of women in long dresses with white aprons and little caps stand in a doorway chatting. Now I'm at the second floor door. No need to knock or open the door, I just move through it. I'm looking around. Rather dreary furnishings." *Oh, my! It's been so long!*

"Okay," said Dorothy. "Can you tell me what is happening?"

No, I want to experience this moment. Don't make me talk!

"He was at the standing desk, writing, and he turned around and saw me and smiled with surprise. Oh, my, what joy! Now he's come to me, smiling that wonderful, disarming smile...and we hold each other in a long embrace...we stand at arm's length to look and talk and laugh. But wait, he's still at the desk. Part of him is still working at the desk, and part of him is with me. I don't understand. He's still working. Am I visiting with only part of him?"

"It's his astral self that sees you," explained Dorothy. "Go on."

"'I miss you, I love you.' He tells me this. 'This isn't as easy as we thought it would be. I've prayed for help. Are you the help?'"

"Yes, help is on the way, I tell him." *Help is coming. Soon. He will come soon, won't he? Not well, he's not well at all.* "He's too pale. He's been sick too long. A finger is wrapped up in bandages—again. I sense this is a chronic condition from writing and playing too much. He works too hard, but he is also very patient.

"Another thought comes...I sense trouble. He isn't replacing the inner energy he expends on his work—it's starting to affect the physical...strange, now my body feels it too. My head hurts. Oh, and my arms and chest." *Hold on. Help is coming. Trust me.*

"He's gone back to the desk. I suddenly begin swirling swiftly around him like some kind of ghostly dust devil, round and round. I feel like a musical trill playing out in motion as I race around another soul. But he's not another soul, really. I feel...this is really crazy...I feel we spring from the same source." *Can that be? How can that be?*

"Okay, Lina, move on now...."

I want to stay here.

"Relax. Breathe slowly, take long, deep breaths."

"A dark room, not his home. The child is crying. He's in pain. He seems about five or six years old. Maybe younger. It's a distressing, terrified cry. His face is covered with angry red sores like over-scratched insect bites. He's so little."

"Is anyone else there?" asked Dorothy.

"He's in bed attended by two men. One, his father, is seated nearby. The other is a doctor...who stands nearer the boy. Ah! My upper arm! It stings! I don't...oh! He's placed a leech on his left arm! The boy has seen it and he's terrified. From where I hover above the bed...I see his fear...and feel his pain, but I can't seem to do anything about it! We're both helpless and...and I'm getting frantic! This is...oh, no! He's terrified. Terrified!"

"Relax. Take deep breaths. You needn't feel the pain."

But I do! Take that thing off! Take it off NOW! "The doctor is moving to take it off. He's mumbling something about taking it off. Did he hear me? How could he? Awful, disgusting practice. What an uncivilized world. He's wiping away the blood...he's leaving the room with his medieval medical equipment." *The quack!* "I sense the presence of another doctor—do they strike in pairs? He's telling the father that...he's frail to begin with, so...the illness could go either way. I sense the doctor is not confident of his own methods and wants to prepare the man for the worst...knowing it would be through his own incompetence or lack of knowledge.

"The father stays a while to calm the boy down. Then the child falls asleep. Bad dreams. I spin around his body again. He mustn't die! He *will* get well. I feel how exhausted his body has become in such a short time. He's only a child. Why am I whipping swiftly around his body? Is it some method of helping him? It still hurts." *I want to stop now...get away*

80

from here.

The scene vanished immediately. Dorothy brought Lina back to the 20th century slowly, in measured tones, counting to ten. On ten, she suggested to Lina to open her eyes, feeling rested. Lina blinked, rubbed her arm and waited as the images settled in her memory. She wanted to remember as much visual detail as possible. After ten minutes of quiet, she rose and followed Dorothy into the kitchen.

"I don't understand," Lina said as they sipped tea. "I seemed to be there, but only as a spirit."

"That's right," Dorothy said with quiet confidence. "Your spirit visited his."

"You mean it wasn't a past life recall?"

"Yes and no—it was an actual visit into that time and space from this time and space."

"How is that possible?"

Dorothy smiled. "With God, everything is possible."

VIENNA, October, 1791.

A chair crashed to the floor.

"Wolfgang!" cried Franz, reaching him just as he collapsed to the floor near the fortepiano. Wolfgang, still conscious, hung limp in his arms.

Panic seized Franz. "Wolfgang! Can you hear me?" he demanded.

"My God, I must be tired," Wolfgang murmured. Mustering his energy, Franz picked him up and carried him to the bed. He sat down, himself exhausted from the strain. Frowning and slightly out of breath, he held his hand to Wolfgang's ashen face. He felt helpless and uncertain.

"Just lie still for a moment. Don't try to talk," he exhaled.

What to do? Go for a doctor. No, I can't. Who will stay here?

A wistful smile played on Wolfgang's lips. In a weary, breathless voice he uttered, "You're trying...to decide...whether to stay here...with me...or go for the doctor."

Franz was not surprised any more to hear Wolfgang repeat his own thoughts. It happened all the time now.

"You're right. I am," he said evenly as he stood up and

81

slowly pulled off Wolfgang's shoes, grateful that he was at least conscious. Wolfgang closed his eyes and winced. For several moments, the only sound in the room was their breathing. Wolfgang turned again to Franz.

"Stay here...with me," he whispered. "Don't you know yet...that you're better for me...than ten doctors...don't leave."

His unusual shortness of breath was beginning to alarm Franz. Calling a doctor was a gamble, he felt, no matter how much confidence others had in their abilities to heal. Franz had never had much use for them or their strange notions. Wolfgang was only a little less suspicious of their methods and general efficacy, in spite of his experience with them virtually all of his life. In any event, they had learned to do without a doctor, usually for lack of money.

But this was different. Wolfgang had never collapsed like this before. God knows how long he'd been weak and un-well without saying a word.

"Sit with me while...I rest," Wolfgang sighed.

"What happened?"

"I...don't know...feel strange...here." His hand touched his chest.

Franz laid his hand over Wolfgang's and squeezed it re-assuringly. In silence, Wolfgang turned and gazed out the win-dow. Watching him, Franz sensed his anxiety and frustration. It seemed to Franz that in the few years he'd known him, Wolfgang's strength was gradually waning. To be sure, he was growing weaker, and it seemed that with each passing week he was less and less able to complete his carefully measured amount of daily work. If they both were not acutely aware of the precise amount of work he allowed himself daily out of habit, they might not have noticed his growing inability to complete it. And now, this.

Fortunately, Franz thought, I was here when it hap-pened and not off in Baden wasting time watching over Constanze. Undeniably, Wolfgang was not well. They had both continued to lose weight. But this new ailment was not some-thing easily assessed. This was more serious than day-to-day hunger. Not as easy to put off worrying about.

Franz shut his eyes.

So many times in the past few months he had had to fight off a growing sense of bitter frustration and anger from their increasingly destitute situation. They were unable to find the right kinds of commissions. The excuses from Wolfgang's former patrons were numerous and inventive....

His thoughts wandered back to the stationer's shop where he bought manuscript paper and quills. Whenever he entered the shop, a twinge of envy seized him. The well-stocked store smelled of fine, fresh goods. Everything was laid out in careful order. Johann, the proprietor, was a prosperous, healthy, jovial man with a good future. If he had any problems, Franz had decided, they were most likely manageable ones. He had a young, pretty wife, too, whom Franz occasionally saw helping in the shop. They seemed happy. And, Franz mused, they had enough firewood in winter and enough food all year. They had succeeded in finding a niche in society's assigned economic flow. Someone wanted what Johann had to offer. *He was needed by society.*

Who needed Wolfgang and Franz? Apparently no one. No one was knocking down their door....

Franz had asked his father for money, without success. It then had occurred to him to steal—if not money, then food. After working out a plan, he had finally decided against it. What if he were caught? This was a real possibility, for Franz realized he would not be at all adept at stealing. Wolfgang would have been sick and alone, instead of just sick....

Wolfgang's mental state had begun to deteriorate. His cheerful moments were infrequent now, and more a frenetic effort, punctuated with the chilling offhand, ironical comments that revealed his profound depression and increasing feelings of hopelessness.

Maybe this illness has come on in anticipation of another cold winter, thought Franz, scratching his head and looking back at the deepening lines on Wolfgang's face....

He was already crushed by Constanze's infidelity. It had cut deep into him. And *Die Zauberflöte* had come to be a mixed blessing after the Masonic community shunned it....

Bastards! All of them!

Franz stood up, turned away from the bed and stood gazing out the window. Wolfgang heard the movement and opened his eyes. He stoically studied Franz's bowed shoulders. It had never occurred to Franz that Wolfgang read in his eyes his growing frustration. He saw before him the young composer frustrated at not being at least moderately prosperous or recognized as a promising new talent. He saw him wishing his career might have begun to blossom by now.

Maybe, Wolfgang wondered, maybe it has been selfish of me to take him on as assistant these three years. Certainly his association with a sickly, out-of-vogue composer must be holding him back. He would deny it, of course, but there was no denying his career was at a standstill. He hardly ever worked on his own music. And he lived in poverty in the bargain.

If I were not around, thought Wolfgang darkly, *if it weren't for me....*

Franz wanted to shout and cry at once. He turned and approached the bed.

"Where is the pain?" he coaxed quietly.

"In my ankles...and hands...and my head, naturally," said Wolfgang meekly. The headache was getting worse by the minute.

Franz looked at Wolfgang's hands. They were swollen. He looked at his ankles. Swollen. What to do! Wolfgang turned onto his side and curled up, closing his eyes against the growing pain in his head.

"Don't leave," he urged again, closing his eyes.

"I'll be right here," Franz assured him. "Right here."

An hour later, Franz was rushing around the apartment trying to prepare a compress. The headache had gone from bad to worse, for now Wolfgang was vomiting. Franz tried to move quickly but with care, all the while fighting panic. He ran back into the bedroom and carefully placed the cloth on Wolfgang's forehead. Tears ran down Wolfgang's face from the intense pain in his jaw and neck. Franz, who had run outside and sent a boy to fetch Dr. Closset, noticed with alarm that Wolfgang was slipping into semi-consciousness.

A knock came presently and Franz showed Closset into the bedroom. The doctor wasted no time in examining the patient. He pulled a stick-like instrument out of his bag and applied one end of it to Wolfgang's exposed chest to listen. Franz watched every move. The young, gaunt doctor with the silly goatee grunted and looked at Wolfgang's face again. Then he slowly, carefully felt his swollen hands and put away the stick.

Franz was inclined to think of him as a quack, but he also realized this man was all Wolfgang had to help him now. It was a frightening notion at best. Closset pulled out a paper packet containing some green powder. Giving it to Franz, he said, "Mix this in water or wine and have him drink all of it. It's for the headache."

"What is it?"

The doctor's face grew stern and questioning as he peered at Franz through his monacle. "Don't worry, my good friend, it should help him immensely," he replied with a trace of indignation.

Meekly, Franz took the small envelope. Closset left immediately, after leaving instructions to call him again if Wolfgang got worse. After showing the doctor to the door, Franz hastened to prepare the powder in water. He tasted it and winced. He hesitated.

Be sensible, he told himself. It's bitter and it smells, but it's better than nothing at all.

He took it into the bedroom and gently coaxed Wolfgang, who lay moaning in semi-consciousness, to drink the mixture. That done, he spent a few anxious moments wondering whether to cover him or not.

Better to cover him, he decided anxiously, don't want him to catch a chill.

He sat down on the floor, pulled up his knees, and waited. Moments later, he reached for Wolfgang's still, swollen hand. He sighed heavily and leaned against the bed, exhausted.

Wolfgang wakened gradually, blinking in the sunlight streaming in through the window. Could it have been so many hours, or maybe days? he wondered hazily. He looked around the room. His hand felt warm. It was Franz. He was sitting on the floor, leaning against the bed, asleep.

"Snai," he said, gently pulling his hand out of Franz's grip. "Wake up, Snai." He touched his head. Franz stirred. Suddenly, with a jerk, he looked up at Wolfgang, who regarded him with weary cheer.

"What are you doing on the floor?" he asked, smiling weakly.

"Oh! You're...are you...how do you feel? Better?" stammered Franz.

Praise God! Oh, what a relief! exulted Franz. He pulled himself up and reached across the bed to examine him more closely. Wolfgang looked much better despite the dark circles under his eyes. But he was smiling, so the headache was obviously gone. And the swelling was down.

"Oh, my, what a relief!" he cried.

For a moment they were both silent.

Please, God, let this be the end of it, thought Franz. *Let this be the end of sickness in this house.*

THE AMERICAN MIDWEST, late 1940s.

The relentless rhythm of the train played a hypnotic accompaniment to the swiftly changing moonlit landscape. Yet Willy's eyes were heavy and his head gently nodded forward. Fragments of thought again meandered through his consciousness.

As a child the railroad had exhilarated him. The sound of the wheels...racing across the miles...the thrill of speed....

But I wasn't alone then....

The darkened coach section was nearly deserted on the late night express to Chicago. Willy sat near the rear of the car, leaning lazily against the faded red upholstery, gazing out the window, clutching his book.

...so late, the night...eyes tired...page after page...the rhythm...the wheels...the night....

The book dropped to the floor.

You weren't alone then, and you aren't alone now.

Willy startled to attention as a young woman slid effortlessly into the empty seat opposite him and curled up under a wide, midnight blue shawl of many hues. Her long black hair was pulled into a single loose braid that trailed down her shoulder. She smiled easily as she handed him the book.

Who are you?

Think back, she responded.

She turned her eyes to the flickering lights of a distant town. Willy followed her gaze. The pearlescent moonlight shone on smooth clouds. The town disappeared as the train sped on. Willy looked again, and blinked. She was still there. He reached for a cigarette.

And the rhythm of the tracks, she offered. *It's a train, not a carriage, you see.*

Tracks!...tracks!

Now how do you think you got those switched?

Beats me, he responded stiffly, lighting up the cigarette.

So you won't tell me who you are, tell me what you're doing in my dream?

Trying out my next vehicle, before the fact, so to speak.

Vehicle, huh? Willy thought he had an idea of what she meant, but chose not to pursue the subject. *What's your name?*

It will be Lina. It was Franz. It's been many others.

Lina. A welcome serenity settled on him as he studied her closely through the wafting cigarette smoke. *Lee...na.... So you've decided to take my advice and take another life.*

You told me I've waited long enough. 'It's time to rebuild,' you said. Tell me again, what will I learn in this next turn?

Trust. In yourself, in love, regardless of the consequences. You will find a way to remember Franz and Wolfgang and then forgive yourself.

How will I remember...that life? Lina frowned.

Everywhere on the planet, people are beginning to wake up and think for themselves. They're asking questions about their true nature, their origins, their destinies. It's a perfect time to delve and heal old wounds. You can come into this move-ment, and when you do, it's highly likely you'll remember!

And if I don't?

I'll show it to you.

How?

Come, come, Franz, use your head! I'm already here! We'll find a way, and when we meet, I'll lend you my library card! He laughed. Lina indulged in a smile.

I have a question for you. She leaned forward as she spoke. *I'd like you to answer without thinking too much about it first.*

I'm listening.

Did you accomplish everything you set out to accomplish? The last time, I mean, she asked.

The last time...scenes of a distant, foreign city disturbed his mind's eye. He slowly put out the cigarette as she contin-ued.

We haven't talked much about those days specifically. I'd like to know.

Frowning, Willy turned his gaze toward his reflection in the window. It was a pale reflection, given the one dim light within the car. His reflection was not Willy, however, but an-other. He sighed deeply, then responded slowly, tentatively at first:

You know, it was difficult, very difficult, to get anything accomplished with that small, overworked body. It was so...worn out. By poor nutrition and almost constant disease...and by neglect. All the travel and little enough exercise or fresh air. Seems ironic now, doesn't it? Fed only water until I was six months old...didn't walk until I was three. Then near the end...the hunger, the consumption, and those stomach aches! Seems it never let up. And so cold in winter.

He stopped and closed his eyes to quench the stinging. Lina reached over and touched his hand. He took her hand and at that moment more memories flooded in.

You were so good to me.... Do you know how good you were? Still, it was an enormous relief to quit that life at last. The incredible sweetness of going home after so hard a life. And the serenity. You know, it never ceases to amaze me...the feeling, I mean. Well, after all the physical pain, and the mental anguish, to feel this exquisite tranquility, and the love...every time.

He closed his eyes to remember more vividly. At that moment, a sweet presence permeated his being.

And what of your work, then? she persisted. He opened his eyes and, for the first time, looked long at her face. Love illuminated her eyes.

I could have done more with a healthier body.

You mean a body that could keep up with you? she smiled knowingly. *The soul energy was high, wasn't it? Too high, I think.*

Those excruciating headaches...I was beginning to blow my circuits, drawing in too much soul energy. More than my share, I believe.

Maybe not. This was such a special project, our soul fragments were maybe overzealous in transmitting energy too quickly, too often. Lina paused before asking yet another question. *Has this American life been any better, Willy? You still feel pale and anxious.*

I'm not sick! And the opportunities here are ten times what they were in Vienna.

Vienna had no heart! Willy was surprised to hear bitterness in her voice after all these years.

Let's not talk about that, he offered as he turned his eyes toward the window. His reflection was complete now; only the eyes remained the same. They were still Willy's eyes. And they were Wolfgang's eyes, too.

How about your musical progress? Were you satisfied with that?

I don't think I was ever satisfied, laughed Willy. *Those primitive instruments sounded...primitive! We all knew it, didn't we? They were constantly out of tune, and poor tone quality was the standard. The only redeeming element, now that I remember it, was the acoustic liveness of the concert halls. The sound in most of them was...what? Luminescent? Yes, that's right. Luminescent.*

Willy stopped to ponder the word, then continued.

Even with that, the music I heard in my head was not what I heard in concert. Almost always. Even when I played it myself. But now! Now I have pianos and orchestras with two hundred years of work on them. I've found an extraordinary new spectrum of sound and tone color. Imagine what I might find in another two hundred years!

But you haven't composed!

Yes I have, Franz! I keep my compositions to myself...in my head where they belong. When I need them, I play them.

You're not frantic to get them down on paper? The way you were then? I remember how you needed to clear them out of your head!

There is no urgency to write anything down now, interrupted Willy. *That's over, at least for now. I've said what I wanted to say via composition, for a while. As for now, I thoroughly enjoy the compositions, the orchestral textures and aural colors of other minds. I want to speak through them now, at the piano, do you see? Besides, composing would have meant more headaches. One headache at a time, I always say.*

What do you mean? What kinds of headaches?

Oh, the usual. Publishers and recording companies and copyright thieves and theatre managers. Shall I go on?

I think not.

No one in America today is interested in American composers anyway, and most wouldn't understand my work if I wrote something. Hell, they're still trying to understand my performances! Do you know there are some critics who say I don't fully understand Mozart? That I play him all wrong! What sweet irony that is! Willy threw back his head and laughed out loud.

What presumptuousness! How can they claim to know the right way to play Mozart? Did they ever hear him play? Indignant and not at all amused, Lina pulled her shawl closer around her.

They have now. When they hear Willy Kapell play Mozart...

...they hear Mozart play Mozart. It's so simple. How can people be so devoid of intuition, of imagination?

Willy leaned forward, smiling.

The audiences enjoy my Mozart performances. It's the critics who are unimaginative. Except I must say in all fairness, there was one reviewer in Scandinavia who said I had Mozart's smile. Isn't that curious? He recognized my smile.

Which reminds me, was there substantial spiritual growth in that life?

Willy's eyebrows arched as he sat back again to ponder. At length, he reached for another cigarette and responded thoughtfully. *I was beginning to understand, and develop, patience. With myself, with others, with circumstance. But it was only a dawning of understanding.*

The train slowed down as it passed through a small town, dark except for streetlights and, now and then, a lighted window. The train bell rang sadly in the distance.

I had an opportunity to love unconditionally, he said pensively.

I know.

You were one of the ones I loved unconditionally. It wasn't difficult. Others were not so easy.

Those others are better for having known you. We all are.

Willy leaned his head against the window to glimpse the moon again. *These persons we loved so wholeheartedly. Where are they now?*

Living other lives in other places.

Tell me, my friend, will I remember this meeting when I wake up? Willy asked as he put out his cigarette stub.

Parts of it, possibly, if you wake up suddenly. Certainly not all of it, though you will know we had a long discussion. That's how astral encounters go. You may remember only the feeling of this conversation. The barest hint of how you feel now, here. And it will linger all day long.

The train picked up speed again as it pulled out of town. Lina tucked her hands under her shawl.

What do you hope to accomplish with your music in this life? she asked.

Startled at his ever-increasing memories, Willy looked up and studied her eyes. *You asked me that once before. On a hill. At night. A night like tonight, as a matter of fact....*

You said then you wanted to create joy in the world.

And you said you would help me.

I remember.

Willy whispered. *I want to perform with heart, and soul. And poetry. Sometimes it happens, and sometimes it doesn't. In many ways, it's more difficult being a performer than being a composer. It's more immediate. Once a performance is done, it's over, and if you haven't reached the listener, then you must try again later, if you're lucky enough to have the listener again later. You know, I often dream colorful ribbons of light stretching and billowing from higher realms to earth. And when I play, the ribbons vibrate.*

I've seen them. It's quite a spectacle. They vibrate with sound and color.

And I want to experiment with tone colors on these newer instruments. The possibilities are enormous, you know.

Don't be too demanding on yourself, Wolfgang. You've had a strict, disciplined training in at least two lives now. Your musical life will collide again with your personal life. Be patient with yourself.

I have work to do.

You had work then, too, and your body couldn't keep up. Nor could your personal life. You had two sons who rarely saw you. You still live for music and everything else is secondary. You don't understand how others can do without music. You walk into a room and if there's a piano anywhere near, you're at the keyboard within minutes. Music is second nature to you, as it is with all our soul fragments. But as much as you crave music, your presence and attention also are craved by those who know and love you.

I see colors when I play, did you know that? In my head. It's like painting a living canvas with sound.

Lina sighed. *I'm afraid we have a tendency to take on too much, or pursue one grand and glorious project too passionately. Then we work too hard and die young.*

I know I'll die young.

How do you know that?

I consulted a reader. She said I would die when I reached thirty.

What? How could she do that? She should at least have left the date open!

It doesn't bother me. Willy shrugged.

I hope you didn't pay her!

You're rather upset, aren't you? It isn't even your life she ended....

I resent some fortune tellers. Their audacity! Predicting in absolutes. No one really knows what's going to happen in any situation. Personal choice is what really determines.... I'm losing contact.

Contact?

The energy is fading. It must be my anger. I've broken the connection.... That'll teach me! Willy, think of me often, as I think of you!

You can't go yet. I have more questions! Damn!

Lina's image faded and disappeared. Willy blinked and rubbed his eyes. He laid his head back to watch the moonlight dance across a field of grass, wondering how much, if any, of this conversation he would remember.

VIENNA, November, 1791.

The darkened room glowed again as Franz entered with the candle and laid it on the nightstand by the bed. He wished there weren't so many windows in this corner room. It wouldn't be so cold in winter if there were fewer leaks to let in the chill air. Wolfgang was on his side, eyes wide, staring at the yellow wall, a look of mingled fear and determination on his face.

He rolled over and watched Franz sit on the bed to place a cool cloth on his fevered forehead. As usual, Wolfgang came immediately to the point.

"Don't pine over me when I'm gone. It's important that you carry on," he whispered.

"Why?" Franz frowned. He was tired of hearing Wolfgang talk of death.

"It isn't right. You're young. You have your whole life yet to live."

"And you don't?" Franz replied as he pulled Wolfgang's stray hair out of the way of the cloth. His face was more pale and fevered than usual. Franz again noticed the deepening lines around his eyes and mouth.

92

"Please, Franz." Wolfgang winced as he tried to move.

"I'm sorry. You're right, go on," said Franz contritely. He smiled and settled quietly for what he expected to be a more serious exchange than he was ready to hear. He looked down and began absent-mindedly rolling the edge of his sleeve between his thumb and forefinger as he listened.

"Then you'll take care of yourself?" Wolfgang persisted. He grasped Franz's arm. "I am concerned that you might not. I know you too well. Franz, I need your assurance that you will continue. Don't give up just because I'm gone. Do you understand?"

"I won't give up," said Franz half-heartedly. Wolfgang released his grip.

"Liar," he said quietly.

Astonished, Franz looked up at Wolfgang, who stared evenly at him. Franz blinked.

"Don't you think you're taking this illness too seriously? Yes, I'll admit you're very sick, but you're certainly not going to die. You're not!"

Wolfgang sighed heavily as he turned to stare at the wall again. Franz is denying the reality of the situation, he thought, and as much as predicting that he *will* fall to pieces when I'm gone.

"Don't look away...please. Look at me," said Franz, suddenly apologetic. Wolfgang turned his solemn gaze on him again.

"When you talk of death, when you talk like this, it...frightens me. It does us no good to talk of what will or will not happen...."

"Franz!"

"Wait! Let me finish. But if you want to give me last minute instructions, if doing that will make you feel better, then do it. I'll do whatever you ask. But you aren't going to die!"

Franz's eyes pleaded with Wolfgang: *tell me you aren't going to die!*

Soft murmuring voices from the tenants below carried up to fill the silence of the room. Someone was whistling outside where the snow muffled the sound of the few carriages that infrequently rumbled by.

"Bring the manuscript. Let's work," Wolfgang said in a neutral voice. Franz grimaced. Suddenly the discussion was closed. Suddenly they were to begin work. Well, it was just as well.

"Which one?"

"The Mass."

"Why are you trembling?" Wolfgang's hands shook.

"You!" Wolfgang exclaimed in frustration. "*You* make me tremble. Cover my hands. They're cold again." Franz took his hands in his own and rubbed them. The flame of the candle flickered, sending shadows flying against the high walls of the room. Some day they would have rooms full of candles burning as long as they needed the light. And mirrors, lots of mirrors. Some day.

"Do you love me?" asked Wolfgang quietly, intensely. Franz stopped rubbing.

"Yes, of course. You know I do."

"Then *love* me. Listen when I tell you I'm dying, for I know it. I know it only too well!"

Wolfgang's blue eyes, weary with pain, yet urgent, held Franz's gaze. In them, Franz saw something he had ignored before, something he could ignore no longer. His heart began to hurt. His breathing grew shallow.

Wolfgang is dying.

In a single moment, Franz grasped reality and he could not shut it out again. He remembered his mother—his young, pretty mother with her loving smile and singing voice—suddenly dead. He was only a boy when she died. He loved her and she left him.

And now.

Wolfgang was suffering only to find death at the end of his agony. And Franz could only watch—powerless. And in the end, they would be alone, separated.

The fear rose in his chest and engulfed him. He stared wide-eyed into Wolfgang's eyes, their hands joined but motionless.

Wolfgang studied Franz, wondering, as he beheld his suddenly pale face, if he had done the right thing. He hands slipped around to squeeze Franz's cold hands. Yes, I've done the right thing, he decided. I'm tired of facing death alone. I need someone to help me die.

"Shall we continue?" he asked.

Franz heard Wolfgang's voice calling through a vortex of grim loneliness. He called back as though in a nightmare, "What...what did you say?"

"The Mass."

"Oh. Yes." Franz tried to climb out of his confusion of thoughts. "Right away. I'll...I'll get it." He struggled to move but his legs were leaden. Suddenly he was paralyzed with over-whelming grief.

"Oh, God! Wolfgang!" he cried, stricken. Wolfgang leaned over and clutched him with all the strength he could muster. Franz grasped him, holding fast as he hid his face in his shoul-der. Wolfgang's eyes welled while Franz held onto him as though love and fear alone might save him.

"Oh, God!" breathed Franz. "What are we going to do? What are we going to do?"

Loving Mozart demanded all of his strength and soul and heart.

The snowflakes beyond the window fluttered aimlessly to the frozen ground from a gray and leaden sky.

IV.

I measure his heart by mine.

—*La Clemenza di Tito*

VIENNA, December, 1791.

It seems I'm always alone in this room.
Franz stood up and stretched. Wolfgang's slow, labored breathing filled the room. It kept Franz awake. Thus he had been sitting in the dark, contemplating. Such a strange, dark room. It had not been his idea to move the ailing Wolfgang to Frau Weber's home, but he could protest little over Constanze's willful insistence on appearances now that all of Vienna knew of his gravest of illnesses. She was, after all, his wife. Wolfgang had shown little interest in where he was, so long as he could work on the Mass, which had become an obsession. Franz felt it a minor victory that he was allowed to stay with Wolfgang at the Weber home, even if it was only because they preferred that he be the one exposed to whatever contagion had seized Wolfgang. For though Dr. Closset pretended to know what afflicted Wolfgang, he was secretly baffled.

Franz reminisced. He had known Wolfgang only three years, more or less, and it seemed to him always that he had known him for three hundred years. More than that.... But of course that was nonsense. Was it just that he was such an intense person? That so much seemed to be happening all the time, even when nothing really was? Franz sat down again and flexed his fingers.

I'm so alone, already.
The mass for the dead was taking all of Wolfgang's strength. It was draining him from within and from without. It was killing him. Little by little. Franz looked at Wolfgang as he slept fitfully. He never let up, even now, as sick as he was. If he couldn't sing his music, he would hum it. If he had no breath to hum, his hands would move as if playing a keyboard. And Franz continued to write. To him it was more terrifying than heroic.

Then Wolfgang would fall asleep suddenly, almost as if his body finally had declared, "Enough!" With Wolfgang asleep, Franz had time to rest and think, and stare into the darkness, listening to the hypnotically rhythmic breathing and gasping. Franz had felt, recently, a strange stoic emptiness growing within himself. It bothered and intrigued him. Was he gradually hardening himself to the situation? He hadn't wept in many days. How many days had it been? How many days had Wolfgang been ill? Seven? Ten? Too many days. Not much time, actually, to stop and think, except recently, like this. Too much to do between taking dictation, fetching things, cleaning, feeding—or trying to....

What will I do when he's gone?

A winter wind blew forlornly outside. It had never occurred to Franz to leave this room. Eybler had been by twice. Constanze, less often. Franz had hoped Wolfgang would not notice that she rarely came to see him. Nor did he attempt to ask her to show some compassion for the man who loved her still. Her sister Sophie came often, sent by their mother in another part of the house to report back on his progress, and to run errands. Sophie was rather timid about approaching Wolfgang, fearing, she had said in innocent confidence to Franz, that he might have the plague. "Wolfgang understands," she had whispered naively.

In truth Wolfgang had grown less and less interested in his surroundings, other than his work. He no longer smiled. His eyes were lusterless, his face wan. Surely it was the effect of the continuous pain in his head and joints. Still, it seemed he wanted only one thing—to finish the mass. Franz found that strange in view of the fact that he had virtually ignored it in the four or five months since he had received the commission. Now, suddenly....

How I miss your smile....

Today he had beckoned him. Franz had put his ear to Wolfgang's mouth, as he no longer spoke with much strength.

"You must...continue...composition...studies...with Salieri," Wolfgang had told him between breaths. Franz had raised his head and looked questioningly into Wolfgang's eyes. Salieri? He wanted nothing to do with the bastard. Why, Salieri had been responsible, almost single-handedly, for Wolfgang's lack of commissions and performances in Vienna for the last—how many years now? At least five. NO, he didn't want to study with a swine like Salieri!

Wolfgang beckoned again. "He is...the only...master...left in Vienna.... Haydn is...gone...no one else...after I die.... You must...if you are...to succeed," he urged patiently. He had read Franz's mind again.

Franz stood up and wiped the sweat from his own upper lip on his sleeve as he considered. It didn't take him long to decide. He did not wish to upset Wolfgang, who was still watching him closely. He leaned down again, this time to Wolfgang's

99

ear.

"If that is what you want, then I will do it."

"You will...learn much," murmured Wolfgang. Franz smiled faintly. It was more of a wince than an encouragement.

"How does your head feel?" Franz asked. Wolfgang frowned and shut his eyes in reply.

Franz stood up and sighed, his mind almost a blank. He walked to the wall and raised his arms above his head, placing his palms against the white wall. His eyes shut tight and he began, finally, to weep. Quietly, so as not to disturb the brother he was about to lose to God knows what, for in spite of it all, he really didn't know what came after death, and he wasn't really convinced it was nothing more than a frightful void.

He wept for the incessant pain Wolfgang felt.

He wept for the futility of their work on this mass of the damned.

He wept that Wolfgang would send him with his blessings to Salieri, for his own good.

"Franz...," Wolfgang called out of the darkness, loud enough for Franz to hear across the room. Surprised, Franz stopped sobbing and hastened to the bed, wiping his tears with his palms.

"Yes? I'm here," he heaved, wondering how Wolfgang found the strength to call so loudly. He leaned over the bed, his ear near Wolfgang's mouth to await the answer.

"Let's work," he said.

"Right away." Even in the dark, Franz's hands moved with sureness to the drawer. His hands found a new candle and the holder. He lit the candle in the fire of the stove. The candle flickered wildly on the nightstand as Franz gathered the only pieces of paper left. The inkwell and pen were already on the little table, waiting. Franz leaned over the bed to listen.

"For the 'Benedictus'...this theme, listen...," whispered Wolfgang. Franz strained to hear the notes, faintly sung in the quiet of the night. It was difficult to string together the disjointed statements of the single theme after one hearing.

"Again, please," said Franz quietly. Wolfgang repeated the theme, his voice almost too guttural for the separate tones to be distinguished. Franz concentrated on the sounds. Then he sat down and began writing swiftly, blocking out all other thoughts but that melody. He studied the notation momentarily while Wolfgang watched patiently, then Franz leaned over the bed again to sing it back to him.

Wolfgang grunted disapproval and Franz again placed his ear near Wolfgang's mouth.

"The first interval...is a sixth...not a fifth," he instructed. Franz sang it again. Wolfgang nodded faintly. Franz sat down again and corrected the notation. As he wrote, a wave of grief invaded him and for a moment he hesitated, closing his eyes.

Not now!

He opened his eyes, wiped a tear away with his sleeve, and then stood up to hear the next section.

"The second theme...listen," and Wolfgang sang again, straining to sing the entire melody in one breath. His voice was fainter than before. Franz moved his ear closer and frowned. After two more efforts by Wolfgang, Franz sang it back to him. Wolfgang nodded approval and Franz again sat down and wrote it out. The two themes, statement and answer, were perfectly matched in an almost pastoral beauty and balance. Franz marveled to himself that such an elegant and exquisitely blissful melody could issue from one so overwhelmed with pain and fear. From what Elysian reserve did he draw these sounds, he wondered.

Franz stood up again for more, but Wolfgang had fallen asleep. Franz hesitated, studying Wolfgang's tired, swollen face. He pulled the quilt close around his shoulders and continued his watch.

He cannot die. I love him too much.

He absent-mindedly laid the paper and pen aside and pinched out the candle flame. He sat down again and clasped his hands together in front of his face. The stove fire crackled in the darkly silent night.

The next morning, Franz woke up groggy and tired to find Sophie shaking his arm. He stirred stiffly in the chair.

"Herr Sussmayr, my sister asks that you come to breakfast if you wish," she said evenly in a high childlike voice. "She has prepared many things. You must be hungry. Come!"

Franz stretched slowly as she spoke. When her words finally sank in, he scrutinized her face. Constanze must be feeling domestic. Why not?...it was her home. But why should she suddenly want to feed him after days of neglect? He could smell coffee.

"Please, sir. Otherwise the food will go to waste," she

continued. "You are hungry, aren't you? Wolfgang is asleep. He will not miss you."

Franz scratched his head vigorously with both hands. At the mention of the name, he got up and leaned over the bed to check on Wolfgang, who still slept. Franz put his hand against Wolfgang's face.

Still hot. Still swollen. No change. No change! Damn!

He had so hoped for an improvement by morning.

"Sir?" said Sophie, inquiringly. "Is he better?"

"No," replied Franz quietly. "He's the same."

"Will you be coming to the kitchen?" she persisted.

Franz sighed. He *was* hungry. And Wolfgang was the same—and he seemed to be fast asleep. Franz had been in this room continuously for so many days he'd lost track.

I'm hungry, thought Franz. Really hungry.

"I'll be along," he told the young girl. She left. Franz was indecisive again. I suppose it will be all right to leave him for a few minutes, he thought. He left the room and was surprised to feel the cool air of the rest of the apartment. It was refreshing. So was the breakfast, which Sophie so generously and quietly served him.

As Franz relished his meal, Constanze entered the sickroom and moved quickly to the head of the bed.

"Wolfgang! Wake up, it's time for your breakfast," she whispered to him. She carried a small cup of broth. She laid back the quilt from his chest to help awaken him and he stirred, groggy but glad to see her by his bed.

"Stanzerl...," he murmured.

"Yes, it's me," she spoke as if to a child. "You will take some broth for me, won't you?"

As she spoke, a cup of broth touched his lips. Yet Wolfgang was interested only in her.

"Come, Wolfgang, open your mouth," she coaxed. He choked only a little before the next swallow came. And the next. And another.

Then she was gone.

Not a word of farewell or comfort, thought Wolfgang numbly. Not even now, here. She has grown to hate me. He winced. There is that bitterness again—bitter and metallic. The taste of death.

By the time Franz had returned, Wolfgang was motioning that he was about to vomit again. Franz ran for the bucket and assisted Wolfgang in leaning over the side of the bed.

Wolfgang was weary and, now, nauseous as well. But he continued to work. Franz sat leaning against the bed, writing. He used the bed as a desk in order to hear Wolfgang sing or speak.

Wolfgang studied Franz as he wrote.

I'll miss him.... No, don't think about it. Can't. He's so young and naive. How will he fare? He's like I was, too trusting and generous and innocent to challenge life properly. Someone else will have to be his mentor or he will surely...no, don't think about it. If there were any way on God's earth that I could help him get along...but I'm dying...dying? I'm not ready to die! Not yet. Oh, God, I'm so afraid! Don't think about it, I warned you not to think about it. You'll frighten him too! Stop it. Think about the music.

"Franz, listen...there's more." *I don't want to die!*

Franz was looking at him now, waiting. Wolfgang hesitantly dictated more music and instructions on how Franz eventually was to handle its orchestration. He began writing again as Wolfgang watched.

I'll miss him. Will he miss me?

"Snai," he called out quietly. Franz looked up and automatically brought his ear close to Wolfgang.

"I love you," he sighed. "Never forget...I love you."

At first, Franz was motionless. Abruptly, he turned and said without hesitation, "I want to hold you." His voice verged on breaking, for he had already sensed Wolfgang's tryst with fear.

"Then do."

"It will hurt you," protested Franz.

"How much more...can it hurt?"

Franz laid aside his work and reached across the bed, gingerly slipping his arms around and under Wolfgang's slight form. Almost at once Wolfgang began to feel a familiar vibrant energy. It coursed through his agonized frame, relieving the relentless pain and crowning his dark thoughts with peace and quiet resignation. Franz's hold tightened and the pain receded as the energy swelled. Bittersweet tears welled in Wolfgang's eyes as he realized the mutual peace and love of their friendship soon would come to an end. He lay limp, too weak to raise his arms; instead, he turned his head toward Franz. He had a thought.

"Listen to me...carefully," he murmured. "I won't leave you...when I die...."

"What are you saying?" puzzled Franz.

"I will be with you...if I can."

Franz hesitated. He wanted to believe it, and he wanted to make Wolfgang happy. No arguing. No doubting, even though he surely didn't know what he was talking about.

"Come to me in a dream," Franz said suddenly, unexpectedly.

"Yes...in a dream...like we did before...do you remember?"

"Before?" asked Franz cautiously, grateful for the new animation in Wolfgang's face.

"You met me on a hill...and told me...you had come to...help me.... I thought then you...were an angel...sent to help...after I had prayed.... Do you know...I met you...not long after I...prayed for help?"

"Truly?"

"And before that...as I worked once...I sensed a presence.... Now I know...it was your presence...." Wolfgang paused to catch his breath. "I will come to you, too...." Franz laid his head gently on Wolfgang's chest.

"Will you tell me what it's like?" His eyes began to well up.

"Oh, yes...I'll tell you...about God...." Wolfgang's eyes brightened briefly. "And I'll give you music...like I do now...." Franz felt Wolfgang's hand touch the back of his head. He had found the strength to reach up and touch him. Franz began to sob.

"Don't leave me...please," he cried despairingly.

"Franz...I won't ever leave you...I promise.... *Believe that*," Wolfgang said with new conviction. "I will come back to you...one way or another...I will!"

Wolfgang sighed. Suddenly, death was not so fearsome to him. What had changed? What was different now from a few moments ago? Could it be this elemental knowledge that death was not the end? That he would, somehow, have the power to return?

Wolfgang had fallen asleep after the exertion of that moment.

Franz spent the rest of the day talking in low whispers with a few well-meaning friends. Those few who had heard how seriously ill the great Mozart really was had come to see him. On one or two occasions, Wolfgang was awake to see his visitors, who stood idly around the bed smiling earnestly and trying to make small talk, but looking glum and uneasy in the face of Wolfgang's advanced state.

Toward evening, Wolfgang's fever blazed anew and Franz became alarmed. He called for Sophie to find the doctor, and a priest. She returned hours later with the news that Dr. Closset was on his way and a priest had told her he might come.

"What do you mean 'might'?" Franz hissed as they spoke in whispers in the hallway outside Wolfgang's room.

"Forgive me, Herr Sussmayr, but none of the priests wanted to come," she answered timidly. Somehow, Franz scared her.

"Why? Did they say why?"

"Yes."

"What did they say?"

"That Wolfgang is no longer a Catholic and that they— the priests—have no longer any obligation to him, they said," she recounted quickly. Franz unnerved her. More than once he had shot her a disapproving look for not moving fast enough, or for failing to return with the proper item.

"The self-righteous swine!" Franz was incensed. "So who is this priest who 'might' come?"

"I don't know, I didn't ask his name. I think he will come. He seemed nicer than the others."

"Thank you, Sophie. Do let me know as soon as he arrives...*if* he arrives," said Franz bitterly.

I wonder if the Masons have any appropriate rites, he pondered, not that they would come either. Not after *Zauberflote*.

He returned to his chair by the bed—and waited.

VIENNA, December 5, 1791.

"Wolfgang? Wolfgang!" breathed Franz, reaching across the bed to grasp his arms. "No!"

A single candle flickered, though the air was still. Franz quickly laid his head on Wolfgang's chest and listened, but heard only the quickening beat of his own heart.

It is over. No more pain....

His head felt light. A dull ache rose in his chest.

The terrible struggle was over. For so long Wolfgang's steady, labored breathing had filled the room. Now, almost imperceptibly, the gentle gasping had stopped.

Franz had sat slumped, half asleep in a chair by the bed. He stood up, stunned and confused. The pain in his chest had reached his tightening throat. His arms hung, idle and heavy at his side, as he stared at the still, slight figure on the bed. The awful reality of death hovered like a gray mist, stifling even in the cold, nearly dark room.

He needn't have died if I'd been more watchful!

He closed his eyes, and remembered. "When I'm dead," Wolfgang had whispered to him between breaths, "you must leave here...immediately...or they'll surely kill you, too."

Franz had said nothing. He hadn't known what to make of Wolfgang's notions of poison. He had nodded solemnly, studying Wolfgang's exhausted eyes, looking for the truth, finding only fear and pain—and the despair of one betrayed.

He could feel the sweat penetrating his shirt. He reached helplessly for Wolfgang's still hand, holding it between his own thin, cold hands.

"Wolfgang...."

Numbing despair washed over him like a cold wave, a feeling so pervasive it blocked all but his bleakest thoughts. He sank back into the chair and held his head in his hands.

Please, God, now let me die.

Minutes passed.

Franz reasoned: Maybe Wolfgang was right. Maybe someone was meaning to kill him, too. Then let it happen. No. Not like this. If I am to die, it will be quickly and by my own hand.

A chill swept over him.

Got to leave! Or the poison will find me!

His legs shook as he groped toward the door. He looked back.

A numb calmness mercifully came as he surveyed for the last time the scene of so many long, remorseful, desperate days. The small bed stood between two large dressers. Wolfgang's small, wasted body barely raised the quilts. On the right, in the corner of the room, more quilts lay on the floor where Franz had spent so many fitful nights. The stove fire had burned throughout the ordeal but now it, too, was cold.

His eyes caught sight of the clock by the candle, two

106

a.m. Franz turned, opened the door noiselessly and slipped through the narrow opening.

Minutes later, sounds of urgent voices preceded the entrance of two women and a man, at first quickly, then slowly as they perceived death's presence. Sophie began sobbing into her hands. Constanze quickly and purposefully surveyed the body, then left immediately, satisfied that it was finally over.

Franz appeared in the doorway, steadying himself against the doorjamb. He brushed shoulders with Constanze as she left the room. Sophie fell to her knees at the bed as Baron Van Swieten pulled the quilt over Wolfgang's face. Sophie's sobbing filled the room as Van Swieten approached Franz where he stood alone, pale and exhausted.

His eyes watched Van Swieten's mouth as it moved, but he didn't hear the words. His eyes met Van Swieten's and fixed there.

Leave here! It may be him!

The baron had turned, slowly shaking his head, and approached Sophie. Franz slipped out into the dark hallway and down the narrow stairs. He emerged onto the street. The sudden cold chilled him to the bone. He remembered that he had not been outside for many days.

Go home. Pack. Leave Vienna.

Several hours later he stood at the carriage house window, waiting for passage out of Vienna. It was still dark when he boarded the diligence, grateful to learn he was its only passenger. It lurched to a start and he closed his eyes in a strange confusion of relief and regret. Trying to ignore the hard pain in his heart, he did not open his eyes again until he was well out of the city. He glanced through the small curtained window. The morning sun was stretching its first pale rays across a bare field of old snow to illumine the thick, dark woods beyond. Thoughts crowded his mind against his will.

He's gone.

It's too late to save him!

I'm alone.

Don't think about it now!

Impulsively, he reached up and drew the curtain over the window, shutting out the growing light. He slumped over and tried to die.

He only slept.

ALBUQUERQUE, 1985.

"Are you ready?" asked Dorothy.

Once again, Lina lay on the bed, waiting. "As ready as I'll ever be," she replied.

Outside, the late afternoon light was fading into evening. The house was still as Dorothy's soft, relaxing voice again took Lina into hypnosis. Lina let herself go, at first hesitantly, then in complete trust and hope. It felt right after all.

"You will be directed by your inner self, your highest guidance, to a time and space in which you will become immersed, but not emotionally involved," said Dorothy slowly. "As you open the door, you will see in your mind's eye and be able to speak of necessary information, be it dates, names, places and events, all that is necessary. Be patient with it, allow it to flow. On the count of three you will open the door and move to this time and space. One, two, three...."

Silence.

"What are you seeing?" asked Dorothy. "Take your time. I am with you and I believe you are there."

"He seems to be on a low cot," reported Lina. "It seems unlikely. A low cot...and he's coughing. He's having a spell. It's night."

"Are you there in this conscious state or are you there as you recognized yourself in another body?" asked Dorothy.

"Yes, I feel I'm in a male body. I can see the stockinged legs. And I seem to be down on the floor next to the cot. It seems strange. I mean the cot and all...."

"It's okay, don't try to make sense of it," said Dorothy.

"He's down," said Lina sadly. "He's depressed and that's all I can really pick up. His head is burning."

"Fever?"

"Yes, now my head hurts, too," replied Lina.

"You don't have to incorporate any pain from this time. Release it. You are protected from emotional strain. Is there any conversation that you hear? It will be in another language, but that's all right. You can bring it into your language," said Dorothy.

"It's coming very slowly," said Lina. I'm anxious, Lina thought. Too anxious to let it happen, to see what's there. "Oh, no! He wants to get up. I'm helping him up. He wants to work. He needs to finish his work. I don't think he should, it's not a good idea, but I'm helping him to the table. He's holding his head in his hands...it's such a small cramped room we're in...he's asking me to get him various things. His music. All the while, I'm thinking to myself, 'He needs to lie down, this isn't good for him, he'll only get more ill,' but I continue to help him get set up to work. He's asking for the music...I believe he's working on a concerto of some kind.

"I'm tensing up," Lina announced precipitously.

She saw the stove. It seemed to be the most important, most central element of the room. She noticed a second cot, and her puzzlement continued until she realized they were placed close to the stove. Sleeping in the bedroom would take them too far from the faintly warm stove. Wood was expensive. And scarce for them. These were desperate times. But they had each other, and love. A strong bond. Very strong bond of friendship and love.

"Things are just stacked here. Nothing's really arranged the way a woman might arrange something. One room, to the left, seems strangely empty. It affects him, and me—this kind of environment is not conducive to his...creativity. His mental state is affected by chaos, by living in what looks like a storage area, really, in that room. In all these rooms. And it's so dark and cold. I don't know about the other room, to the right of the stove. I can't 'see' it. We both miss having a real home, you know, as opposed to just a place to live—a pit stop. It's a shock. He's never been without a real home. And that's what's making him sick, too. It's a kind of heartsickness. And it seems the only time he gets relief is when he's working because he can forget everything when he's working."

Lina stopped.

"Okay, let's move now," interjected Dorothy. "Another suggestion. We are moving forward in time to shortly before his death, perhaps a few days, or even, necessarily, a little earlier than that."

Lina immediately felt a tightening in her chest and a vague reluctance to continue.

"You're still with him," continued Dorothy. "And because you have a broader view from your vantage point, even though you're having a little difficulty focusing, you're seeing it little by little. And when you're ready, and you have some focus there, think of what you see and what you're experiencing."

Lina struggled as the gradually intensifying emotions distracted her ability to focus. She decided to sort them out.

Frustration.

Impatience.

Helplessness.

Desperation.

Fear.

Grief.

Seconds passed. Lina gasped. She saw the pathetically small figure lying under the quilts on the bed. Still, very still. The sound of labored breathing filled her head. She remembered this scene from a meditation, long ago.

"Where are you?" asked Dorothy patiently, slowly.

"I don't know," replied Lina, clearing her throat. It was continuing to tighten, making it difficult to speak. "I don't think we're back in that place, with the cots."

"Okay, you've moved."

"I don't know where it is. I know there's a bed. It's another one of those dark rooms. I know something has happened...but I don't know what...and I'm grieving inside already...because it looks like he's dying and...*there's nothing we can do about it!* That's it, you know...it's such a strong feeling...."

She had to stop. Tears were welling in her eyes. Her throat threatened to close entirely. Dorothy waited quietly.

"It's like we're up against a wall, trapped! He's going to *die* and there's nothing we...can do...."

Tears rolled down the sides of her face and into her hair.

"When you say...." Dorothy began.

"Nothing!"

"...'we,' is there someone else there?"

A shadowy figure appeared in the periphery of Lina's inner vision. "A doctor. But they're useless." Her voice was sad with despair. "There was so much still to be done. And now, I don't know...it just seems...it's an accident. It shouldn't...this wasn't planned. It shouldn't have happened. And, oh, God!...I felt maybe...I should have been able to control...to control things that affected his life and his work. I mean, I was there to take *care* of him, and this happened! Oh, God, I should have been able to *avoid* it...."

110

"All right, now...."

"...and I *didn't!*" Lina was sobbing.

"...let's go with that. You seem to be picking up a great deal of guilt in this time period. Was there some promise that you felt you had made to take care of him?" asked Dorothy.

"Yes! I promised *him,* and I promised the others, and...I don't know, something slipped through or somebody got past me and they've killed him!"

"Okay, they've killed him," Dorothy cut in evenly. "So you feel there was...."

"Somebody's *killed* him!" cried Lina in horror and confusion. "And I don't know *who!*"

"This is a very good time, then...," began Dorothy. Lina was gasping. "Wait, now, a very good time for your soul to release the feelings of guilt. You were there to help him. You did what you could. You were not responsible that others misused their energies, were not loving and caring. You were. So you must release the guilt. Now. For his sake, which is your soul monadic source. For your sake, for the sake of all others. It is best now to release this feeling of guilt and let it go. You are not guilty of not fulfilling your promise. You were there on his behalf and yours, and on behalf of the world, for the music, for the challenge. And this you worked to complete after his physical demise. Take your time. Let it go."

Several minutes passed as Lina again attempted to sort her feelings and let go. Gradually her breathing slowed. The tears and anguish slowly faded, but the newly unlocked feelings of profound responsibility remained.

Dorothy continued. "Can you see who was responsible for his death if there was foul play? Are you looking at that?"

A new set of thoughts emerged to confuse and confound her. She wrestled within herself momentarily, unbelieving, before responding.

"It just couldn't be her. No. I don't think she's smart enough to do it," Lina said distractedly.

This is craziness!

"His *wife,*" she announced. "I keep seeing his wife as the one. I don't think she could do it. Maybe she would...I don't know, maybe it was someone she was having an affair with, maybe he did it. No, no. I have no idea who did it."

But I do, and I can't believe what I'm seeing. This can't be right!

"Okay, but someone, you feel, was responsible?" asked Dorothy carefully.

"Yes. Umm, I don't know if there was...it's hard to get an overview feeling...." Lina paused. Then, "I think *she* did it! She's not there. I don't see her there. She doesn't spend any time by his deathbed."

No, this can't be!

"Maybe that's just a personal prejudice of mine, but I...I think she did it. I'm probably wrong, I'm just...."

Oh, God, let me be wrong. Not her! That would be too terrible. He loved her so!

"Maybe that's how I feel because, uh, of the poor wife she's been up to now. Maybe she was a better wife in the earlier days of their marriage, but now she's not attentive at all. She's not around and even if she didn't do it, I feel she did it. If she did it...it was with her neglect. I don't know if she personally poisoned him, but I think what I'm trying to say...."

What am I trying to say? I see her. I see that she did it, but I can't admit it. I can't....

"I'm accusing her...I'm accusing her. Maybe she's not...maybe she shouldn't be accused."

"Lina," said Dorothy softly. "I have a picture in my mind. I see what you see. Mozart never suspected her either. She was, literally, the last one he ever would have suspected. He was too devoted to her. At the time, she spends, as you say, practically no time at his side as he's dying—and yet this very short time that she did, and it was unlike her, she raised his head and...didn't she offer something to his lips? This is what I'm seeing. Were you there? Were you in the other room or not seeing this?

"I see somebody offering him something," said Lina. She saw a woman bent over the bed on his left. "...and suddenly he's got...something in his...system that is making it...worse."

Suddenly, Lina felt herself moving gently in a horizontal, oval orbit above the bed where she lay. It was a curious lightness of being, unlike anything she had ever felt before.

"Let's move on," said Dorothy. "Is there anything else that you need to look at in this lifetime? Think about it a minute. Look and see. Anything that would be helpful...."

"I want to know why he was doing this. Why this lifetime. I want to know how. The word 'experiment' keeps coming to my head. What kind of experiment was it? What was it all for?"

"Go to a higher place for that information. To the Akashic door, and there—when you spoke of the 'others' that you had given your word to that you would take care of Mozart—those others, we will call the Elders. There you will get your questions answered. Go to that door knowing that you are now on another level, and you can ask these high beings for some answers. Know that they will correspond with you in thought form that you must pick up. It will not be in a way of words. You must be able to understand and put it in your own words, and then really you are understanding it within yourself. You, then, are with those high souls who will answer your questions with love and with great compassion. Feel free to ask."

A long pause filled the room as Dorothy sat at attention and waited in the darkness. Thoughts began to "occur" to Lina. She received them in awe and verbalized them as they came to her at a steady pace.

"We came to give the world beauty," she began in a smooth, rested tone. "Musical respite. He was a direct channel from the musical center, the musical heart, of the higher planes...with all the mathematical implications, or manifestations, that lie beyond the normal consciousness or comprehension of an Earth-bound soul. He tapped right into it, and was able to pull that into the music—his music. There is a place where all this harmony is...."

She struggled to find the words that adequately described the sense of order and rightness.

"...is natural, and beautiful, and logical...," she continued, at once realizing these words were inadequate.

"...and where harmony and rhythm and melody are integral to all other aspects of existence and...to God...but we on the Earth plane don't...can't...hear that...but, through Mozart, we have a direct line to that, through his music, and that's what is meant by his 'genius,' his 'divine spark.' He showed us something we couldn't otherwise hear or see or feel within us because we are clouded here. The intensity of the process cost him his physical well-being...but he knew this, and accepted it."

The thoughts kept coming, yet she felt herself unable to translate all that she absorbed.

"He wrote enormous amounts of music because of the nature of the way he received it. His consciousness was not always aware of what he wrote down. Often he would not realize what he was writing until after it was written...then the fine, pristine mathematical structure and the effortless beauty of the melodies were a surprise even to him at these times. This is not to say he was only a receptacle. He worked hard all his life to learn and perfect the mechanics of composition because it was necessary to the experiment. It was his part to do, as well as to draw on the experiences of all his lives, and the beauty of his heart, which imbued, colored, inspired the music in its finished state."

The last thought came in a rush. Lina was beginning to feel like a spectator as she listened to her mind and mouth attempt synchronicity.

"The term music is a confining one, because in our true reality, it goes beyond what we know as music here. There, we *are* music. There, we live in it more fully. There, it nurtures us more fully. Here, it heals us—its healing here is a hint of its activity there...."

Lina realized there was more, but it was coming too swiftly now. She couldn't keep up, so she stopped.

"Would you ask, for our mutual benefit," ventured Dorothy, "of the elder brothers and beings, if some of the musical spheres involved, and our listening to it, and Mozart's being able to channel it through, are in line with the chakric openings of the New Age?"

"Like anything else that requires the consciousness to blossom, his music will provide a bridge. But only to those who are ready for it. To those who are not ready for it, it's just pretty tunes. For those who find that they can accept his music for what it truly is, they will recognize it and it will help them in that way. It will act as a bridge between their existence and the true reality. And that is why he did it. In order to help us recognize the true reality.

"The music focuses on a *remembrance* of a home that we have temporarily forgotten. Earth is only a lower vibrational dimension—a valley of mists. During our Earth visit, music smooths the edges and calms the heart. It is...hope.

"Like the work of all true artists, the music of many composers is a bridge between the true reality and the lower vibrational dimension. Certain musics have certain purposes, such as peace, harmony or healing. This music was a cosmic experiment brought about by many entities working together to channel healing sounds through a high vibrational connection with the entity Mozart. That entity possessed (and possesses) tremendous soul energy which was used at that time.

"All the music of this entity leads to mental and spiritual balance, and beneficence among men and women. For those who are whole of mind, it will establish a firmer oneness with their Source. This new unity results in kindness and generosity toward others.

"For those who are not whole of mind, the music is a miracle in that it happens necessarily in that particular part of the brain that wants balance. It is especially effective for those with multiple personality or neurotransmitter disorders, and general retardation.

"For those who are spiritually lost or uncertain, it will provide comfort whether or not they attempt to find their way back. Yet for them, it can stand as proof of God's existence, or, at the very least, an orderly force in the universe. The purpose of these sounds is multi-dimensional, extremely complex and, above all, healing."

"How does it heal?" asked Dorothy.

"The earthly body is mostly water. In this sense the body acts as a conductor, resonating to vibrations made around it. The sounds trigger, in the human form, a profound awareness and response on the cellular level. Also, there is a focal point of spiritual balance within each entity which is centered in the solar plexus area. From there the sounds radiate to open the chakras and to alter the molecular structure as needed. These vibrations similarly affect other living beings as well as basic Earth elements. One does not need to appreciate, or even pay attention, to this music to be healed by it. It plays on our minds and bodies like a beautiful light.

"Spiritual evolution on the Earth plane is enhanced and accelerated by these vibrations, both on an individual level and collectively."

"Can you give an example?"

"In the concerto form, the interplay between the solo instrument and the orchestra reflects, as it were, the interplay between the soul and the group soul, or the group soul and its Source. The subconscious recognizes this. The conscious understanding responds with acknowledgement, and then with *joy*."

KREMSMUNSTER, December 5, 1791.

When Franz arrived in Kremsmunster, the sun had disappeared behind the shadowy white mountains. The black carriage jolted to a stop. Moments later, the door opened and Franz stepped out stiffly into the night air. The short, round driver handed him his bag and, slapping himself for warmth, quickly escaped into a nearby tavern. Franz hesitated, standing in the light of the tavern window, his shadow long on the snow before him.

It would be so easy, he thought, to simply walk into these hills and lie down under a tree and.... No one would miss him, no one even knew he was here.

He resembled a ghost, unmoving in the road, contemplating how ridiculously easy it would be. Except....

Except that Wolfgang had asked him not to. He had exacted a promise. Like a breath on a breeze, the memory of that promise came to him now.

He picked up his bag and trudged down the white, eerily moonlit street. Fifteen minutes later, he arrived at the home of Father Pasterwicz. Franz stopped short.

Why am I here?

What will I tell him?

He approached the house. It seemed so many years ago that Pasterwicz had introduced Franz to Wolfgang.

It must be me, then, Franz reasoned, who will inform Pasterwicz of the death of our friend.

He knocked on the door and stared out at the cold, snow-covered ground while he waited. He looked up again at the dark window of the door. A light approached, gradually lighting the ice crystals on the window into hundreds of yellow diamonds. Franz blinked. The door opened slightly.

"Yes, who is it, please?" a woman's voice said quickly in a country accent.

Franz tried to speak, but his voice caught in his throat. He cleared it and tried again. "It's Franz Sussmayr, madam, here to see Father Pasterwicz. I've come from Vienna this night."

"Wait here," she said, and the door shut. Franz closed his eyes and pursed his lips. He began to sway, so he opened his eyes again. His stomach hurt. He remembered he hadn't eaten since the previous day. Moments passed before the door opened wide. "Come in, sir, come in."

He stepped in and dropped his bag.

"This way, please," said the old woman. Franz followed the light of her candle down the narrow hall and into the sudden, welcome warmth of Pasterwicz's modest library.

"Franz, my son, what brings you here at this unusual hour? Please forgive me, I would have come to the door, but my bad hip has been acting up again, you know how it is!" Pasterwicz laughed until he saw Franz's face in better light. As his mentor spoke, Franz surveyed the familiar room. The firelight glowed orange on the shelves of books that lined all four walls, and on the bright brass and warm, dark, polished wood paneling. A respectable fire burned in the hearth by Pasterwicz, who sat wrapped in blankets, holding a book, as usual. Franz had never known him to be far from a book or a score of some kind.

He looked at the hearth again. He sank slowly into the chair opposite Pasterwicz, and leveled his exhausted gaze at the old priest.

Pasterwicz frowned. His brightest music student at Kremsmunster had always been a kind of mystery to him, for he lived life intensely, but said little about it except through his music. He remembered their first meeting—the slight, tow-headed child of thirteen asking for music lessons on first arriving at the monastery school where the Dominican priest taught. Even then, he was taken with the boy's intelligent, yet pale face and vulnerable, compassionate brown eyes. Today those eyes were frightened.

"What's wrong, Franz?" he asked evenly. Then, instinctively, he added, "Where is Wolfgang?" A moment passed before Franz answered in a voice as quiet as the woods outside.

"He's dead, sir."

Pasterwicz closed his eyes briefly, and said nothing at first.

"Dead?" Even more alarming than the news was the look of desperation on the young man's face. Pasterwicz waved the woman out of the room before asking, "Tell me what happened."

"I don't really know," began Franz slowly. "He was fine. I mean, not really fine. He's never been in good health. But he was all right, except for the coughing, and his stomach. And the headaches. Then about ten days ago he took ill in a most sudden and violent way. He collapsed, you see, and I...." The tears started to burn his eyes.

"Take your time," counseled Pasterwicz, reaching to touch his hand. Franz turned to the fire.

"At first we thought it was just another one of his fevers. But the days passed and he didn't improve." Franz took deep breaths as he spoke. "His stomach rejected everything...and his headache never stopped. He got so weak he couldn't lift his arms...and his breathing! For days his breathing was...steady and gasping and...and then he just died. Last night. He just stopped breathing." Franz suddenly turned to Pasterwicz with an inquisitive and demanding expression, as if expecting an explanation.

"Were you with him then?" asked Pasterwicz.

"Yes." Franz sighed heavily and sank back into the chair.

"Was it a peaceful passing?"

"...Yes...." Franz looked again into the old man's eyes.

What profound sadness, thought Pasterwicz. "Franz, help me stand up."

Franz stood up slowly, obediently, assisted him to his feet and handed him his cane. Pasterwicz steadied himself with it and then, quite unexpectedly, pulled Franz toward him and held him around the shoulders with one arm. He held him tightly. At first Franz was confused, his mind was so clouded with weary misery. The closeness of another person soon took its effect, however, and before he could stop himself, he was sobbing bitterly into the old man's broad shoulder. His arms circled around him and he held on as if to life itself.

He cries as though his heart would break, Pasterwicz thought, wincing. Never, in all his long years, had he heard such sobbing from man or woman. Franz had always nurtured a strong passion for life, and being so long with Wolfgang had intensified it. He had envied them for their close friendship, but now he realized there could be a dark side to such intense associations, for Franz's grief was agonizing.

When he felt Franz had cried himself out, he let go of him and motioned for him to sit down again. Pasterwicz lowered himself into his own chair. For a while they sat, saying nothing. The old man studied his visitor.

"There's something you're not telling me," he said at last. He knew Franz too well.

Franz occupied the chair as though he had been tossed there. Tears stained his drawn face as he looked up, wide-eyed.

"Did someone kill Wolfgang?" inquired Pasterwicz. He had always known Mozart had jealous enemies as well as those who didn't like his brilliant and effortless musicianship or, for that matter, his enlightened brand of non-religion.

Franz clutched the wooden arms of the chair. "I think so," he exhaled, "but I don't know who...or how. Wolfgang told me he had been poisoned, that he could...taste it still...but I didn't believe him. Then he told me to leave Vienna immediately after he died...he knew he was going to die...he said to leave because they probably would try to kill me, too—whoever 'they' are. I didn't really believe him, you see, because I didn't believe he would die. But he did die...." His voice trailed off.

"Who killed him, Franz?" persisted Pasterwicz sympathetically.

A low sob came from Franz as he leaned forward to hold his head in his hands. "That's just it. I don't *know*. All I know is if I had been...more careful...I might have prevented it from happening, don't you see? I should have been with him at all times. But I wasn't. No, I wasn't...and they got him...and someone has poisoned him...and now he's gone. He's *gone*. Do you see? It's as good as if I killed him." Franz was shaking now. Pasterwicz shook his head sadly and rang the bell for the housekeeper.

"Listen to me, Franz," he said, leaning over to touch his head. "Listen here, you did what you could. You couldn't be with him at every turn. That's not possible, or reasonable. You have to stop this destructive thinking right now before it eats away at your very soul," ...and it will, he thought.

"He was my brother, and my friend...and now he's gone. He was all I had. What will I do?"

Pasterwicz frowned, suddenly feeling helpless and ineffective.

The housekeeper appeared in the doorway. He motioned to her. "Anna, get us some warm brandy. Franz, will you drink something warm?" Franz shook his head. Pasterwicz looked up and motioned to her to bring it anyway. She nodded and was gone.

Franz suddenly stopped shaking and sat up straight.

"Sir, I need a place to hide," he said stiffly.

"Of course, Franz, you will stay here for as long as it takes," said the old man. He reached over again and touched his hand.

"Thank you. It's good to know I have you to turn to. My own family, you know, is not...."

"Now, let's not get into that right now, shall we? Tell me, have you eaten today? I know you too well. You and Wolfgang could go for hours and hours without food and never complain."

"We had no choice," said Franz quietly.

"Yes, but you were still happy, weren't you?" said Pasterwicz. "I could see that. And I know Wolfgang loved you quite a lot. I remember running into him...let's see, when was it?" Pasterwicz saw Franz look up with interest. Encouraged, he went on. "Must have been a year ago last spring sometime. You were gone somewhere. Were you in Baden in the spring? With Frau Mozart?"

"Probably," Franz replied. Anna appeared with a tray. Pasterwicz took both cups and handed one to Franz.

"I saw him at a tavern, dining alone. So I sat with him. He was happy for the company, as usual. I asked for you, how your studies were coming along. That's when he told me you had stopped writing your own music in order to help him with his. He was so pleased, and proud of you, as if you were his own son. I'll never forget how his eyes shone when he spoke of you and his wife. 'Life's companions' he called you both.

"But he missed you both terribly. I'm afraid he was too passionately attached to his wife, although maybe I'm wrong. I wouldn't know, would I?" he chuckled.

"She broke his heart, Father," Franz uttered coldly. "He loved her too much...beyond reason. She couldn't make him hurt her or be angry with her, no matter what she said, or did. He was compassionate and full of love...for her, for life.... But she shut him out of her life. You don't know, do you? She has been living with someone else."

Pasterwicz shifted nervously in his chair. He didn't want to hear this. It was none of his business, but he didn't stop Franz because he obviously needed to get it said.

"How did Wolfgang feel about that?" he asked politely.

"He never said a word," Franz sighed. "But I saw it all in his eyes, the hurt, the disappointment, the humiliation. At first, you see, she only flirted with others, but never around Wolfgang. Mostly in Baden. That's why he sent me with her— to watch over her. To prevent...but then she started seeing someone in Vienna, I don't know who. It doesn't matter." Franz started slowly, unconsciously, to wring his hands.

"If she was being kept," asked Pasterwicz, no longer able to contain his curiosity, "who had the children?"

"Her mother," answered Franz. "It was all so unfair. She had her whole grasping Weber family behind her, including that loathsome guardian Thorwart, to twist his arm into signing another stupid contract. And what could he do? He had no one, and he knew nothing of real business or the law."

"A contract, Franz?" Pasterwicz prompted, his interest growing.

"It was a travesty, really. It said that if Wolfgang insisted on remaining a musician and composer, instead of seeking steadier work at some kind of government post with what they called a 'real' income, that he must pay the Weber family a set amount to keep Constanze comfortably set up. Wolfgang had protested at first, but Thorwart threatened to make it public that he could not support his own family...so Wolfgang signed it.

"That happened before I knew him. Still, he wouldn't let me try to do anything about it because he still loved and trusted her! That's what I don't understand. He didn't complain, because he loved her so. He said the contract was not her idea, that she would tear it up at any time, like she did the other one. But she never did."

"The other one? What other one?"

"Before they were married, Thorwart insisted Wolfgang sign a contract agreeing to pay a certain amount if he did not marry Constanze within a set time. After Wolfgang signed it, Constanze tore it up. But she didn't tear up this one. He couldn't, or wouldn't, realize that for some reason, she had drifted away from him. He never let on. Then I made it worse. She came to hate me."

"What do you mean? Why on earth would she hate you?"

"At first, she...she was...attracted to me. When I shunned her secret attempts, she...." Franz hesitated.

"Yes?..."

"She began telling her friends...that Wolfgang and I were lovers," muttered Franz. "I cannot understand what drives anyone to spread such venom and lies."

"How did she behave now, in Wolfgang's last days?"

asked Pasterwicz.

"I don't know, I hardly saw her. She rarely came into the room, and when she did, she hurried away as quickly as she could manage. But that's only because everyone thought Wolfgang was contagious. Everyone was afraid they'd take ill with the same thing...the fools. They're probably burying him right now, quickly, and without a proper funeral, just because they think he's...." He looked away from Pasterwicz.

"Come, Franz, you need some rest," said the old man. "Anna will show you upstairs. And take in some extra quilts. It's going to be a cold night, I can feel it." He rang for Anna again.

He turned to Franz and said, "Franz, listen to me. Only God knows why things happen the way they do." He slowed down to enunciate for more emphasis. "It is not for us to question. It is for us to follow the will of God, do you see that? I want you to stay here as long as you need to, and to remember this, and pray on it. And pray for our Wolfgang, but also take heart in knowing he is happier now than either you or me." He paused to see how his words were affecting Franz, who stared at the floor in stoic exhaustion. Anna arrived. Pasterwicz shook his head and murmured, "God bless you, my son."

Franz blinked, rousing himself from the chair, and slowly followed Anna out of the room. Pasterwicz watched him pensively, then turned his gaze toward the fire to grieve quietly for Wolfgang.

ONE WEEK LATER.

Franz couldn't remember when he'd felt this aware of his physical surroundings. The chilly air seemed to help. He had found a wooden bench in Pasterwicz's deserted garden and spent the afternoon in immovable solitude. The ground here was covered with a re-melted snow that formed a crust of ice inches above the wet earth. He remembered as a child taking enormous delight in the sound and feel of that icy snow crackling and crunching under his boots.

Now he sat motionless staring at the clear, cold rivulets under the ice as they snaked toward a stone gully leading around the house, out of sight. Franz closed his eyes and heaved a slow sigh. His mouth set in a frown.

Wolfgang's health had never been good. Franz had noticed immediately that he had a blithe disregard for his health, although he worried a great deal about the health of others, particularly Constanze. As long as Franz had known him, Wolfgang had suffered frequent and terrible headaches, stomach pains and frightening coughing spells. His strength had seemed to dwindle gradually through the months that Franz had known him, until at the end Wolfgang had nothing with which to fight back. He was helpless.

Franz sighed heavily. A cold breeze came up. He pulled his greatcoat closer around him. The sun was setting. Soon the rivulets under the icy snow would freeze for the night. The cold, dark night. Suddenly he caught his breath. He saw Wolfgang walking briskly along the flagstone path not fifteen feet away. He seemed lively, healthy—happy. He was in a hurry. He half turned as if called, laughing and waving but not stopping. He looked better than Franz had ever seen him.

The sight faded. Franz was too weary to get excited over a hallucination. Soon he began, again, to weep.

The sunlight faded with the setting sun; the blue shadows of the snowbound landscape deepened as the night advanced on Kremsmunster's beautiful countryside. In the Pasterwicz kitchen, Anna peeled potatoes with swift strokes as she asked the Father, who had just sauntered in, to fetch Franz "before he freezes to the ground."

"Has he been out there long then?" asked Pasterwicz.

"All afternoon," said Anna, faintly insulted. "The man's haunted, I'll warrant you, plainly haunted. His color's bad, he never eats, he doesn't sleep...."

Before she was finished, Pasterwicz had gone to get his wrap. All afternoon indeed! He promised me he would take care of himself, thought Pasterwicz. He promised!

He gasped at the cold breeze. A storm must be coming, and the sun had long since set. Poor soul, what am I going to do with him?

"Franz! Come inside, my son," he said. "You'll catch your death out here." Pasterwicz put his arm around him and slowly pulled him up from his crouching position. Franz had stopped sobbing, but his eyes were red as he looked up. Pasterwicz held him up as they walked back to the house. Franz's stiff limbs moved slowly, and he noticed a stinging feeling in his hands as they gradually approached the house with its golden yellow lit windows.

Squeaking mice behind the wall of Franz's bedroom woke him from his half-sleep. With unfocused eyes, he glanced around the room to see if he was alone. Yes, Anna was gone, though his headache was not, nor his fever. His gaze wandered aimlessly along the ceiling and down the opposite wall to the pale green curtains on the window. The wind had worn itself out, but the snow had begun falling again.

Snow. Covering a barren land of barren people, like me, Franz mused dejectedly, doing nothing but waiting to die. He rolled over to face the wall. Suddenly, the wall began to spin. He clutched the bed, at the same time feeling the headache worsen with dizziness. When the spell had passed he cautiously let go of the bed.

Please, God, let me die.

He drifted, gradually, into sleep.

He was back home in Vienna. In that peculiar way of a dreamer's knowing, he realized his pain was gone—the pain of his headache and the pain of losing Wolfgang. Somehow, it all had subsided as he strode into the room looking for his copywork.

But he saw immediately something was amiss. He squinted. Nothing here is as I left it! Why, the furniture is gone, the fortepiano is, too. Everything's missing! I must have waited too long before returning to Vienna, and now the authorities have taken everything to pay Wolfgang's debts. Damn!

Franz ran into the bedroom. Nothing there either, except some portraits on the wall...and the bare floors. Where are the rugs? The walls were a different color, too. And these portraits....

Portraits? Franz thought in haste. Who put those there? They don't belong to me, or Wolfgang. He heard footsteps and spun around, intent on demanding an explanation.

Their eyes met and held. Lina knew immediately it was a vision, because she could see the wall through him. Still, his eyes were as real as anyone's she'd ever seen. They were sensitive and troubled. He was dressed as if waiting to go onstage in some period play.

As she had caught him by surprise as she walked through the door of the museum, her first impulse might have been to scream and pass out or run away, but she was held frozen by those eyes, so compelling and so—familiar.

Franz did not move. Transfixed, he found quiet compassion and earnestness in the eyes of this strange apparition. He was only vaguely aware that her legs were showing below a skirt that was too short, and she carried a leather pack hanging by a strap from her shoulder. Her eyes were familiar.

If he could remember where he'd met her before, or her name, he would ask her if she knew what had happened to his belongings. He noticed her hand grasp the doorjamb behind her skirts as she leaned back against it. She seemed to be surprised. He reached out, opening his mouth to speak.

Then he awoke.

"Lina, where did you go?" Kathy called from the other room. Lina didn't respond. Her mouth dropped open as she stared at the air where he had just been. He had just been there, and he melted into thin air. Poof, like that. A real, honest-to-God ghost!

"Kathy!" she called excitedly, as she backed out of the room, still staring at the spot.

VIENNA, December 21, 1791.

Franz arrived in Vienna on a cold, snowy night. The hollow clatter of the diligence was muffled by the fresh blanket of snow on the streets of the city. The night glow reflecting from the streetlights had enchanted him as a child. Now it all seemed very nearly like death to Franz. The city was dead and cold, even as life itself was no more than waiting for death.

On descending from the conveyance, he took his bag and trudged through the snow to another carriage to be driven home. He would not look at the city as the carriage passed through the wide avenues of the central district and into the narrow winding streets nearer his neighborhood. He was tired, and the city disgusted him. When the conveyance finally stopped in front of the gray building, Franz hesitated.

"Sir?" started the driver as he half turned to peer into the carriage. Franz looked up at him as if seeing him for the first time. "We've arrived," he said.

Franz looked again at the building before stepping out. His legs felt wooden as he fumbled for money and paid the driver. The carriage moved off into the gray and white night.

Franz clutched his bag nervously and turned toward the building. It was still there. With slow, heavy steps, he entered the walkway and turned to face the stairs.

Nothing will ever be the same. Nothing.

Somewhere in a nearby neighborhood the sound of a Christmas hymn broke through the stillness of the falling snow. Franz glanced at the sky and then began the long climb to the door. The rail was cold, as was the latch. The apartment was dark and still. Wearily, he closed the door behind him and dropped his bag where he stood. He leaned against the door as his hands slowly withdrew into fists. He felt weak.

What am I doing here? Why did I come?

Then he remembered. He had wanted to return. He had begun to feel like a burden at Pasterwicz's, and had insisted on leaving as soon as he recovered from his illness. Pasterwicz had let him go with misgivings. Not that he was fearful for his life. No, Pasterwicz had made sure of that by writing to certain friends in Vienna regarding any rumors of a similar attempt on Franz's life. He was not about to let Franz return to his own death. His fears were not laid to rest entirely by the responses he had received, however. One told of the general suspicions of foul play in the death of Mozart. But it was mere gossip with no real evidence or even a name to whisper.

More alarming to Franz and Pasterwicz was a report that attributed Wolfgang's early death to his supposedly heretical life. He was a Freemason, they were saying, and worse, a fallen-away Catholic. As such he had invited demons into his compositions, which many thought were unplayable—too many strange harmonies. Then the demons killed him. Why else, they were asking, would he have been carried off on the fifth of December—Krampen Eve—the night the devil began his roamings throughout Vienna, according to the ancient Austrian tradition? For this reason, some Viennese were crossing themselves at the mention of Wolfgang's name. Others insisted that he never should have received a church burial. Still others said his body still had demons, and for that alone he had been buried quickly.

Some insisted they knew the real reason for the quick funeral. One of Mozart's doctors (for Closset had called in an associate) had secretly admitted that he didn't really know what had killed him, but that whatever it was, it might have been contagious. The quick burial was for the safety of everyone involved, he said, safety from a new, potentially serious epidemic. "That's a stupid lie," Franz had said quietly. "He was not contagious."

"That's not the issue," Pasterwicz had cautioned him. "Imagine what they must think your part was with these so-called demons."

Franz didn't care. He half-heartedly hoped someone would make an attempt on his life. By making his life shorter, they would solve his problems.

He stepped carefully in the dark toward the desk and fumbled in the drawers for candles. After a few minutes, he succeeded in lighting one and jamming it into the brass notch on the desk. He pulled himself into the chair and gazed at the flame. His head shook faintly. The desktop was neat and cleared of work. The blank staff paper sat in a neat pile, waiting. The pens waited in the jar. Franz glanced toward the music room and assured himself that Wolfgang's chests were still there. He had half expected the arch-Catholics to have burned them by now.

He stood up and approached the cabinet, where he found a half bottle of wine. Popping the cork, he took a long swallow and tossed the cork into the corner of the room, then wandered into the bedroom. He finished the bottle in a few more swallows, grimacing—the wine had long since gone to vinegar. He fell across the bed, still in his greatcoat. In minutes he was asleep.

The candle flickered, sending shadows across the room in a wild dance of light. Then the flame was still again. Snowflakes gathered against the windows until they completely covered the glass.

Franz's eyes opened, then closed. Then opened wide. He lifted his head and found himself at home. On Wolfgang's bed. In that innocent split second of time between half sleep and full consciousness, he felt truly at home, not yet aware of the events of the past two weeks. Then he emerged to waking and disappointment. His next sensation was of a powerful hunger.

He slipped off the bed and sat down on it as he tried to rub the sleep from his eyes. He looked toward the window and noticed it was late afternoon. He felt pain in his stomach. A half-hour later he appeared on the white, icy streets heading toward the Silver Serpent. He had pushed aside all thoughts of life and how he expected to live it. He was hungry.

The Silver Serpent had become a favorite place for Wolfgang and Franz. Its dark wood paneling, heavy wooden tables and low ceilings gave them both a feeling of protective warmth and coziness they did not get in the airier, white-walled apartment. The Silver Serpent, Franz had once decided, was as close in atmosphere to a real home as they had had. Their troubles were forgotten here, especially as they got progressively lightheaded on one of Josef Deiner's heady beers or local wines. Here, too, the heavy glass panes effectively held back the cold winter. Franz sat at the usual table close to the hearth and concentrated on his meal of sausage and potatoes.

"Franz." A hand touched his shoulder. He looked up to behold the kind face of Josef Deiner. "Franz, we missed you." Josef hadn't noticed until now, peering into Franz's face, how much his eyes resembled Wolfgang's. The same gaze: wise and smiling, yet somewhat melancholy. And now the same look of exhaustion, too.

"Are you all right?" he inquired. Somewhat shaken to see a friend, Franz reached across the table where Josef had sat down and took his hand. The innkeeper of the Silver Serpent was one of their most faithful friends.

"Are you all right, Franz?" Josef repeated.

"I don't know," Franz admitted, feeling the tears sting his eyes. He fought them back. The last thing he wanted to do was break down in front of Josef or anybody nearby. "I think so."

"Do you know the Webers are looking for you? They say they need to collect Wolfgang's music. They say Constanze is frantic, that she thinks you might have left town and taken everything. She's suddenly become very possessive about his music," reported Josef. He squeezed Franz's hand reassuringly. "I knew you wouldn't do that. But, to be honest, I didn't know what to think. Where have you been?"

"I had to leave, Josef, I had to. I couldn't stay here so I went to Kremsmunster."

"You couldn't stay here? Why?" Josef persisted.

"Please don't ask me anything more. I'm not well, Josef. I...," Oh, God, he thought. This is hell. So many questions! "Tell me about the funeral, will you?" he countered.

Josef studied his friend for a moment, frowning. "It

was held the next day at St. Stephen's, nothing elaborate, mind you. In fact, it was a very meager funeral. I was very surprised, but if I hadn't been there myself and heard the funeral arrangements with my own ears...."

"Heard what?"

"Well, I don't like to repeat such things, but I think you should know. When Van Swieten asked Constanze how she wanted to handle the burial, she told him, 'There is no money, do what you wish.' He said she spoke as if she didn't care whether he was buried at all. In fact, her sisters and mother were telling visitors she was ill, when I know she was up and about. I saw her, she was fine. I imagine she only wanted to avoid everyone, but I don't understand why she wouldn't make the effort to attend her own husband's funeral. At any rate, she couldn't, or wouldn't, pay for the funeral, even with her family's help. That's when Van Swieten started looking for you. When he didn't find you, he decided to arrange the funeral on his own. That's how he got on the wrong side of the Emperor."

"What do you mean?"

"The Emperor got word that Van Swieten, his own court librarian, was taking on the responsibility of burying a fallen-away Catholic and, more seriously, a Freemason. He ordered Van Swieten to have nothing to do with Wolfgang's funeral, that it could not be a holy sacrament. When Van Swieten ignored his warnings, the Emperor released him from his court position. All who knew him, and who heard of it, were shocked. Still others had seen it coming for a while. A known Freemason cannot survive at the pleasure of the court for long."

"What did he do?"

"There was nothing he could do about being fired, but he sorely regretted having had to buy Wolfgang such a poor funeral. It was nearly a pauper's funeral, but not quite. Bad enough, however. If only you had been here, Franz." Josef was sobbing quietly now.

"Why did he buy so cheap a funeral?"

"It was all the money he had on hand. You know how difficult ready cash is to get on short notice. And they wanted to bury Wolfgang immediately."

"Did he get his own grave?"

"No."

Franz frowned. He knew what that meant—an anonymous burial in a communal pit with at least three others. "Then

129

I don't suppose there's a marker," probed Franz.

"No, and no one has said anything about getting one. Constanze's family still claims she is ill with grief, although I've seen her at the market. I don't know what she hopes to gain by these deceits. It's a disgrace." Josef was wiping his tears with his apron.

"Can you show me where he's buried?"

"I'm sorry, Franz, I don't know where he's buried. I haven't been out there yet. No one has."

"Will you go there with me? Tomorrow? We'll find it together."

"We needed you, Franz." Josef was stubborn. "Why did you leave?"

Franz sighed. "I had to go, Josef. The city was suffocating me." He would not talk about Wolfgang's admonishment to leave Vienna immediately. If it came up, he might tell Josef later. But not now.

The next day Josef came for Franz in his brother's fine carriage. Fortunately, it had a foot heater of warm coals. The carriage rumbled along the Schulerstrasse, past the Stubentor gate and into the whitened countryside. Finally they arrived at St. Marx Cemetery and alighted. The sun shone brightly that afternoon as they proceeded solemnly through the gates in search of the keeper, who pointed the way to the burial pit used two weeks prior. It was now covered with earth and snow. A new pit had been dug to the east of it.

Franz was numb with cold as they stood next to the long rectangular patch of earth, discernible only by the rise in the snow that topped it. All of the cemetery, with the exception of the gaping brown pit not far from where they stood, also rested under a covering of snow. Josef stood by silently, lost in his own thoughts.

Franz stared stoically at the white grave. Wolfgang had spoken once of the peace he anticipated in death. Franz glanced at the blue sky, and the leafless countryside. Where was he now? In God's heaven? In man's limbo? In hell, as he so often had predicted with a laugh?

Franz sank to his knees in the snow and crossed himself. Joseph also knelt. Franz closed his eyes, hands clasped to his heart. His clear, steady tenor voice carried only a few yards as the snow muffled his words. He prayed:

130

"Pater noster, qui es in caelis;

"Sanctificatur nomen tuum; adveniat regnum tuum;

"Fiat voluntas tua, sicut in caelo, et in terra.

"Panem nostrum quotidianum da nobis hodie;

"Et dimitte nobis debita nostra, sicut et nos dimittimus debitoribus nostris.

"Et no nos inducas in tentationem. Sed libera nos a malo. Amen."

With each word, he seemed to gain a peace unknown to him in the past several weeks. Finally, he opened his eyes.

Josef watched him anxiously. Franz gazed calmly at the mound of white before him. Impulsively, he reached down onto the whiteness with his bare hands spread wide on the snow, as though, in some oddly mystic way, the white chill and the gentle rise of the grave could prove to him that it really had happened. That Wolfgang was really here, cold and sleeping under the snow. That he wasn't home working and worrying where Franz had gone to, or wondering, with the others, why he had left Vienna so suddenly. "You didn't tell me, you!" he would have said sternly, before grabbing him by the shoulders for a relieved, forgiving bearhug. Now, in this oasis of peace that he felt, Franz would seek an answer for his friend's death.

"Franz," Josef said tentatively, touching his shoulder.

"It's all right, Josef. I only wanted to...feel the earth." He stood up, dazed but dry-eyed. "I wish I had some flowers," he said, suddenly embarrassed. "Something white, like this snow...like his soul."

"They'd only freeze out here," said Josef, watching the wisps of Franz's hair whip lightly across his pale forehead.

"Let's go, Josef." Franz turned and walked away. Suddenly, he knew it was no use. There would be no answer to his question here.

After returning from the cemetery Franz went to a tavern where he would not find friends, nor they him. He sat alone and drank until he lost count of the glasses. Then he bought another two bottles of wine, stuffed them into his pockets and quietly meandered home, holding the walls along the way with cold fingers to avoid slipping on the icy streets and walkways.

He didn't bother to light a fire in the stove. He drank the first bottle by the light of a single candle. The room was as cold as a tomb as he leaned on one arm across the worktable, quietly singing to himself and tracing quill marks in the candle wax.

At one a.m., he put aside the half-empty second bottle, took off his greatcoat and hung it on a hook. Slowly, fumbling, he slipped off his waistcoat, and his shoes. He pulled at his jabot, then unbuttoned his cuffs and shirt. With a heavy sigh, he stood up and staggered around the room in his stockings, opening the windows. He opened the last of the windows in the bedroom and then sank down onto the floor under it. He huddled himself into a ball and covered his head with his arms. A tune from *Zauberflote* floated through his consciousness and he sang softly: "We walk by Music's power, cheerful through death's dark night."

He closed his eyes and fell asleep.

A startlingly chilly breeze on his bare chest awakened Franz. Disoriented, he groaned and tried to move, but found that his stiff and cold body resisted. His head felt leaden. Stunned with agonizing pain, he felt too paralyzed even to cry. He pulled himself onto all fours and crawled toward the bed, where he pulled the quilt down. He turned his back to the bed and the quilt circled him. The room spun. His head began throbbing as though it would burst. Waves of sharp pain enveloped his skull and body.

"Oh, God, " he whimpered. The words brought a violent cough, followed by another and another, each wracking his chest with fiery pain. His hands instinctively clutched his chest.

Pneumonia. I've caught pneumonia. Why didn't I die? No! Don't say that. Suicide is wrong...then why did I do that? What was I thinking? It doesn't matter, the pneumonia will surely kill me now. Oh, Franz, you fool!

He tried to stand up on his stiff legs, but they weren't ready to hold him and he fell on the bed. Slowly, he crawled under the quilts. He lay there for hours, imprisoned by pain, helpless. At length, he prayed. Then the coughs and sneezing began. Toward evening, he heard a knock at the door. He tried to call out but could not without coughing. Afraid that the caller would leave, he reached for a book and pushed it to the floor where it sounded a crash. Yes, someone is home, don't go! Josef Deiner opened the door gingerly and stepped in. Franz was coughing.

Josef found him in bed. "Oh, my! Franz!"

A quick survey of the apartment told him what had happened. He immediately hurried to close the windows. He started a fire in the stove and then ran out to find someone to fetch a doctor. "Not Closset," whispered Franz, who wanted nothing more to do with Wolfgang's doctor. Then Josef covered Franz with as many more quilts as he could find in the disarray of the bedroom.

For days Franz agonized between life and death, as if deciding. Dreams merged with reality as he came and went in his delirium. Once, he thought he saw his sister Anna Maria sitting by the bed working needlepoint. He reached his hand out toward her, but realized it must have been a dream. He called out. But no sound came from his mouth.

On the morning of the fourth day, the fever broke.

NEW YORK, November, 1952.

Willy was finally alone. He hadn't had time to think of it since it happened. Now he walked along Fifth Avenue's wide leaf-swept sidewalk as he tried to piece together what he could recall of the young woman by the wall. Yesterday's concert had been one of the most energy-concentrated events of his career. Though he had performed Mozart in past years, it still felt new to him, and to his public—a public that was more accustomed to hearing him blaze through the fiery, finger-bending Rachmaninoff, Prokofiev or Katchaturian concertos. He was somewhat annoyed and impatient that people were still calling him William Katchaturian Kapell, as if that were all he was capable of performing. So he had worked hard, and concentrated even harder for this concert, and it was a good performance. But it wasn't over yet—he still had a matinee performance tomorrow.

After the applause and curtain calls, he found that, as usual, a backstage crowd had already gathered to greet him, shake his hand, slap him on the back, hand him a glass of champagne.... As always, it was a heady, chaotic blur of smiles and perfumes and one or two photographer's bulbs popping.

Beyond the riot of lights and noise that seemed to imprison him, he had glanced across the cables and drapes of the large, blackened backstage. A young woman, maybe in her early twenties, arms akimbo, stood against a wall and gazed intently at him. Today he could remember only the eyes. They were familiar and intense and knowing. They smiled on him. While everyone else had tugged at him or shoved programs at him for an autograph, she just stood there calmly, watching him. He had been unable to pull himself away to ask her if he should know her.

She might have come over to where I was, he thought as he pulled up the collar of his overcoat. Maybe she'll be at tomorrow's performance. If she is, and I see her, I'm going to talk to her if I have to walk on someone's chest to do it. If she's there....

The following day, after his final bow, and again surrounded by a crowd, Willy glanced around backstage. She wasn't there. Concealing his disappointment, he gradually inched his way through the fans and friends to his dressing room. Making his apologies, he shut the door, tossed his jacket and sank into a chair before the mirror. He reached his arms high in a backward stretch and let them fall. He loosened his tie, scratched the back of his head vigorously, then settled into a pensive posture as he closed his eyes.

He smiled to himself. It had been another good performance. He was hot tonight! The Mozart was finally, truly his! He opened his eyes and glanced at the mirror.

He started. The young woman with the eyes stood behind him, a look of radiant admiration lighting her face. Willy sat at attention, eyes riveted on her. He already knew she was no typical starstruck fan looking for whatever that sort seemed to need. But what did she want, then? Her dress was quite unusual. She wore a brilliant blue shawl over a moss-colored dress. Her hair was a long dark braid flung casually over one shoulder.

"Who are you?" he asked tentatively, turning around to face her. Her smile widened into sunshine.

"You don't remember me?"

Willy frowned briefly as he tried to remember. Under normal circumstances, he would have lost patience with that answer and had her thrown out. But.... He looked around the room. No one else....

"We're alone," she said. Her voice was even familiar. Then she laughed, as if pleased at having pulled off a fast one. "Willy! Don't you remember your own Lina?"

Something snapped. Willy's eyes widened, remembering Lina. Lina! Sometimes he would wake up from a dream with that name in his head and a feeling of well-being. Lina. What it meant he never could decipher. Dreams were such fleeting things. But here she was, and he had an overwhelming urge to embrace her. He stood up.

"Lina?" he probed. "From the train?"

She reached out and took his hands in hers. "The same!"

"Oh!" he gasped, closing his eyes to absorb a stunning flow of vibrancy that seemed to pass between them through their clasped hands.

"I *knew* I knew you!" he exclaimed exuberantly. "You are my own. You're my own soul. How could I forget you?"

"But you haven't forgotten. You do know me. The older your Earth life, the more one can forget. But you have remembered!"

"It's been so long, so long since the last time," he said distractedly, still feeling the electricity in their hands.

"We meet almost every night," she said. "When you sleep, we meet with our other soul fragments. Those who are in Earth lives, and those who are not. Do you remember now?"

"No," he said, pulling one hand away to touch her face. "I don't. Tell me how, where."

"There is a part of us that never needs rest. Some call it the higher self. During the deepest moments of sleep, our higher selves leave our sleeping bodies and meet," Lina explained. "You've heard soldiers talk about falling back to regroup? Well, everyone falls back to regroup...at night. Oh, Willy! You've finally done it! You're playing your own music with confidence!"

"You're going too fast for me. What are you talking about?" Willy blinked at the sudden change of subject. Now he recognized her eyes. They were his own eyes.

"The concerto tonight," Lina replied excitedly. "It's your music."

"I don't understand. What do you mean *my* music?"

"Oh, Willy! *You* are Mozart. Mozart is you. One and the same," she explained slowly. "You were reluctant to play any Mozart. You denied that part of yourself because of what happened to Franz after you died, but now that's over. You've conquered your fears and doubts and regrets! And you've inspired Franz to do the same!"

It was too much too fast for Willy. Before he could say

a word, a knocking at the door preceded its flying open. Lina vanished as Willy's manager and several friends burst in.

"Listen to this, Mitropoulos wants to perform more Mozart with you. I told him we'd work out the details later. Right now you need to come with me and meet some friends I brought over...."

Willy awakened from a reverie and saw that he was seated before the mirror. He stared at his intruders in detachment. Fans and hangers-on began edging into the room, waiting to speak, hoping for an autograph, or just watching the famous pianist intently, wondering what manner of man this was who could bring them so close to such spacious, unearthly beauty.

Thirty minutes later, they all had left. Willy looked longingly around the room and sighed. Had Lina been real? Or was it exhaustion catching up with him?

Whatever it was, he would keep it to himself.

V.

No more hope, there's no forgiving!
Sick and tired am I of living.

—Papageno, in *Die Zauberflote*
Opera by W. A. Mozart, 1791

VIENNA, December, 1791.

"Franz, can you hear me?" Josef's voice came as if from a far distance. Franz turned his head toward the voice and strained to focus. His mouth seemed paralyzed. He felt a hand take his own. "Praise God, he's responding," cried a woman's voice. Another hand lifted his head up and a spoon touched his lips. "Franz, take this now, open your mouth."

He centered his efforts on opening his dry mouth. The muscles of his face ached as the warm broth touched his tongue. Another spoonful followed. And, gradually, another. Franz pushed back on the hand holding his head. No more. The hand slipped away. He fell into another fitful slumber.

Franz felt warm hands slowly, deliberately rub his own. They were a woman's hands—small, narrow fingers. He opened his eyes to a slit. Dim candlelight illuminated the yellow walls of the bedroom. It must be night. He turned his head, slowly and with effort.

"Oh! Franz! At last!" Anna Maria's hands were instantly holding his face, touching his hair. "Oh, thank God, I've been so worried!"

"Maria...." He recognized his sister. "You're here...."

"Josef sent for me." She peered intensely into his bleary eyes. She lowered her voice conspiratorially. "I've been so worried...you almost died, Franz! You've been unconscious for days. But you're fine now. You're going to be...."

Franz looked at the ceiling as she continued. You almost died, she had said. *Almost....*

"...when I heard I came immediately. What with you being all alone in Vienna now, but don't fret, because when you're better, Franz, and if you'd like, you can come home with me. Papa says he doesn't mind. He's not the bear he once was, you'll see. Oh, Franz!"

"Where is Josef?" he asked heavily.

"Working. He promised to come by tomorrow morning again. He comes every day. He's such a good friend. Have you known him long?"

"A few years. Maria, hold my hand, will you?" Franz was suddenly seized with a strange, anxious melancholy. "Don't go...please."

"Of course," she said. "Do you want to pray with me?"

My God, he thought, has she been praying over me for days? He wanted to laugh and cry at once. She had been praying that he would live, while he had been praying that he would die. What miserable irony! Wolfgang would have loved it. He looked at his sister. He didn't want to pray, nor did he want to hurt her feelings.

"Will you pray while I listen?...My throat...." He looked at her again. His little sister, with pale, delicate blue eyes, and a big heart. He wished her a better life.

"Yes, of course." Maria smiled hopefully and hesitantly lowered her head on the bed, still holding onto his hand, and began reciting in a sweet voice innocent of the world's deceits. Franz stared at the white sculpted scrolls on the ceiling. His head still hurt, but he was warm—even the room was warm—and there was a quiet consolation in that. To be warm in the middle of winter was good.

The music running through his head now came to his fullest attention, blocking the hum of Maria's solemn recitations. He had awakened with the music drifting through his consciousness—an old-style partita by Johann Sebastian Bach, a long dead northern German composer known only to a few. The partita was one with which Wolfgang had fallen in love, and which he had played often enough for Franz to remember. Its simple melodic line was like a prayer to him.

He offered it up to whatever force had power over the rest of his life now, for he felt sure God had abandoned him.

The next morning, true to his word, Josef trudged up the steps to see how his friend fared. Maria's face told the whole story. Franz was going to live. Josef gave a sigh of relief and crossed himself in thanks. It would have been a tragedy for both Wolfgang and Franz to perish in such a short space of time. Yet it seemed one could not live without the other. Yes, there were still ominous obstacles in the way of Franz's recovery. It was clear he was taking Wolfgang's death extremely hard. And Josef wasn't sure just how long, if ever, it would take him to recover from the blow.

As long as he'd known Franz, all of two years, he'd been impressed with his seemingly unending devotion to Wolfgang. The slight young man with the sad smile never called attention to himself, never imposed on any scene, domestic or social. But he was, nevertheless, always there. Always at hand. And

Wolfgang seemed to have grown accustomed to his quiet, assuring presence. He had come to depend on his loyalty, and whatever spiritual support he certainly must have given him. They were, essentially if not in fact, inseparable. And Wolfgang had known it. He was spoiled by Franz, he admitted to Josef once in a thoughtful moment when Franz was away at Baden. Wolfgang had leaned on him, relied on him, occasionally taken him for granted, teased him mercilessly, but he loved him. Josef had never seen any two men radiate brotherhood more than those two. And now this...such a tragedy!

Josef tiptoed into the bedroom and approached the rumpled bed. Franz was wide awake, staring out the window. He turned but did not smile.

"Josef," he said quietly. "My friend."

Josef took his hand in his own. "Welcome back," he said, shaken at what he saw. He couldn't help but stare. Franz's face was aged and colorless.

"I hear from Maria we've had visitors."

"Yes," replied Josef, looking away. "Constanze's attorney has taken Wolfgang's manuscripts. Every scrap. Letters, music, poetry. I'm afraid there was nothing we could do. She has a right, you know. But I do wish you had been awake. I keep thinking they may have taken something that was yours."

"Letters," said Franz. "Did they take my letters to Wolfgang...from Baden...when he was in Berlin. They were there. So many. Are they gone?"

"Yes, if they were in his bundles...I'm afraid so. What will happen to them? I don't know that it would help to try to get them back...."

"No, it doesn't matter. I...don't know what she'll do with them. Probably burn them." Franz looked at the window and closed his eyes. "It doesn't matter. I don't imagine it's important any more...." Suddenly his face darkened and he turned to Josef. "She'd better not destroy the music! I won't have that! She'll have to deal with me if she tries to destroy the music!"

"I don't think she'll do that," Josef hurriedly offered. "She's hoping to stage some benefit concerts, from what I hear. She'd be insane to destroy her source of income."

"Ummm...." Franz couldn't remember what he'd done with the letters Wolfgang had written to him. Were they in the dresser? The cabinet?

140

He sighed.
It no longer mattered.

ALBUQUERQUE, 1985.

Dear —,
I can hardly believe how things are coming at me. This letter is going to be a visit through the looking glass, so get yourself a cup of tea first, then read on.

There has been no chance, until today, to listen to the tape recording of the deathbed regression with Dorothy. I heard it today. Then I played it to Dorothy over the phone to get her opinion.

There is a curious sound on the tape that neither of us can explain. From the point where I report floating above myself, up to the point where I begin to discuss the music's purpose—in other words, all through the actual deathbed scene—there is an audible, continuous, labored breathing in the background. At the time of this regression, Dorothy and I were the only two people in the room. In the whole house! Her husband was away on business. The breathing continues even as Dorothy and I speak, and we weren't breathing like that anyway. They are short, gasping inhalations alternating with longer, slightly more audible exhalations at a rate of about twenty-five per minute. The voice is definitely a tenor.

Don't worry about me. I'm not unnerved by this. I think I know what it is. In fact I'm sure it's the sound Sussmayr must have heard for so many days and nights, shut up in a silent room, alone for hour after long hour, and in his remorseful condition! God, it must have been awful. Hearing the sound of Mozart's gasping breaths must have burned itself into his soul's memory forever—so much so that it released itself during this very cathartic regression.

I still have so many questions. Is this the healing process? Do memories like this fill our souls, waiting to be released? What happens when they aren't released? Physical illness, maybe? Who can answer these questions?

I'm keeping a journal, you know. Got to. Too many things are happening. Write soon and let me know what you think of all this. Keep me grounded.
L.

Dear —,

...I've started writing. I suppose it will be a book, eventually.

I didn't expect it to be this unnerving. It's a daily struggle.

Even as I write, I ask myself, do I really want to do this? Sometimes I cry as I type. Then my hand moves, or I feel a gentle, unobtrusive squeeze of my hand. So I continue for a while. And then I stop and find something else to do. Something mindless, like housework. I'm only avoiding the book, you see. Why should I open myself up to what will surely be more ridicule than I can handle? And then a thought pops into my head that this book is about a new way to look at death— death as a temporary separation and not the end of the world. And what I've learned about the purpose of music is certainly worth a few felled trees, isn't it?

It's like an itch I have to scratch, this writing. Between eleven p.m. and two a.m., mostly. Then I begin doubting again. Then thoughts and memories come. Did I mention the flashes of the other life coming to me during the day? They're like glimpses of snapshots taken in a place I don't readily remember, but that I know I've felt before. It's feelings, mostly. Feelings. But with pictures to back up the feelings, which are more important. Today, for example, I was sitting still—a rare occurrence—and in my mind's eye I saw hands wearing thin, maroon-colored gloves on which the fingers were cut off. Strangely enough, I also knew why they had been cut off. It was to allow the fingers, which were very cold despite the gloves, to hold a thin reed-like pen. Both hands were on a desk. One held the paper, the other wrote swiftly. Musical notes. Occasionally pausing to warm the hands over a candle flame. Then back to work.

They wore all of the clothes they owned in order to be warm in winter. There was no firewood because it was expensive. And the woods were too far away, and off limits. The nights were the worst. The days sometimes had sunshine, which was warm, and free.

I remember reading something H.G. Wells told the writer Joan Grant about her past life memories. Joan Grant wrote of him, "He [Wells] listened with the eagerness of a child who hears a fairy story it knows is far more true than facts. 'Keep it to yourself, Joan, until you are strong enough to bear being laughed at by fools—but never let yourself forget it. And when you are ready, write what you know about.... It is important that you become a writer.'"

Sometimes when I type, I feel that extraordinary "presence" I told you about. A tingling warmth for a few seconds. Not long after, the words begin to flow quite easily. Sometimes I can't type fast enough to get all the thoughts down. One night it was a long passage about the special relationship between Mozart and Sussmayr. How their friendship developed, how they interacted. And then the thoughts stopped as suddenly as they started. That was it. Dictation was over. Or whatever it was. It wasn't bad, actually. Certainly not like the regressions where I was swept up in emotions and feelings I had no control over. Dictation is better, but without the regressions, I would never know the depth of love between them. Us.

Lina

VIENNA, January, 1792.

By the end of the second week, Franz had memorized every crack and stucco wave and curl on the ceiling and walls of his bedroom. He knew by heart the lines of the four-poster bed, the colors of the light and shadows around each window, and the outline of the sun's rays streaming each afternoon into the room. His mood darkened from boredom and the pain of intermittent headaches that allowed him no real rest. His chest still seized with pain when he coughed, and little that Maria did seemed to relieve his melancholy.

Josef came by less often, it seemed to him. When he did visit, he was little enough company, Franz decided morosely. He acted more like a mother hen than a friend, and he had an annoying habit of sitting by the bed looking solemn. *Basta!* And what bad news he managed to find and bring! Franz got to where he could hardly stand to hear what he had to say. First Josef told him the manuscripts had been taken away. Then he confirmed that Wolfgang's letters to Franz had been taken as well.

"Stolen, you mean," Franz had muttered.

On another visit, Josef reported that he had inquired at the Webers' about Franz's letters to Wolfgang and had been told they were there and there they would stay.

On the following visit, he told Franz that Constanze had hired Josef Eybler to finish the requiem mass that Wolfgang had worked so desperately over. Franz had shrugged at first, but a vague hurt crept into his heart on hearing the news. Despite his own disinterest in ever seeing that heartbreaking work again, it seemed like a stab in the back to both himself and Wolfgang that Eybler had gone along with a purposeful flaunting of Wolfgang's own wish that he, Franz, finish the mass—a final wish at that, and one Wolfgang had expressed to Constanze and anyone else who came to his bedside.

"He must have guessed she would ignore him," Franz concluded. He blinked. "Now you're talking to yourself, Franz.... Well, why not?" Not since school days had he talked in solitude.

Walls. Windows. How he wished he could leave this room....

The requiem mass was not even close to done when Wolfgang died. Franz remembered one scene vividly—papers on the floor, papers on the bed. Franz, tired and sleepy as ever, bent far over the bed with his ear to Wolfgang's mouth, straining to hear his faint whisperings: this chord broken on its reintroduction, first in that key, then change to this one. Don't forget the triplets will come next...remember to do that....

Wolfgang's weak and swollen hands lying, useless, on the pages of his work....

Franz sighed.

Impulsively, he sat up in the bed and the room immediately swayed. He clutched the bedclothes until the room stopped spinning. Moments later, he carefully swung his legs over the side of the bed and, little by little, lowered his feet to the floor and carefully stood up. He had not been out of bed for at least two weeks.

"Maria?" he called, and waited. No answer. She was gone.

He reached for the door and stepped gingerly, one slow step at a time, into the main room. The sun shone into the room with an irreverent brilliance. Franz winced. He was still incredulous that life could go on as if nothing had happened. The sun still shone. People still laughed on the street below his window. Life went on.

Franz drew up slowly to the fortepiano and sat down

144

with relief. He closed his eyes and caught his breath before placing his hands on the cold, wooden keyboard. His still fingers ran up and down the black keys, playing an old cadenza he'd written in school. His left hand fingers slipped and missed. He stopped to flex them, and to run some scales, at first slowly, then faster and even faster.

Instinctively, when his hands were ready, he began to play a sonata by Wolfgang. One of his favorite pieces—in C. His hands now tripped lightly across the keys as the music trickled into his head and soothed his senses. It had been so long...so long. He played on, his hands and head gaining confidence with each measure. The piece, he suddenly realized, was so lighthearted, so full of joy and love. His heart leapt as he played on. What glorious love there was in these sounds!

His hands stopped.

"Not for you," he whispered to himself. He stood up and stumbled back into the bedroom where he fell on the bed to stare vacantly at the ceiling as he wrestled against another fit of coughing. His hands formed fists.

You've got to stop doing this.

"Shut up."

It makes no sense. You're creating a hell on earth.

"So much hurt...."

The pain will disappear.

"Go away! Stop!"

Suddenly Franz was frightened. Whose voice was he responding to? He stopped and waited. The voice was silent.

"God help me! I'm losing my mind!" he cried.

AUSTRALIA, Fall, 1953.

The piped-in music was beginning to get on Willy's nerves. He frowned as he sat alone in the nearly deserted restaurant reading the previous day's journal entry. His Australian tour was almost at an end, but he felt only impatience and frustration, rather than any sense of accomplishment or completion. Was it that, for the solo musician, there was no freedom to fail? This, he had lived with almost from the beginning. How and where did one draw the line between artistic excellence and human error? he would argue. Why must every performance be perfection itself regardless of human or circumstantial variables? And another thing, how do these managers pretend to put a dollar value on such a chimeric event as a performance? No, I don't want to get into *that,* he thought.

He wanted another cup of coffee, but there wasn't a waitress in sight. He lit another cigarette and wrote, "Feeling impatient. Again." He returned the journal to his coat pocket with some hesitation, left some bills on his check, and made his way slowly to the front door. Suddenly he felt anxious. He pushed the feeling to the back of his mind long enough to exit the building. As he emerged onto the street the feeling rushed over him again in full force as he wondered where to go next. He wasn't sleepy, yet for lack of a better notion, he turned and headed toward his hotel.

He felt cornered.

Wasn't it already enough that he had pushed himself— his mind, his body—to his limits for his art? What more was required? And for what? Why was he here? Was there more?

"What am I doing here?" he said aloud as he paced swiftly down the rain-shiny street. Then he suddenly remembered the psychic he'd visited several years ago.

"You will not achieve that which you wish to attain in this life," she had said cryptically. He hadn't paid as much attention to that comment as he had to her other prediction. She'd said he'd die violently at the age of thirty. And here he was, just turned thirty-one last month. Was that what was bothering him? He was overdue for his date with death?

Nah!

Well, maybe a little.

Wait a minute. Is it dying, or missing what I really want, that's bothering me? What *do* I really want? To knock myself out making money for everyone else?

He reached his hotel room, flipped the light switch and dropped his coat and jacket on the chair near the door. Suddenly weary, he shut the door with his foot and, loosening his tie and kicking off his shoes, sank down on the bed to rest.

He dreamed he was coughing. Harsh, wracking coughs that tore through his chest like roiling hot coals. The cot on which he rested was hard and not at all comfortable. Long, strangely cast night shadows flickered on the white walls of the small, cramped room. The stale air was bitterly cold, yet no fire burned in an old ceramic stove that stood nearby. His head throbbed.

146

The pain was especially unbearable when he coughed.

"Franz!" he rasped between coughs. "Come here!"

But Franz was already there, crouched next to the cot in the near darkness of the single candle. He looked tired and old.

"I'm here." His gentle tenor voice was tinged with weariness.

"Help me up," Willy told him. It was time to work.

"What? Work now?" protested Franz in mild alarm. "You're not well, Wolfgang! Please, reconsider! You need your rest...." But Willy recognized the look of resignation on his friend's face. No amount of arguing was going to change his mind, and Franz seemed already to have realized this despite his protest.

"Help me up," Willy cut in as he began coughing again. He was bringing up blood and there was that peculiar odor of infection on his breath. Worse, his head felt as though it would explode with each cough. He stopped to hold his head with both hands. "Is there any more wood?"

"Yes, are you cold?"

"To the marrow...."

Franz helped him to the worktable. The cold was numbing! Moments later a blanket appeared around Willy's shoulders. The candle on the worktable lit up a neat, empty tabletop.

"I need the concerto," he said patiently, grimacing as he turned slowly to look at his young assistant.

"One moment, just one moment," replied Franz, as he placed a precious piece of wood in the stove. Willy noticed that the stove stood between two doorways. He studied Franz. He was thin, pale and unkempt; his eyes seemed unfocused. It seemed to Willy this Franz needed eyeglasses for his work, but had none.

Why am I pushing myself like this? Willy wondered as he watched the young man start a fire in the stove.

Because it helps the pain in my heart go away. If I lie still and examine my thoughts, the hurt comes. If I work, the hurt is forgotten, for a while. Do you see?

And what am I avoiding? he persisted.

Rejection, came the answer. *And disappointment. By my wife, my family, my public.*

Willy leaned over and held his head in his hands while

147

Franz rustled through the manuscripts in a cabinet and brought them to the table. Then he brought fresh quills, and stood still, looking down at him. Their eyes met.

"Do you need anything else?" Franz asked evenly, not taking his eyes off him.

"Who are you?" asked Willy quietly. Franz's eyes widened.

"Where am I?" Willy continued. Franz gasped. Willy's eyes wandered past him to the open door of the stove and the meager fire within.

He awoke with a jerk, then settled into stillness as the visions of the dream played out in his mind's eye. This one he would remember, so he had to lie still and try to remember everything. Instinctively, he reached for his head. It still ached. He glanced at his watch. It was eleven-fifty.

Strange dream...and in only twenty minutes. Maybe I'll go for a walk.... Nah, maybe I won't. It's too wet. Maybe I'll just lie here and think this dream out.... Never had a "period" dream before. Or one where I seemed to be someone else...someone else. Someone named Wolfgang. With a friend named Franz...and carryover pain. Bizarre.

Then there had been that intense inner need to cloud the mind with work...such an overwhelming motivation. Work to forget...work to get it out of his head...work to mask his feelings, work, work, work. Is that what *I'm* doing? Is that the message of this dream?

There's more, I think. The work seemed important for what it brought to him...how to define it...a kind of inner catharsis of mind and spirit, not unlike the sense of completion I often get at the piano. Intriguing....

Feeling more tired than before he fell asleep, Willy eased up onto the edge of the bed and continued sorting his feelings.

The young assistant. He could still see those eyes leaning over him in the darkness. Familiar eyes. Full of love and concern. And anxiety.

Small hands.... Those small, graceful hands reaching to hold his aching head. He still smelled the burning candle, and felt the bitter cold in the room.

Rain began pouring hard outside, replacing the half-hearted drizzle of the early evening. The bathroom light gave the room a lonely cast similar to the sad candlelight he'd just dreamed. Willy involuntarily shivered.

"Get some rest," he said aloud. "Worry about this dream later."

In ten minutes, he lay in dreamless sleep.

THREE DAYS LATER.

Despite her preference for the dark—she said light bothered her closed eyes—Willy liked her air of simplicity and honesty and so was less wary, though her price was a little higher than most. She came well recommended, so he didn't complain about her methods or her price.

Now they sat in two large wing-backed chairs in the semi-gloom of her cozy, book-lined office. She sat upright. He relaxed in his chair. As she prepared herself, he puzzled that her method was less dependent on the tarot than on simply closing her eyes and "seeing" what came to her. She had requested only his name, and though it was all the same to him, he was impressed when she began telling him things about his personal life that she otherwise had no way of knowing, for even if she had read of him in the papers, he was not a local boy and little of his personal life had yet, if ever, appeared in feature stories.

"So. You are here to ask about a disturbing dream?" she finally asked. Willy noticed her eyes no longer fluttered open, as they had when they first began the session, and that the quality of her voice had changed so that she had an almost imperceptible Oriental accent now.

"Yes. I am."

"Please tell me your dream." Willy took a breath and began recounting the dream he'd had of the two men working in the cold night.

"It seemed so...real, that I knew it must be more than a dream," he concluded.

"In this you are correct, my friend," she assured him. And we think you know what it is."

"I don't understand."

"We see a previous 'reading' given some years back. You learned then what this means. You were once a brilliant and prolific composer."

Willy stopped and frowned as he tried to understand.

He remembered the reading, but the details were faded in time. "Are you talking about a previous existence?"

"We are."

"Who's 'we'? If you don't mind my asking?"

"Of course not. We are a group of entities who speak through this woman seated before you."

Willy's eyebrows shot up. Maybe I shouldn't have asked, he thought.

"It is a reality that is new to you, but one you will, in time, find logical," continued the pleasant voice of the sleeping woman. "Do you have another question?"

Willy reached up to scratch behind his ear while he pondered whether to ask his next question or just leave. His curiosity winning out, he asked, "Are you saying reincarnation is a fact?"

"We are."

"Oh." Well, there you have it, he thought sarcastically.

"It is another reality that is new to you, but...."

"Yes, I know, one I will, in time, find logical."

"Yes, this is true."

"And you're saying I lived before, as a composer?"

"Yes."

"When?"

"By your calendar reckoning, almost two hundred years ago, in the time frame you refer to as the late 18th century."

Now he remembered a reader telling him the same thing, several years back. He had lived before, she said. He would die violently before reaching age thirty, and he would have a fine, if meteoric career. All of that. He had been so intrigued with the predictions of the future that he had disregarded the notions of the past.

"Do you have another question?" The voice interrupted Willy's thoughts.

"Can you tell me more about that lifetime?"

"You completed the mission for which you engaged that life."

"Which was...."

"To bring joy and beauty to the world through music."

"I see. What was my name?"

"Wolfgang Amadé Mozart."

"What?"

"Wolfgang Amadé...."

"Yes, I heard you, but I can't believe what I heard!"

"Why not? It is the truth."

"Yes, but Mozart? He wasn't just brilliant, or prolific. He was damn near divine—inhumanly perfect!" If anybody was going to be a reincarnation of Mozart, it would certainly have to be at least Horowitz....

"Look at your hands," directed the voice.

Willy looked at his hands. He had always regretted having small hands.

"What do you see?"

"Hands! I don't know what you're getting at!"

"The hands of Horowitz are not small." The voice was gentle and firm.

"So what does that prove?" Willy asked. "Wait a minute, did you just read my mind?"

"To answer your second question first: yes, in a way. To answer your first question second: the cells of your body carry the memory of previous forms and can and will express certain, although not all, physical characteristics. Your eyes, for example, resemble Mozart's. And your hands are similarly small. Talents may carry over, if so desired or needed. Your performances are as exciting and expressive as were his."

"Jeez! This is crazy. Why did I have that dream, then? And if Mozart was crazy enough to want to come back after what happened to him, why would he come as an overworked pianist?"

"We think you know the answer to these questions. Look within."

"Can't you just tell me? I'm new at this."

"Very well. You have returned to explore new harmonies, rhythms and tone colors. To be near music, not as a creator of music, but in the next process, as an interpreter of music. You are more the middleman now than before, as Mozart also performed. Yet lately, you feel there is no advantage to living out of a suitcase and playing in every large and small town in the world. Or continuing at the mercy of critics every time you perform. However, you also know you don't play for the critics. You play for yourself and for your audiences. It is your wish and intention to pull your listeners up with you into the joyful heights of music. And when you feel you have failed, you are especially hard on yourself because that is your nature in this personality. It is felt that knowing who you were in the

151

past will have the effect of easing these self-defeating emotions in the present and allowing those energies to continue to strive, without self-reproach, toward what you call perfection."

"Is that...."

"There is more. It is also your soul's intention to show your audiences the wealth of compositional talent that blossoms in their own gardens. You would teach American audiences to break their dependence on the music of European countries, to look toward and support their own composers. You are aware of cultural imperialism, having suffered, as Mozart, in the shadow of the ubiquitous Italian musicians. It is no accident that you are the first major American-born, exclusively American-trained pianist of consequence."

Willy blinked.

"Yes, Mozart had Salieri to deal with, I remember," he mumbled to himself.

"Salieri is your father."

Willy stared in disbelief. Harry Kapell was Salieri? Harry, the Russian/Spanish immigrant, the World War I veteran of the trenches who worked so hard to build his bookstore business? As long as Willy could remember, his father had as strong a love of music as of books. He played the classical radio station continuously. That was where Willy first heard the music that he loved so much.

The woman spoke again. "Recall also that Harry supported your music career unfailingly. He paid, uncomplaining, for your piano lessons even at a time when the family could scarcely afford it. And he finally managed, on his meager income, to buy you a piano."

"He helped me get started. To make up for...."

"Yes. To make up for the maneuverings that resulted in Mozart's poverty and professional eclipse. We find it most amusing that after Salieri's and Mozart's struggles over the post of Kapellmeister, you both have returned as Kapells today."

"Very clever." Willy frowned. Some cosmic pun.

"Unmistakably so. Such is the way of remembrance—physical, emotional, spiritual. More important is the unspoken understanding brought through experience."

"What do you mean?"

"What had hindered in a past life was corrected in the present life. While you took to music immediately as a small child, no one forced you to it until you were ready. Hence, you

152

were ten years old when you began serious study. Not eight, nor six, nor three, like Mozart. You would not be used, nor cheated out of a normal childhood and a normal physical and emotional development."

"It seems to have worked," conceded Willy.

"Harry Kapell saw that it did. He was a good father. He was there for you. Some call this karma. The medium is fatigued; we will stop now."

"But I have mo...."

"Good day."

The young woman blinked as she came to.

ALBUQUERQUE, December 10, 1985.

Dear —,

Have you seen your seven friends in your dreams yet? How ambitious to want to see all your spirit guides at once! You probably already have and don't remember it. It's not always easy to remember. In fact, I remember probably one in a hundred of my astral visits. When my soul grows up, in a few thousand years, I will remember more and more. But even though I don't remember them, my daytime feelings give away a lot of the flavor of these visits. Some days my mind keeps wandering back to the same person or idea—unintentionally. Then I know I've spent most of the previous night with that person or idea. Or sometimes it's just a feeling. And it can be a dark one. I don't imagine all astral visits are pleasant.

Well....

So....

Reincarnation, I've decided, is at once a comfort and a threat. Knowing we get a second chance—or many chances—and knowing we must come back *here* to work it out, are like the bright and dark sides of the moon. But it's hard internalizing it. We weren't taught reincarnation as an alternative reality when we were young. We got heaven and hell, period. To me, it's a benevolent god who offers new chances to learn and make it all up to one another, even here, in what surely must be the snakepit of the universe.

Does Herbert Spencer ring a bell? He wrote, "There is a principle which is a bar against all information, which is proof against all arguments, which cannot fail to keep a man in ever-

153

lasting ignorance; that principle is contempt prior to investigation." Hold that thought.

I want to tell you about something that happened to me. I'm not sure what miracles are, but this may be one. I need your opinion. Before going to bed the other night, still down in the dumps, I stopped to notice that my full glass of ice water reflected the red light of the digital clock numbers so the water looked like watery blood. With that joyless thought I flipped off the light and fell asleep. It was about ten thirty p.m. In the middle of the night I awoke with, of all things, a light case of hiccups. At first I tried to ignore them, hardly believing I could get hiccups in my sleep, but they persisted (I have *never* awakened with hiccups, ever). I looked at the glowing clock; it was one fifty a.m. I flipped on the light and looked for my water. It wasn't there. It was about seven feet away on my desk, to the right of my typewriter, the water half gone. Annoyed rather than amazed, I got out of bed, got rid of the hiccups with one swallow, and fell back in bed. I looked at the spot where I had left the glass before going to bed. There was a fresh ring of water there! But that's nothing compared to the glass being in a different place altogether after my waking up...at one fifty a.m.

Still with me? Later that day I had to type a letter and looked up the day's date. I began typing and then stopped. The date was December fifth. *Mozart died on December fifth.* What's more, I'm absolutely, positively convinced he died at one fifty a.m. (I have read where his sister-in-law said twenty-six years after the fact that he died at five minutes to one. She was *wrong*—don't ask me how I know. I just *know*.)

Okay, so what, you ask. Well, what if I were to interpret this event as I would interpret a dream? What do hiccups mean? A modified form of crying? At one fifty a.m.? Okay. And a glass of water half filled—a story half told? The glass was to the right, or write, of the typewriter—dreams are famous for double entendres. A glass/story that is moved to the right of the typewriter? Am I moved to write about this story? To tell the other half of the story? Think about it.

There's more.

Last night I had about eight people over for our book readers' gathering. All in all, it was an enjoyable evening, as usual. Ray usually reads books about social change; Kay takes notes; Lyle reports on political or espionage books; his wife,

154

Jaclyn, reads complicated treatises on time or chaos or mathematics; Vickie finds the widest variety, everything from humor to Joan Grant; Jim finds books on nature and environmental issues. And, of course, we all discuss each book thoroughly and with much animation.

As everyone was leaving, I overheard Vickie telling Kay a dream she had just had that night about Mozart. Vickie is a delight. If Americans were ranked by the amount of wisdom, not money, they possessed, she'd be an aristocrat. But she's not stuffy or arrogant; in fact, the two of us carry on like kids whenever we meet, laughing and joking.

Oh, yes, her dream. Well, I'm still curious about it, even though we didn't get to talk about it much. She had to move her car so Kay and Ray could leave. I told her I'd call her the next day to discuss it. What I did hear is this: She is at a concert of Mozart's music in Vienna. It's a premiere of "Eine Kleine Nachtmusik"—she didn't know the title, she hummed the tune for me and I recognized it. It means "a little night music," which is already appropriate for a dream!

Just before she left, Vickie said, "There was something about his death that wasn't right, and that no one knows about." You can imagine how agitated I am to learn more of her dream.

L.

Slightly Delayed PS: Vickie wrote down her dream for me. Here it is:

"I dreamed that I was in a large concert hall waiting for a premiere of one of Wolfgang A. Mozart's works. I was a member of a chorus sitting to the right of the stage where the orchestra was to be. My mom was in the front row and I was in the next row. I turned to my left and suddenly I was sitting on the right of Mozart and his wife Constanze was on his left, holding a baby. I felt a very close relationship to Mozart as though I were his wife or lover, but I felt a little confused when I saw Constanze and realized that *she* was his wife. I felt strongly that the baby was or should have been mine and Mozart's. I asked to hold it, but Constanze seemed resentful of me and didn't want to give it to me. She treated it as if it was very fragile. Mozart said something to the effect that 'of course I could hold it' and he passed it over to me. It was very small and fetal-looking with pale, transparent coloring, and was not

155

very 'full of life' as a baby should be. Suddenly I was in another room with the baby. Constanze had faded away and Mozart was in the background. I put the baby down on the carpet by a table and began to play with it by moving its arms and legs. As I did this it began to take on more life. It 'fleshed out' and became pink and rosy. It began to kick its legs and wave its arms and I was very pleased with the way it looked. Then the baby peed all over the golden carpet beneath."

Vickie also said there was a choral section in the music. Since "Eine Kleine Nachtmusik" isn't a choral work, the chorus was symbolic of a group effort. A little night music might possibly refer to my glass-in-the-night experience, which I am now interpreting as a definite suggestion that I tell the rest of the story with my typewriter. The chorus indicates I will have a lot of help doing it.

Kay says a baby in a dream is a new project or idea. In this case, the project is the story I would write of the truth of Mozart's last years. The baby was unformed in Constanze's hands. Nor did she want to have the real story of her husband's life revealed, having spent fifty years after his death constructing a myth about those final years. Fifty years—all that time she had to decide which of his many letters to let the world have. She left an incomplete, unformed picture of him.

Then the dream baby—the project—is given over to Vickie, and it begins to grow and fill out. Mozart wants her to take the project to fill in the truth, which is half formed—his intentions are clear. And the toxins that leave the baby via the urine represent the purging of my guilt and grief through this project, and the unfortunate effect that guilt has had on my spiritual foundation (carpet).

Fascinating, isn't it?

She had the dream Friday night. She knew—so her soul guides knew—that she was coming to my house Saturday night for the book gathering. So they gave her a dream message for me. Kay says, "It happens." Vickie feels the dream was for me. I believe so, especially since my own ability to remember dreams lately has been very much diminished, I don't know why. Grief?

I told her about the glass in the night and the regressions. I had to, if she was going to understand how she was my dream messenger. I know Vickie is very spiritual, but she also has a healthy skepticism, as do I, about a lot of things. Like

156

fifty percent of today's New Age scene. Still, she seemed interested, and urged me to go on when I offered to stop once or twice. I hadn't realized until then how long and circuitous a story it is to tell. I wonder how I will write this story. Or if I want to. It's so *personal.* The pain. The love. All of it. Nobody's business but my own. Why should I share it? Except that I see such a sublime story of overcoming incredible odds through love. But will a jaded world care? These feelings are real and maybe too close to the sleeve for public taste—the American public, it seems to me, avoids feelings. And, besides, I can already hear them complaining, "Why is everyone's past life always Cleopatra or Marie Antoinette? No one ever claims to be the cleaning lady!" Poor Sussmayr. He was a cleaning lady if ever there was one! Still, I don't think I want to tell this story to anyone. I'd rather send it anonymously to an Aquarian archive somewhere and forget it. Mozart will just have to shelve his glass-in-the-night tricks. This isn't going to happen.

Lina

VIENNA, January, 1792.

The fire crackled and rumbled gently in the stove. Maria had placed a small pan of brandy on top to warm for Franz. Outside, another winter storm had begun with snowflakes as big as flower petals falling all around Vienna.

Maria and Franz sat quietly by the stove, listening to its audible warmth. He studied her as she mended a tear in one of his shirts. She seems rushed, he thought. Or maybe that's how women sew—rapidly. Never really noticed...or maybe my presence, up and sitting here with her for the first time in weeks, makes her nervous. Maybe that's it.

"Do I make you nervous?" he asked quietly. She stopped abruptly and looked at her brother.

"What a strange question! No. Of course not," she said calmly. "Why should you?"

"You work so swiftly," he observed.

She lowered her head smiling and continued sewing. "I always work this fast. Blame it on Step-Mama."

"Why? Was she fast, too?"

"Yes, she worked constantly. She used to tell me that if

she was to get any time to herself at the end of the day, or even in the middle of it, she'd very well better work fast or she could just count on working into the night, too."

Suddenly, a knock came at the door. Franz turned briefly toward the door as Maria put down her mending and stood up to unbolt the door.

In stepped Josef Eybler, covered with snow and cold air, carrying a bundle under his arm. As Maria quickly closed the door again, he placed the bundle on a table and threw his coat and hat on a nearby chair. He greeted Maria with a smile and a nod, then glanced briefly at Franz. It was the first time the two friends had seen one another since before Wolfgang's death. Maria discreetly gathered her mending and left the room, closing the bedroom door behind her.

Franz was standing up to greet Josef in the proper Viennese fashion when their eyes met. Josef's mouth was set firm as he fought back a flood of grief. He hesitated, looking at Franz's lusterless eyes. He stepped forward and carefully, slowly, clasped Franz in a sad embrace. Wordlessly, Franz fought his own grief as his friend and colleague held him for several moments. Suddenly Franz heard a loud sob. He pulled back and regarded his grief-stricken friend.

"I'm sorry," stammered Josef. "I'm so terribly, terribly sorry. We loved him so much." Franz caught his breath swiftly. Josef was a year older than Franz. He, too, had spent many long years in a boys' monastery school. Often, Wolfgang had ribbed them for being "a pair of unforgivably innocent rubes in the unforgivably jaded city of Vienna."

Josef had preferred to continue composing church music, while Franz had abandoned sacred music for stage works. Josef disliked theatre intrigue and politics. Still, they had found enough in common, including a mutual admiration of Wolfgang, to become good friends. One thing about Josef that Franz had immediately noticed and respected was his genuine religiosity. Wolfgang and Franz, more often than not, found the Mass difficult to endure for more than an hour at a time, whereas Josef seemed to draw strength from it. Impressed, they often had exchanged silent glances on seeing Josef so genuinely moved.

"Sit down, Josef," coaxed Franz. "Sit down, please."

Josef sank into Maria's chair, wiping his tears with the back of his sleeve and peering at Franz in mild embarrassment. Impulsively, he leaned forward and took Franz's hands in his own.

"Is there anything that you need?" he asked intensely.

"Just a little company now and then." The two young men spoke in tones as quiet as the snowfall outside.

"You know I tried to see you...it must have been two weeks ago...and they told me you were very ill and couldn't see anyone. In fact, they said you very nearly died." Tears streaked Josef's face.

He looks terrible, thought Franz.

"You are better now, no?" continued Josef. "How do you feel?"

"I'm going to live," Franz replied without emotion. Josef thought he sounded disappointed.

"What are you going to do now?" asked Josef.

"I don't know. I haven't thought about it."

Silence.

"What happened? Why did he die?"

"I don't know."

"I didn't realize he was that ill."

"He wasn't."

"What do you mean?"

"I...don't know. I suppose I mean that it happened so quickly."

"I've heard talk of poison. Did someone...."

"I don't *know.*"

Josef stood up and warmed his hands near the stove while Franz stared pensively at nothing in particular. "Don't tell anyone, Josef, but I tried to kill myself."

"Franz, don't say that!"

"I don't remember making the decision to do it, Josef. It just happened. I can't explain how. I was very drunk and they say I opened all the windows and fell asleep on the floor under the bedroom window. That's how I came to be so ill. It's all a big joke. But the real joke is that I'm still here, don't you see?" Franz looked away from Josef's inquisitive, puzzled gaze. He couldn't take cross-examination.

"Have you been ill ever since he died?" Josef asked.

"I think so. Maybe," said Franz numbly.

"Maybe?" questioned Josef. He was beginning to worry about Franz's mind.

"I don't actually remember." Now there was a hint of impatience in his voice. A log collapsed inside the stove. The brandy Maria had put on top had begun to spice the air with its scent. Josef absent-mindedly took a mug and poured some out.

"Well, then, you wouldn't know any of the news around Vienna," he ventured. He found a spoon nearby and stirred the simmering liquid as he spoke. "Did you know, for example, that Albrechtsberger has succeeded Wolfgang at St. Stephen's?"

"He's a worthy man...fine musician," said Franz of Josef's teacher. He was beginning to get sleepy.

"He told me you had gone to see him at four a.m. the night Wolfgang died. Do you remember that?"

Franz grimaced as he tried to remember.

"No." He was at once embarrassed and curious. "Why did I do that? Did he say?"

Josef spoke softly. "He said you told him Wolfgang had wanted him to know of his death before anyone else in Vienna so that he might apply immediately for his position at the cathedral. Albrechtsberger was touched by Wolfgang's thoughtfulness, even during his own sickness and death. But he was also worried about you. He said you looked so much like a ghost that it was frightening at first. Of course, visiting at that hour, anyone might immediately assume it would have to be a ghost. No one else would be out at that hour, except late-night carousers."

"I don't remember...."

"You told him this would be your only opportunity to tell him because you were leaving Vienna immediately. Albrechtsberger tried to talk you out of it but he said you didn't seem to hear him."

Franz strained to remember such a conversation. He looked helplessly at his friend and shrugged slightly.

"Ah, well. It's all in the past now anyway," Josef said with a sigh. "The only concern now should be that you regain your health, eh? Here, this brandy is almost cool enough to drink now. Do you want the spoon?"

"No, thank you." Franz did not want the brandy either, but he took it anyway, so Josef would not be hurt. The mug felt warm against his palms. He took a sip and listlessly watched Josef's fingers entwine nervously as he continued.

"Franz, there's something else I want to discuss with you. I don't know if you were aware that Frau Mozart had asked me to finish Wolfgang's last commission." Josef noticed

160

that Franz's fingers tightened around the mug.

"I was not aware," Franz whispered evenly.

"I want you to know something. Frau Mozart told me she desperately needed the rest of the money it would bring. But it had to be completed before she would get anything for it. So I took on the job to help her, not realizing that you had been working on it with Wolfgang for quite a while already...I didn't know." Josef looked apologetic. "Frau Mozart didn't tell me this when she gave me the work. I heard it later from her sister, Sophie."

"Josef." Franz raised his hand to silence him. "You did the right thing in taking the job. Don't concern yourself so...."

Better you than me, he thought.

Josef continued, still obviously discomfitted. "She was having trouble finding someone to work on it. Sophie said Frau Mozart had asked Albrechtsberger and Abbé Stadler to finish it. Albrechtsberger said he didn't have time and Stadler didn't feel he could do it justice, so, out of desperation I suppose, she came to me. I don't know what's going on in her head, but it's rather obvious that she's...she's avoiding you."

"She's avoiding me because she doesn't like me, Josef."

"What?" Josef was shocked. "Why not? You were her husband's best friend!"

"Josef, my friend, it's a long story and I don't know that you'd want to hear it."

Josef swallowed uneasily before speaking again. "I see. Franz, about the mass. I need your help. I can't finish it. There's something about it. It's too much. I don't know what Wolfgang wanted and if I simply write what I'd like, it will sound like...well, like two people wrote it. Two people of vastly different styles. Your style is much closer to his. Your handwriting is even like his, and if this work is to be passed off as one person's work, we won't be fooling anyone if I do it. Beyond that, and more difficult to explain, is this. There is something about this project that is completely out of my reach. I can't explain what, precisely. I ask only to be released from it. I've told Frau Mozart all this and that I cannot finish it."

"I see. What else did you tell her?" asked Franz, bracing himself.

"That I'm giving it to you. You're the only one who should do it."

Franz shut his eyes, suddenly feeling very old. "Oh,

Josef!" he moaned.

Josef sat very still as Franz paled before him. Several moments passed before either spoke again.

"I don't know that I can...," whispered Franz at last.

"But it's only a mass...." Josef began to wonder if he should have waited before bringing this project to him. But Frau Mozart needed the money now, and she was impatient to get it back completed as soon as possible. Josef had already taken too long with it.

"Yes, a mass...for the dead. For Wolfgang. He wrote it for himself. Don't you see? It killed him...as much as any poison. It will kill me as well...if I finish it. Too many...thoughts of death. Oh, Josef!"

"But he wanted *you* to finish it, did he not? Wasn't he concerned that you finish it? That's what Sophie said."

Oh, Sophie!

"Yes. I told him I'd finish it. It was the only way to calm him. It was almost as if he thought finishing it...might somehow rescue him...get him within sight of God. I don't understand why...or how. I don't think I ever will." His eyes began to sting.

He knew he had to do it.

Josef winced. Franz was visibly exhausted by this news.

"I'm sorry, Franz. I shouldn't have come to you with this so soon after...I'm sorry," he said. He reached over and took the mug from the table and placed it in Franz's hands.

"Please, take a drink of this. It will help."

Franz lifted the mug and swallowed some brandy. Josef took the mug and placed it back on the table. He gently helped Franz to his feet. Together they walked slowly to the bedroom where Josef helped Franz into bed. He'll be asleep soon, thought Josef as he crept to the door. Maria emerged from her room.

"Franz has gone to bed," he informed her dejectedly as he donned his coat and hat. He turned to the bundle on the chair and hesitated.

"If Franz decides he doesn't want anything to do with this, please send it by messenger to Frau Mozart, will you?"

"Yes, sir."

"And send for me if he needs anything. Will you do that?"

"Yes, of course, sir," she assured him.

"Thank you," he said absent-mindedly.

162

Then he was gone.

Franz heard the door close behind Josef. He turned onto his back and stared at the ceiling.

It's finally happened. The Mass is mine again...now it will kill me, too. Well, isn't that what you've wanted? To be dead? To be done with this lonely, miserable life? Now it begins. And ends...how that accursed mass grew to haunt Wolfgang! When it is done, he said, I will be dead. And so it was. And so it will be...with me. I promised Wolfgang I'd finish it. But I also promised him I wouldn't give up and die.

I have no choice.

ALBUQUERQUE, 1987.

Dear —,

The opera company is wearing me out with one disappointment after another. Not that it matters. The bank account is empty (no salaries unless the board comes to our rescue), and our board president found a good job on the East Coast and left within a week. Also, we've been asked to vacate our heretofore donated office space; we found new offices but we have no furniture so I'm working on the floor out of boxes. Do these sound to you like direct cosmic hints to chuck the opera gig and go to accounting school? Hints that any further maneuvering to save this company is, as our choreographer keeps mumbling, like "rearranging the deck chairs on the Titanic."

Oh, well....

On another front, our Spanish comic opera company has been invited to perform *La Verbena de la Paloma* at the zarzuela festival in El Paso this summer. Fortunately, we have production money and have been planning this project for a while now. Everyone is so excited to be touring out of state. They're even providing us with an orchestra—do you have any idea how much money that's going to save us? Fortunately, Dan has been working for months transcribing that old music script onto the computer. Then we're going to have a cut and paste party to create solo and orchestral parts out of the conductor's score because his software does only so much. What a curious combination of high tech and tedium. Printouts and pasteups. Minutes and hours.

Speaking of high tech, have you seen the computer software that makes music directly from a keyboard? I wrote a story on a New Age composer in Santa Fe for the paper, and during our interview he showed me his studio. It was a series of music and computer keyboards joined together through the miracle of a million cables and terminators. But the real miracle came when he played music at the keyboard, and, Voila! the notes appeared on a computer monitor *as he played.* Then he tapped at the computer keyboard and out came a printout of the notes he'd just played! In mere minutes! My mouth dropped to the floor. I was so overwhelmed I could only stand there and stare. I can't help but wonder what Franz the Relentless Copyist would have thought. But then I suppose I know. He would have said, "I was so overwhelmed I could only stand there and stare."

Well, anyway, did I tell you I finally heard a live performance of Mozart's *Requiem Mass* last week? It's always been, for me, a peculiarly affecting work. The first time I ever heard it was a decidedly strange experience. I was a sophomore in college at the time. I was alone in the listening room, having begun a semester-long project of listening to all the Mozart repertoire in the school's record library. Ambitious, yes? I had reached the sacred works, and had put the *Requiem* on the turntable, with headphones in place. I remember the clear Sunday afternoon sunlight streaming through three large windows. Lots of solitude to marvel at the quiet and fearful beauty of Mozart's mass for the dead—but then I began to grow sadder and sadder with each new movement. When the *Lacrymosa* began—it's about halfway through the piece—something bizarre happened. I began to cry! It started as a tightening in the chest, then a tear, then a gush. I laid my head on my arms on the table and *I cried.* Hard. There was so much regret in that music—maybe that was it. The regret. Of course, at the time I didn't know what to think. Now I do.

Anyway, I heard it again last week, live. I was lucky to be able to hear it performed in a vaulted cathedral where the sounds resonate the way they're supposed to. Not one to just listen, I wrote down some thoughts during the concert. Partly because the music was often so scary, writing helped me keep my equilibrium. Here's what I wrote:

"Flinched as the air filled with the first frightening and brooding measures, each newly layered tone building a tragic

164

harmony at once personal and universal.

"Fear and hope alternate throughout the work in a mosaic of dark and light colors. The frontispiece of the Bible on which I write is Raphael's painting, *The Transfiguration.* Like the *Requiem,* it was the artist's last work. It had hung over Raphael's deathbed, just as the *Requiem* haunted Mozart as he died. The painting, like the music, is divided into shades of light and dark, hope and fear. The top half of the painting is all light and beauty—a transfigured Christ admired by two favored mortals—while the bottom half is filled with darkly painted, uncertain and confused apostles and followers wondering and asking one another who will cure a young boy held by his frightened, pleading father. Only the boy himself, of all those around him, knows to look up toward the Christ. Only the one *in pain* knows where to turn. Raphael's message? I believe it's 'anyone can choose to live in light or live in darkness.'

"A live performance reveals so much more than a recording. This music is full of fear. At the end of each movement, I find myself exhaling with relief and slumping back, limp. I also hear hope. Had Mozart, even at the end, still not chosen between light and dark? Or was Sussmayr the one responsible for the dark harmonies and terrified themes? Had one found serenity while the other still grappled with fear?

"This music also shows Raphael's apostles where to turn, but it's shot through with their uncertainty and confusion. The mass, though an epic work, is thus flawed. Was it merely a technical matter of a merely fair composer trying to complete the work of a genius? Or was it a matter of strength of spirit? Did fear battle hope for ascendancy? I wonder: If Sussmayr had looked up toward the Christ like the boy in the painting, would he have co-created a masterpiece instead of a flawed cry for help?"

There. These are my notes. I have thrown them into a box of notes, impressions, and thoughts about recent events regarding Mozart and certain regressions. There should be software that accepts boxes of notes and spits out a good story, no?

No. Why do I care? I don't know. Maybe because I know *I need to do this.* For me, to get it off my chest after two hundred years, and for the historical record. It will hurt—I know this because it already hurts. The memories hurt. But I can sense his presence now, and his intention of helping me tell the story. And I sense his love, and that is what's going to make this work.

I'm going to do it.

Yours in mild panic,
Lina

VIENNA, January, 1792.

Long past midnight, Franz's sleeping body lay motionless in bed, in deepest sleep. Franz himself sat before the stove in the other room. A robust fire blazed within the old stove, filling the room with brilliant light and soothing warmth. Beside him stood Wolfgang, looking young and energetic and compassionate. Franz spoke contemplatively.

Why? Why do you want me to finish it?

You promised me....

But why is it so important even for a promise? It killed you. The memory alone will kill me if I try to finish it.

You know that's not true. You won't die.

Franz looked up, startled at the strength of Wolfgang's statement.

Now listen, I will help, Wolfgang continued, unaware of Franz's surprise.

What do you mean? How?

I'll guide you. Just let your thoughts flow. I will give you ideas, and you will write them down and work them.

Wolfgang beamed with confidence. Franz blinked, less convinced.

You haven't answered my questions. Wolfgang, why is it so important that I finish the mass? insisted Franz.

Suddenly serious, Wolfgang sat down and looked straight into Franz's eyes.

Remember this: Love binds even beyond death. Finish the mass and give it over. Let them see and hear what we can do together, even now. Especially now.

Franz was still. As he struggled to comprehend Wolfgang's words, the latter began to fade.

Where are you going? Don't go! cried Franz.

He felt a rush of warmth surround him, and a nearly tangible feeling of all-pervading love. In a moment, it was gone.

Franz woke immediately. The little bedroom was dark, cold and silent. Even the window glass was covered with snow and ice, blocking whatever moonlight shone outside. In his head rang the sounds of Wolfgang's *kyrie*. It was one of the last sections of the mass he had worked on before death stilled his heart and mind.

He lay in bed for several minutes, clutching the quilt and contemplating how strange it was to wake up from a thoroughly dreamless sleep with music sounding in his head. He sat up slowly, like an old man, and reached for the candle on the nightstand. Carefully he slipped out of bed, while the strains of the melody kept wafting through his head. He shuffled to the stove and opened its door to light the candle on the few fading embers. He gently placed a log in the stove and left its door open.

Feeling a chill, he hurried to place the candle in its holder before going back into the bedroom for his robe and slippers. He glanced at the ice-glazed window. Darkest night.

Lord have mercy, Christ have mercy....

"But mercy never came," he murmured with an air of passive bewilderment. The rushed, angular melody called over and over, each statement followed by an ascending stepwise movement.

Always ascending, thought Franz. Wolfgang had never stopped hoping. And asking. But he had been frightened, too. This music said so. Yes, he was afraid, all those weeks, before forcing me to understand that he was dying. He was alone then. Dying is a very lonely task.

Christe eleison....

He stood up and picked up the candle. Maybe the music would go away if he walked about. He moved slowly so as not to waken Maria, who slept in the music room. Of course, it was no longer a music room, now that all the manuscripts were gone. Josef had moved a bed in there and Maria had turned it into a real, albeit modest, bedroom.... Was Josef also paying all the bills? For example, this firewood. How in the world was he ever to pay him back?

Kyrie eleison....

When he was an altar boy, the *kyrie* had been his favorite moment because he got to ring the crystal-toned handbells. They had made a beautiful cheery sound. And the multitude of candles that lit the altar fell in perfect harmony with those airy soprano ringings. Yellow, crystalline lights together with golden-toned chimes.... But that was years ago and far away. Now Franz just felt very, very old.

The *kyrie* was the only part of the mass written in Greek, he remembered. Classical Greek....

Franz stared in horror at the table. There rested a large leather portfolio tied with a string.

He stepped back.

Damn Eybler! No, I'll have nothing to do with it. Nothing. Not now, not ever. Never. I will send it to Constanze in the morning.

He noticed a slip of paper hanging out one side of the leather cover. Immediately, Franz recalled Wolfgang's bed, covered with many such fragments. They had run out of money and could no longer buy staff paper, so Franz had begun cutting and tearing the edges and unused portions of his own compositions, and a few of Wolfgang's. They also had used pieces of blank paper from letters.

He stepped forward, grasping his robe with one hand while gingerly pulling at the bit of paper, holding it as though it were on fire. It gave way easily and Franz held it up to peer at his own handwriting. "*Domine Jesu*, violins—lightning," it read. He frowned until he remembered.

Wolfgang had told him, "Here, emphasize the strings on the first and third beats, so that they pierce the voices like strokes of lightning." Wolfgang then had indicated a melodically-implied rhythm with one finger. Franz had dutifully written it down in the dim light of one candle.

Clutching the paper fragment, Franz sank into a chair. He held his head in his hand as he bent over, elbows on the arms of the chair.

"I can't!" he cried. "I can't."

You can.

The fire crackled as the log began to burn brightly. Franz looked up slowly, frightened.

What was that I just heard? "You can"? No, no, I didn't say that. Why would I say that? No, it wasn't even my voice. It was Wolfgang's voice! It was! No, it couldn't be, how could it be? But I heard it.

Franz shut his eyes and stopped thinking for a moment. In that moment, the voice spoke again.

168

I love you.

The air stood still around Franz. He swallowed; his head grew light as his hands tingled. The room seemed to spin as his slight body grew heavy. He slumped over against the arm of the chair, unconscious. The crumpled paper floated to the floor.

Maria found Franz slumped over in his chair by the desk. The fire was almost dead. She rushed to stoke it before tugging gently on his sleeve and calling his name. He stirred from a deep sleep.

"Has the priest arrived?" he asked groggily.

"What? Why do you want a priest?"

"For Wolfgang, of course," Franz answered impatiently as he leaned forward in the chair. Then he caught sight of the manuscript. It jolted him back to the present.

"Franz, we don't need a priest any more," Maria was saying. "Have you spent the entire night in this ch—"

"Eybler forgot this," Franz interrupted, pointing to the Mass.

"No, he left it on purpose." Maria was patiently tidying up and preparing herself a cup of coffee.

"Send it back to him. I don't want it here."

"Very well. He said you might want to send it back."

"He was right."

Franz stood at the window, brooding, and idly watching pedestrians along the street below. Oblivious to his mood, Maria hummed as she prepared a small breakfast. Before sitting at the table, she reached down and retrieved a slip of paper that had fallen to the floor.

"What is this?" she asked casually. "Do you need it?"

"It belongs there," said Franz quietly, indicating the portfolio.

"Oh." She untied the string and opened it. "Here?"

"It doesn't matter," he said, frowning impatiently. "Put it anywhere. Close it, Maria, please."

She placed the slip on top of the papers, and closed the portfolio.

Why am I so afraid? Franz wondered. I'm not going to touch it. I've made up my mind. But what about last night? That voice. Never mind the voice. It was only a dream. I must be going mad. Small wonder. I haven't been out of here in weeks. I've got to get out of here.

He found his clothing, laundered and folded neatly in the armoire. His shoes felt large on his feet as he headed toward the door.

"I'm going for a walk," he announced firmly, and before Maria could object, he had donned his heavy cloak and was outside.

His eyes ached in the sunlight. He hadn't seen a blue sky in weeks, nor had he breathed fresh air. Despite a persistent weakness in his limbs, he instinctively picked up his pace as he approached the square, which stood beyond his own neighborhood of shadowy, winding side streets. Horses snorted breathy clouds as they stepped carefully in these narrow roads where the snow remained high and powdery. The snow muffled children's yells and chatter as they played outdoors on the first clear day of the week. Franz glanced up from his hesitant steps along the icy patches. Ahead, he saw the wider, sunnier avenues. There, the snow was more packed and icy than on the cobblestone street from which he emerged. A large fountain stood at the center of the square. As far down the avenues as one could see loomed tall, wide buildings side by side with narrow apartment buildings. On their ground floors were the multitude of specialty shops. Here, and in the street, the Viennese gathered and shopped and visited.

It invigorated Franz to see, once again, the lively commercial bustle and to hear the typically animated voices and loud clattering sounds of the square. He slowed his pace to pick and crunch his way carefully over the ice and through the crowded square. He smiled faintly on overhearing several excited conversations at once as he passed shopkeepers' doorways and small knots of laughing women. They were not intimidated by the cold, or the ice.

Walking over ice and snow was tiring work. Stopping to lean against a wall and catch his breath, Franz watched two young boys shouting and chasing a third around a corner. One fell down, and as quickly picked himself up and raced after the others. An old man with a load of wood on his back shook his fist at the lad for nearly knocking him down.

Franz decided to avoid the Hungarian Crown, and the Silver Serpent. Too many people he knew would be there, and he wasn't ready to see anyone yet. Not that a few hadn't already sought him out, as had Eybler and Vogl, another friend and colleague. But they were closer friends than most. Everyone else would be politely sympathetic or curious for short explanations. It was all no more than courteous indifference.

Their interest was shallow, Franz told himself. Vienna was shallow. It laughingly took what you had to offer and then let you die of neglect and disappointment.

He walked on. Before long, the Cathedral of St. Stephen loomed before him. The ancient cavernous church, with its overabundance of gilded interior facades, was, in the weak winter sun, as bone cold as the outdoors—and possibly colder. In the dark gloom of the nave several women knelt here and there among the pews, praying or just resting. As Franz walked stiffly down the center aisle, he heard a voice coming from the choir loft somewhere in the higher reaches of the arched ceilings. It was a choir practice, at which the sharp tenor voice of a Kapellmeister held forth in rapid instruction between singing. Franz turned and searched the loft just as the choir broke into a *sanctus* he'd never before heard.

Not bad, he thought as he pulled his cloak closer around his shoulders and sat down to rest and listen. His eyes wandered up and down the vast, ornate altar as he let the music wash over his senses. It had been a long time since he'd heard live choral music.

In Haydn's style, he determined, but not as good. A Haydn student, possibly.

The music echoed through the long, narrow church, sending itself off like light refracting through a prism, as Franz reminded himself that music was an infrequent blessing.

He closed his eyes. At once, his mind's eye focused on Wolfgang's face—with his familiar expression of casual anticipation and amusement bordering on mischief. The open, self-confident smile. Franz strained for more and saw that Wolfgang held a violin. He turned and began to play. Franz saw a theatre orchestra in the background. Wolfgang was conducting a rehearsal.

How animated he was when conducting! At his peak, virtually radiating musical sound as he led the men of the orchestra with courtesy, conviction and extraordinary passion. It took hours for him to calm down after a performance, so invigorated was he by the music and the event. Often, he'd want to go partying.

He was no less excitable at home. Franz remembered

171

the first of what he had come to call Wolfgang's "smash sessions," during which he vigorously tossed and smashed dishes and cooking pans as he energetically conducted and sang with some wondrous music thundering in his head. The noise of the breaking objects was part and parcel of that sound, Franz had reasoned. It was the only explanation. Wolfgang's face had amazed and intimidated him as he realized at once that for Wolfgang, all the world was sound. He thrived on it. In some transcendant way, he *was* sound. And not above experimentation, as evidenced by the broken crockery.

Wolfgang had admitted that these episodes had been one of the reasons Constanze had moved out. Well, I shouldn't blame her for that part, Franz had replied, remembering his own mother's joy in the few possessions her husband had allowed her. Constanze had been beside herself over the loss of her porcelain figurines and other bric-a-brac. Nor, Wolfgang had admitted in retrospect, was his remorse any consolation to her, or his reasoning that everything was easily replaced. Still, the smash sessions continued long after she moved out of his life and into her lover's quieter, more predictable residence.

Franz shifted in the pew as he watched an altar boy light candles for a midmorning mass. Some candles took two tries...and, of course, the boy had to kneel before, during and after each set of candles. Franz had done the same as a boy. In its own minor way, it was like being onstage....

Even before Constanze left him, music was all Wolfgang had. Performing was like breathing. It was his native expression. It was his exhilaration. So often would they take a break from writing to plumb the beauty of a duet for two pianos, or piano and violin, while at once plumbing their own inner voices! Afterward, they invariably were calmer and ridiculously optimistic about their miserable existence and even more miserable prospects. They were refreshed and placid.

I mustn't forget what music means to me.

While Wolfgang often performed chamber music with friends, Franz had preferred to stand aside and listen—for listening to Wolfgang's music was an enthralling, all-encompassing occupation for him that would have been compromised by playing a single part of that wondrous whole (though that, too, had its rewards). At these times, as he stood unobtrusively against a wall or near a window, Franz's face glowed with a quiet joy and exhilaration of his own—a joy that only this music, created by this soul, could arouse. So often, when his eyes were closed, others mistook his interest as minimal. If someone happened to whisper such a notion to Wolfgang as he tuned his viola between pieces, or as he warmed up at the keyboard, he might glance at Franz and then at his nosy informant. Then he would laugh as if at a secret joke. And indeed it was secret. For he alone in the room knew to what heights his music carried the private, retiring young man, whose only request was to be left alone during these performances. Not even Wolfgang dared interrupt his meditations at those times.

The effect Franz's retiring behavior had on his public image was mixed. He knew that those who noticed him had long before formed their opinions that he was indeed a strange bird. Quiet and courteous, to be sure, and not one given to strange behavior or sudden silences like Wolfgang, Franz was more like an unsolved riddle, albeit a pleasant one. He arrived unnoticed, stood in the background, holding the music, handing it out, gathering it up again. And leaving. The women especially were puzzled. Those who bothered to notice—and a few did, for despite a certain slackness of style, he was attractive in a boyish way—found it more natural to mother him than to flirt with him, although some did. Most of the men ignored him.

Still others, notably the theatre folk of Vienna, knew another Franz: the slightly wine-soaked wit of the post-performance party, where his modest nature dissolved easily in the company of performers like himself. When he was surrounded by the friendly faces and laughing camaraderie of so many cast members, his winning smile and engaging manner emerged freely. He was among the creative spirits of his age—the laughing, exuberant, generous and expressive actors, actresses, singers and dancers of the theatre. It was with these joyful souls, whose vision and imagination sparked one another into spectacles of drama and beauty, that Franz felt a special kinship. And for these people he opened his heart and friendship.

Franz lingered in the Cathedral until the end of the choir's practice session and the beginning of the mass. Then, reluctantly, he stood up and slowly made his way into the mid-day sun.

AUSTRALIA, Fall, 1953.

The late winter sun settled on the ocean horizon, streaking the sky with an infinity of color beaming from the other side of the world. Willy walked purposefully along the long, deserted beach. The cool ocean breezes felt good on his face, and the sea shone in brilliant pinks and oranges as it reflected the fiery setting sun.

His hands were beginning to chill. He thrust them into his jacket pockets and made fists while he stopped to gaze admiringly at the celestial spectacle. He felt whole, here near the water and light and air. He had begun to feel trapped, even with the occasional break, like this one—a few days alone in a seaside house to collect his wits and gather his strength again. Alone here, near the bottom of the world, he was able to sort out some of his thoughts.

He had looked forward to leaving Australia almost from the day he had arrived. After three months of back-breaking, exhausting performances with hardly a penny to show for it and nearly as paltry a critical estimation of his worth given by the press, he had had it. And to add insult to insult, this insane business about Aaron Copland had come up almost the first day. It was all so damned ridiculous.

He glanced out again, across the ocean's expanse, remembering the moment he had heard the insulting request.

"Apparently the Australian Broadcasting Commission feels being accused of communist leanings makes one a bad composer!" Willy had said.

"No, Mr. Kapell, we simply would rather you didn't perform his music in Australia, at least until his name has been cleared," came the reply.

"By McCarthy? Come on, get serious! The whole thing's a set-up!"

"That's not for us to judge, Mr Kapell. Besides, we're sure you can find something in your large repertoire to fill the void left by one or two Copland works."

It had taken all of his self-control and patience not to leave the country immediately.

Yet, there were some joys to remember from his tour. The sheep station gatherings at first had been almost a joke to him, playing to people on the fringes of civilization who probably had never heard a live recital before. But he observed their reactions to his performances, and they touched him. He saw the awe and sincerity on their faces when they came up afterward to shake his hand earnestly and thank him. His performances had *moved* them. Only then did he realize there was a lot to be said for their brand of unsophisticated appreciation. To many of these people, music was still a spiritual, almost elemental need. It seemed to touch them at the heart, where it was supposed to. Not like the city audiences, where heartfelt displays of human emotion were almost an embarrassment, if anything, to acknowledge. Where flashy technique and bravura, not profoundest statements of the soul, got the standing ovations. The city performances were the epitome of what he disliked most about playing for money.

His thoughts segued to the psychic, as they had so often since he'd visited her. He had analyzed and re-analyzed her information, and realized that various pieces of his life's puzzle fit more reasonably in the context of what she'd told him. Could she be right? It made sense, even if he couldn't prove any of it—to himself or anyone else. He smiled as he remembered her unseen friends telling him he would come to accept their notions, and it seemed to be the direction he was taking.

He looked out over the surf, the longest one he'd ever seen. Waves fell against wet sand on the beach, which seemed the length of a football field from dry sand dunes to any serious ocean depth. It was unique, to say the least. Australia certainly had its natural surprises.

Longing. Always longing. And separateness. From what? Not just friends and family. Even surrounded by family, the longing persisted. Was it a part of getting older, or was it a side effect of life's attachments?

The sunset was melting away swiftly now. He had walked a long way, and he briefly contemplated turning back. No point in getting stranded on a dark beach on a moonless night.

On the other hand, he thought, stopping to decide, so what if I do?

He raised the collar of his jacket against the breeze and continued toward a campfire he had seen flickering on the horizon.

A DISTANT BEACH.

The world was beautiful and serene in the dusky evening light. The ocean breeze whipped Lina's hair and whispered in her ears as she tended the fire on the beach. Sitting cross-legged, she reached behind her for another piece of driftwood. As she nestled it into the fire, she noticed how the muffled sounds of the breezes around her ears were so similar to the muted rumblings of the fire nearest the glowing coals. These sounds—like the sound of a flag whipping gently in a breeze— gave her a secure yet detached feeling. A feeling that she was alone in the world, yet somehow protected all the same. It was a feeling that all was well, at least in this remote part of the world where the surf stretched far out over incredibly long, flat beaches before falling back into the deep green sea.

How long has it been since you were really content and happy and serene? she asked herself. Once, in the mountains near Creede, Colorado, she had stood transfixed by a startling panorama of towering mountains and a glistening river. There was that same extraordinary feeling of serenity and joy.

How long had it lasted? she pondered. Two minutes? Three? Okay, two minutes. And that was how long ago? Too long!

This life was like living in a convent, with life's most essential thoughts and emotions folded neatly under black folds of propriety and neglect. It was ironic that in a lifetime of direct, intense involvement with numberless people and myriad projects, she still felt such a profound and seemingly unbreakable separateness from everyone around her. She could not conceive of another way of being. Surrounded by so many, yet isolated. Even her family, itself separated from the extended family, distanced itself from her in so many subtle ways. And her husband of twelve years seemed more often a stranger. A marriage of convenience? How did it happen?

How did I get to this? she wondered. How did I get trapped in another life of virtual solitude? How, and for what reason?

The breeze blew strands of hair across her face. She realized her only refuge, lately, had been sleep. In sleep she found herself living in places like this. Spending whole days exploring places she'd never been. Lina looked up at the ocean through misty eyes. How vast the beaches are here! She felt as

176

though she were looking at all this from the other side of a dream. Australia had been in her dreams three nights in a row, but this seemed more real. This must be real.

When she turned and saw him, he had been standing not far from the fire, not wanting to startle her, waiting for her to look up. She smiled warmly and, wiping her tears on the back of one hand, stood up to greet him.

"Willy!" she said warmly, as if she had been expecting him.

He approached anxiously with swift strides onto the dry, grassy sand. They embraced, rocking back and forth.

"Lina!"

"You're really here!" she announced breathlessly, pulling back to hold his face in her hands. She gently kissed him and smiled broadly.

"Are you real?" he laughed. "I thought I was alone out here.... You've been crying!" He took out a handkerchief and wiped away her tears. She took his hand and pulled him down to sit by the fire.

"Sit with me a while," she said. "Before I have to go."

The golden lights of the sunset were gone now, replaced by the sky's radiant afterlight and the gold of the fire. The vast star-splashed sky and dark ocean were all there was in the world now as they sat facing one another. Willy quietly studied Lina's face as she smiled and rubbed warmth into his cold hands.

He murmured, "Your gaze was like a blessing."

"What did you say?" She turned her gaze away from the sunset.

"Nothing really, just some poetry I once wrote."

"I remember it," Lina beamed. "'No matter where you wander....'"

Together they recited, "'My heart with you will be.'"

Willy closed his eyes. The fire's warmth felt good. "I'm tired, Lina, and restless. I want to go Home."

"What's happened?"

"Nothing, and everything."

Lina was still, listening and watching.

"I'm worn out, inside and out. I'm not growing artistically. I'm too tired to focus on the music, and nothing else matters."

His sigh was overwhelmed by the rumble of the fire and

the distant thunder of surf.

"Play only for yourself, and your friends. Forget everything else. And all will fall into place," she said, leaning closer for emphasis. "Remember how the music energizes you—use that energy to balance yourself."

He watched her closely. She wasn't happy either. Something was wrong. Even though her life, he knew, was happening in another time, he wondered if there was any way he could help her other than with words. He watched her mouth.

"I wish I could have come into your life," she was saying. "But it might have been like the last time. I would only lose you again. That would never do. Never do...."

Willy smiled indulgently. "You didn't lose me. I was with you. I made you finish the Mass, remember?" They laughed. There was her radiant smile again, and her tears shimmering in the firelight.

How I love you! he thought.

Lina felt a sudden inner glow as energy flowed around them like a second fire.

"I remember more than you think. Like those sudden feelings of warmth. It happened only a few times. It puzzled me then. But it was you, wasn't it?" she asked.

"Of course it was." He fell silent.

He's exhausted, she thought.

She's alone, he mused.

Her eyes widened as they leaned forward to touch foreheads. She closed her eyes and her tears dropped and glistened on his hands. "It's happened again, hasn't it? I'm still terribly alone. You were supposed to be here," she said.

Willy concentrated.

Give me your thoughts.

They entwined their fingers and became still. Eyes closed, he gathered and concentrated his energy, sending it down his arm and into their grasp. A warmth filled his being as she did the same. It was a special ability they had as fragments of their oversoul. Waves of color billowed out as they continued to build and exchange love and strength. Willy sighed. He felt the incredible healing warmth coming through her fingers. It was an extraordinary feeling to be so completely and unconditionally loved and supported.

Lina wanted to sing.

A brilliant, crystalline white light surrounded them. His

thoughts projected to her—*Take my love and never be alone. When you are discouraged and sad, remember this fire, this night, these sounds. I will jog your hand from time to time. When your hand moves, know that it is me. Remember that. I'll never leave you. We are facets of the same crystal.*

Lina replied—*Take my energy to balance your mind and heart. Remember that this boundless sea of love and support is deep within us both and enables us to create that which we would give the world. Give freely of your art, for in the giving is the receiving. Be patient. With yourself, with others.*

Lina faded and was gone.

She awoke with a start and found herself half sitting up in bed. With a sad smile, she settled back on her pillow. Dawn was beginning to light the walls of her bedroom, but she curled up and fell back into sleep, determined to find him again.

VI.

If you should ever feel,
A light breeze play around you,
My dying sigh
That breath will be.

—*La Clemenza di Tito*

VIENNA, January, 1792.

The blue flame of the fire held Franz's attention more than its surrounding orange glow. It seemed more sublime, he thought, as he sat slouched before the stove with its door open so that he could make use of both the light and its radiant warmth.

Night had long since descended on the city, and Franz sat alone, a vague terror of the night occasionally seizing his thoughts. Maria had been gone now almost a week, and he found he had relied heavily on her, not only for her unobtrusive companionship and, yes, housekeeping, but for her stabilizing presence. It was too quiet without her. And too dark.

The fire was all that stirred now, flickering and crackling as Franz stared unblinking into its warmth. He reached down, picked up the bottle of wine from the floor and held it up to the light. Nearly empty. He tipped it and finished it off, then tried to remember if he'd bought a second. Sighing, he pulled himself out of his chair. Taking a lighted candle, he made his way to the worktable and sat down slowly, wearily placing the candle in its brass holder.

The portfolio of paper scraps and the mass lay open before him. Fresh quills and ink waited patiently, as always. Resignedly, he gently laid his open hands on the manuscripts. He closed his eyes, said a brief prayer and began to work, scanning each page, each scrap, one by one.

Some pages had only fragments of music. The notes blurred before his eyes as he tried to ascertain where each section belonged. Ink blots covered some of them.

Wasn't easy trying to write on a bed, he remembered as he placed another sheet to one side. His hands began to tremble and he stopped.

Stop for a moment, he told himself. I'll work on it only for a little while.

He turned and stared at the window. Darkness. Not even a star or two. Quickly, he looked again at the fire in the stove. It was the only other moving object in his world at the moment.

As he sat in silent desperation, his hand moved unobtrusively but deliberately, as if squeezed by another hand. It took him a moment to realize it. His hand had been very definitely squeezed as it lay idle across the fragments of music. He stared at it in silence. As he watched it, something squeezed it again. He shuddered and pulled his fist to his chest.

What is this? Who is this? Who is here, touching me? He felt a sensation, and then an enveloping warmth that was at once protective and loving. Franz knew immediately.

He stammered tentatively. "I'm not alone, am I? Is it you? Wolfgang? There is nothing in this world that I wouldn't do for you," he continued, feeling stronger. "But I'm sorely afraid this mass will kill me, and as much as I dread living, even now, I dread dying even more. Unless it were to happen quickly. But this mass will kill me slowly. It's too late to bargain with God. To ask Him for your life in exchange for mine. So I will ask only that this project *be finished quickly.*"

He sat in silence while he flexed his hands slowly. Suddenly feeling foolish, he shook his head, blinked and returned his attention to the music spread before him.

I will finish this work as quickly, but as carefully, as I can, he promised himself. I will not think about my fate.

For the remainder of the night, he studied and sorted the slips of paper and the larger sheets. It seemed to him, as he worked, that some fragments were missing. He knew there had to be more, for his memories of those days and nights were also memories of continuous writing. This was not the whole set. What had Constanze done with the rest? She was never very careful with Wolfgang's papers....

By early morning, Franz slept soundly. Nearby, the fragments were neatly ordered on the desk. There they would stay until he got to each section in succession.

Franz reeled into the cabinet, knocking a glass to the floor where it shattered loudly.

Better to sit, he thought, and he focused on the chair. He reached it and fell into it. The room spun. He suddenly felt trapped. He was too drunk.

Oh, God, why? Why did I drink so much so fast? Damn. I'm going to pass out. And there will be no one here to help me. And I will lay on the floor until I wake up. Just like the last time. Only this time I have a shirt on, so it won't be as bad. And the windows are closed. And the fire, where is the fire? Yes, the fire is going. I can feel it coming...so weak...arms so heavy. Oh, heavenly mother of God.

He slumped in the chair. The bottle fell out of his hand

and spilled out across the wooden floor. Brilliant firelight flickered from the stove.

The next day, Franz drank only two glasses of unwatered wine before sitting down to work on the mass. His head was light and the heavy feeling in his heart had abated. Today, he thought, I will work. And with luck I will finish at least twenty measures, depending on what I have to do.

He studied Wolfgang's vocal lines and figured bass, and then his own notes to himself. He hummed some melodic fragments and tried to imagine how the orchestra would sound. He closed his eyes and contemplated the words. Then he leaned over and began writing, at first tentatively, then with more deliberation.

Bravo, Wolfgang. Bravo! I see what you meant. I see what you wanted here. It all fits so easily, no?

His hand moved swiftly now. The notes seemed to pour from his pen onto the rough paper.

Ah, yes, it's coming quite well now. I didn't realize it would be this easy. How it flows!

We can do this, can't we? We will finish it together.

The last thought came unbidden into his head, and unnoticed by Franz, who was too engrossed in the celestial music sounding in his head.

An hour passed quickly. Franz contemplated the entire section, triumphantly tossing the scraps of paper into the stove.

I could sing this in my sleep now, he told himself as he pushed away from the desk and reached for another glass of wine.

It's glorious. Naturally. They're his ideas. All his.

At the thought of Wolfgang, Franz stared soberly into the fire as the papers burned. His thoughts grew dark again.

This empty feeling, I wonder, wherever Wolfgang is, does he feel it, too? Is he suffering like me? No, not likely. Don't be a fool. He's nowhere. Or is he? Didn't I believe, once, long ago, that angels existed? That they sat on our shoulders and whispered beautiful melodies in our ears? And that God was good? That He watched over us all?

I'm such a fool. Such a stupid fool!

He leaned over until his cheek touched his knee. He stared at the floor, watching as his mute teardrops stained the wood, one by one.

Standing by his side, his hand on Franz's shoulder, Wolfgang frowned and sighed. His anguish over seeing Franz in such self-inflicted grief and loneliness shadowed his heart. Also, he hadn't realized it would be this challenging to communicate with him. He sometimes got through to him, but only when Franz was partially intoxicated. At those times, Franz would fall into a kind of egoless, unconscious concentration, and Wolfgang found he was even able to move his hand and pen for him. To Franz, of course, it appeared as if his hand sped along trying to keep up with his mind. And indeed his mind also "saw" the music before it went on paper, for Wolfgang gave him the music there, too. It was a wonderful feeling to reach Franz this way.

Then, encouraged by his success, Franz would pick up the wine bottle and drink more, hoping for even more "inspiration." But the extra wine had a numbing effect on him instead, and Wolfgang ultimately would lose his delicate connection. It was frustrating in the extreme, but he was determined to work as intensely as possible during the receptive periods. He vowed also to continue to squeeze his hand when the opportunity presented itself. Eventually Franz surely would come to regard it as a sign of reassurance.

The room began to fade as Wolfgang lost his own connection with the Earth plane. It was too difficult and dense a frequency in which to stay very long.

Poor, dear Franz, he thought as he kissed his friend on the head. If only he knew he was *not alone*.

The fire rumbled gently. All was quiet within and without.

Franz blinked.

What was that? "Not alone"? Fragmented thoughts again. It must be this wine. I've got to stop. I'm sure if I stop, then.... If I can stop. But I can't consider it seriously, for then the pain would resume, and that would be unbearable.

As day faded into night into day again, Franz worked diligently on the mass, trying not to think of its completion and what might happen then. He wanted only to finish it. But with each completed section, the tragedy of Wolfgang's untimely death loomed larger in his thoughts. The empty bottles by the door grew in number.

Eventually, he turned his attention to the *Lacrymosa*.

185

This was a section that Wolfgang actually had begun himself, in his own hand, while he still had the strength, and was not yet bedridden. Franz frowned as he examined the five measures of melody and several more of figured bass. This was the music that had broken Wolfgang's spirit as he tried to sing it with Schack, Hofer and the rest. He had insisted on hearing some passages, and his visitors had obliged. Franz could hear it still—Wolfgang's breathy, nearly inaudible singing—his last performance. The men had stood around the bed, singing softly so as not to drown him out. Franz had played accompaniment at the keyboard. He would not sing.

He *could* not sing.

The poignant, two-measure introduction, with its searching, wandering melodic fragments, had torn at his soul as he played. The singers had completed only two measures when Wolfgang broke down weeping. During that terrible night Wolfgang alternately slept and stared. Once, he grasped Franz's hand in the dark.

"Don't let me die alone!" he had pleaded hoarsely. "Stay with me! Don't let me die alone! I couldn't bear it!"

Franz shuddered. These were bittersweet passages at best. A memory of a long ago nightmare. The Latin words were dark and hopeless: "Lacrymosa dies illa/Qua resurget ex favilla/Judicandus homo reus." That day is one of weeping/on which shall rise again from ashes/the guilty man to be judged....

Wolfgang had stopped writing at "Qua resurget."

Typically, he had chosen to illustrate these fearful lyrics with hope—a gradually ascending, tragically hopeful plea for mercy. As Franz studied those few yet dramatically powerful notes, he realized all at once that this passage—this interrupted musical thought—was not only the last Wolfgang had ever sung, but the last he had ever written.

He put down his pen and closed his eyes. He sang the five measures to himself and concentrated. He knew the passage should continue rising, but then what? The figured bass told him which harmonies to use, but it wasn't enough. He sang again, and stopped. Nothing came to mind. Moments passed as he tried to concentrate. Nothing. Was it time to stop for the night? He let his thoughts wander. Wolfgang so often had counseled him to think of the words.

"What are the words telling you?" he would ask.

Franz ignored the growing ache in his heart as he

thought out his interpretation of the words.

"Homo reus. Guilty man."

I am the guilty one. I let him die.

Franz swallowed hard and tried to concentrate on the rest of the prayer, "Huic ergo parce, Deus!" In thy mercy, Lord, then spare him. He hesitated, then continued. "Pie Jesu Domine/Dona eis requiem. Amen." Merciful Lord Jesus/grant them rest. Amen.

So, pondered Franz, the words call for mercy and rest. The God of the church may be so generous, but the God of my world is not. As he stared numbly at the pen on the desk, the rest of the passage simply came to him: a melodic line rising to high "a," then a sudden octave drop on the second syllable of "reus." Franz quickly seized his pen and wrote what he had just heard sounding in his head.

Just as suddenly, he heard no more. He stopped and blinked at the blank page. Then he remembered. Hadn't there been a fugue to follow here? Yes, he gave me a fugue subject. But it's not here. Where can it be? Did Eybler keep it? Damn. I can't do this! I haven't the skill.... Wolfgang knew that. Yet he insisted that I finish this.... Why? What is he trying to prove? That I can make a fool of myself? This is madness.

He jumped up from the desk and headed for the door. He wanted to run.

How in the world did he expect me to finish this? The whole idea is ludicrous. I'm just not good enough! I never was good enough!

His hand grasped the door latch as he leaned against the wall. He had to stay and try. Just try. His hand dropped from the latch. He returned to the desk and slowly took the quill. With great heaviness of heart, he dipped it in the inkwell and resumed.

In the final measure of the movement, Franz's melodic line descended in direct opposition to Wolfgang's opening measures.

Two hours later, he put down the pen and stretched his arms upward, flexing his stiff fingers. He stood up to find something to eat.

Will anyone ever be able to tell who wrote what on these sheets? he wondered distractedly. Our handwriting is so similar. Virtually identical. Well, when they play my miserable music and compare it, they'll surely know then.

He rummaged around in the pantry cabinet and found some bread. He took it back to the table by the stove and sat, warming himself and reminiscing. He and Wolfgang had always more or less taken for granted the similarity of their music script. It was merely a fortunate convenience in that his music notation looked consistently like Wolfgang's.

But the signatures! The similarities there were uncanny—the loops, strokes and t's were virtually identical. They presented Wolfgang with another reason to rib him mercilessly.

"So *you're* the one who's been running up my bills all over town!" he had exclaimed.

"Bills, indeed!" Franz had replied in mock indignation, reminding Wolfgang of all the times he'd signed Wolfgang's name to a completed copy of music just to save him the bother. Earlier on, it was their private joke, but near the end, it all came to be of much assistance.

Franz remembered the opera.

It had become a well-known secret that Franz had written the recitatives of the opera, *La Clemenza di Tito,* but few knew that he had written three set pieces of that two-act work. While the good Praguers had discovered the recitatives as Franz's, only the discerning had any idea that he'd written the set pieces. Not that he and Wolfgang had set out to deceive anyone. It had been a matter of necessity. They had received the commission so precipitously.

"With such short notice, I can't do it all myself," Wolfgang had said. "It will be our secret."

"You can't be serious," replied Franz incredulously. "All anyone would have to do is listen to the music and they'd know it wasn't yours."

"Not if I go over it after you're done, to give it more my style. You've almost got my style learned anyway...come, Franz, you know you can do it. Our notation is similar, so the musicians won't know either. I won't accept anything less than yes," Wolfgang had said firmly. "You'll do it."

Franz knew Wolfgang was too ill to do it all himself. He was right, he needed help.

"I'll do what I can."

"You'll do more than that. It will be a masterpiece."

They had completed it in eighteen frantic, heart-stopping days, working on the road to Prague, working in their lodgings at Prague, working offstage at the theatre, working always.

AUSTRALIA, October, 1953.

Willy pushed his bag under the seat, then slowly folded his overcoat and placed it across the seat next to his own, hoping it would discourage others from sitting there. He was dead tired, and nothing was worse than a long flight next to an insufferable gab artist with nothing to do.

He sat back and waited for the long flight to Honolulu, and then San Francisco. Not long after that, home to New York. He could hardly wait. He reached across and, relishing the gesture, drew the curtain shut.

So long, Australia!

He had cancelled his next tour. He needed a rest—a chance to catch up with himself. He needed the time, too, to pursue a personal project that would wait no more. He would convince RCA to let him record a set of works by contemporary American composers. They'd fight it, of course, but he'd insist. Americans had to stop looking to Europe for musical leadership. Good composers were right under their noses—good American composers, speaking in a language that he, Willy, an entirely American-trained pianist, would relay to American audiences—at the piano. It was absolutely imperative that this project be completed.

Once the DC-6 had taken off, he settled in for the eighteen-hour flight. Hours later, after finishing a book and studying several sets of music, he fell into a fitful sleep. It was fraught with fragments of dreams rushing in and out of his subconscious. On waking, he remembered only the last one. He was lecturing a student. "The best fingers in the world won't help you if you have no musical meaning for them to release," he told the student.

He woke briefly to readjust himself in the cramped seat. Dreams never seem to be of any use, he thought with irritation, except to interrupt the blissful oblivion of unconsciousness. Again he sank into the silent wanderings of sleep. Now he dreamed in earnest. He saw the figure of a man standing toward the front of the cabin urgently beckoning him and the others to come. It was so real a vision that Willy protested. It isn't nearly time to land yet! Why is he calling everyone forward? He saw others standing and gathering their things as the figure beckoned unceasingly. No, it's too early, he thought. "It's not time," he said in a loud voice.

189

The airplane hit an air pocket and the jolt woke him. He didn't move. That had been only a dream, but it was so vivid! He was vaguely uneasy now. He didn't try to sleep again; it was obviously more difficult and worrisome than staying awake, however weary he might be. Nor did he bother to look around, as it would offer him the same tired scene as it had the last time he got up.

Suddenly his heart began to pound and he broke out in a light sweat. Anxiety was no stranger to him. He suffered some of the worst cases of pre-performance jitters in the business. But terror? Here? On a flight? Flying usually brought a headache or nausea, but not jitters.

Hours passed. Honolulu had come and gone. Willy read, studied, paced, even visited. But he didn't sleep. He was dulled with ennui and a vague unease, remnants of his anxiety attack.

As they approached the California coast, the stewardess came forward to announce their impending arrival. Then she was gone. Willy had hardly noticed her as he sat half asleep. The flight would soon be over. The fear was gone now. He pulled aside the curtain to see California's golden coastline. Instead he saw fog. Thick, gray fog. He grimaced. *How in the hell do these people expect to land in this crap? Is it a cloud bank? Will we get below it into some visibility? That's got to be it.*

He waited for what seemed forever for the cloudbank to lift—for the plane to descend sufficiently to get out of the miserable soup. Impatience and nerves were his downfall, he knew. He tried to feel neither, but now fear took over again, and concern. It was too late to get up and walk around. He shut the curtain with an impatient jerk and closed his eyes.

"I hate flying," he muttered.

A sound like thunder surrounded him. His eyes flew open to see seats and people flying toward the front of the cabin. Was it another dream? In a split second he realized the worst had happened—was happening, right now. The thought had no time to complete itself before he was tossed violently forward, still strapped in his chair, and slammed into a hard surface. He blacked out.

He seemed to hover above the burning wreckage of the plane, unharmed. He was, to his relief, outside, in the fresh, crisp fall air. What had gone wrong? He saw the completely obliterated airplane flaming against the rocks and foliage of a hillside, along a ravine. *Surely no one had survived that...no one.*

No one, he puzzled, realizing he was dead.

The flames on King's Mountain near Half Moon Bay lit the foggy morning sky. The mountain lay somewhere south of the 38th parallel. Somewhere south of the same parallel in Colorado, in the quiet village of Antonito, four-year-old Lina dreamed of flames against a mountain that night. Her dream self moved in and out of the fires, searching in vain. She didn't know why she looked, or what she hoped to find, but she cried aloud when she didn't find it. She awoke sobbing. It was a sad, anxious cry. She knew it was wrong, that the flames weren't supposed to have been. Not yet.

VIENNA, February, 1792.

Franz knew immediately on hearing the sure and steady knock at the door that it was Father Pasterwicz. Nor were greetings necessary, it seemed, for Pasterwicz took one look at his former student and stepped across the threshold to throw his arms around him in silent assurance. Franz closed his eyes and gratefully accepted the old man's embrace.

Moments later, while he warmed himself by the stove, Pasterwicz studied Franz's face as the latter put some watered wine to heat.

"How are you, Franz?" he asked at last.

Franz had slipped into a chair and covered himself with a quilt. It seemed he could never get warm enough. It was such a wretchedly cold winter and, as always, he had little firewood now that Deiner no longer supplied it. He looked at the priest, surprised as though distracted from deep meditation.

"I'm finishing Wolfgang's requiem mass," he responded diffidently.

Pasterwicz frowned, not quite sure how to react. A requiem mass! He remembered Franz mentioning it before. Why couldn't Wolfgang have started a simple mass instead? Or a cantata? Or even an opera? He didn't remember Wolfgang as being morbid. Maybe it hadn't been his idea. But here it was, a mass for the dead to torment Franz; although he seemed calm enough, there was a haunted look in the young man's eyes that bothered him. Too, he was thinner and paler than the last time he had seen him.

"Is this something you want to do?"

Franz looked at his hands as if seeing them for the first time. "It is something I must do. Wolfgang wanted it completed. So...." He looked up at Pasterwicz. "So I am...completing it."

Pasterwicz knew Franz had a tendency to the quiet understatement—or to simply keeping his thoughts to himself. But he had to know how he was taking it, down deep in what was obviously an unsettled and anguished heart.

"I see...."

"Thank you for coming to see me, Father," said Franz abruptly. "I...it's quiet here, you know, and I don't get out much. It's good to see a friendly face now and again. How have you been?"

"Oh, quite well," replied Pasterwicz, somewhat relieved. "I'm in Vienna for another go at performing my work. And, of course, taking some students. They keep coming and coming, those students. They're like the poor, you know, they're always there." He chuckled.

"You're a good teacher," Franz volunteered. "Your students should be grateful." The clock ticked.

"Do you want to talk about Wolfgang?" ventured Pasterwicz.

Franz sighed. His teacher had no qualms about getting to the point.

"No," he hastened. "Yes. What is there to talk about? He's gone. He's not coming back. I'm alone." He shifted his weight in the chair and leveled his gaze on Pasterwicz. "In essence, we're all alone, aren't we?" Franz continued. "Except...."

"Except?" Pasterwicz probed quietly. He pitied the young man. Only twenty-six years old and the weight of grief so heavy on him still.

"You know I have tried to survive. At first I didn't want to. But I'm still here, and I'm enduring this bitter, unending winter." Franz stopped and sighed. He spoke as if to himself. "It's winter in more ways than only one for me. Sometimes I think I see things that I know aren't there. Maybe it's this music I'm writing. Once or twice I thought I heard...." Franz stopped. He considered: should I tell Pasterwicz? Why not?

He's probably the only soul on earth who cares what happens to me.

Franz took a breath and said, "Sometimes I think I hear Wolfgang's voice in my head."

There. I've said it. Not that it matters, but it's said. Now the good priest will either tell me I'm mad or try to convince me I didn't hear anything.

"It's probably him, then," said Pasterwicz calmly. "What did he say?"

Franz looked up, wide-eyed.

He believed it! And he isn't even smirking. No, he wouldn't do that. He would only worry about me.

Franz cleared his throat. "He told me that, together, we would finish the mass...and then, another time, I heard the words, 'Not alone.' Seconds before that, my scalp felt a tingling sensation. Here." Franz pointed to the back of his head, remembering how he had been bent over his knees on the chair, watching his tears fall to the floor. "I imagine he was trying to tell me he wasn't alone where he is. Wherever he is."

"This is amazing, Franz! Don't you see?" Pasterwicz jumped out of his chair, startling Franz. "He was telling you that *you* aren't alone! That he was with you. That he *is* with you! This is...astounding. You know, it never fails to amaze me when I hear about...." He had begun pacing the floor but stopped now to consider. "Listen carefully, Franz. I am telling you that as a priest I've heard many things from people, in and out of confession. You must trust me, Franz, that what I tell you is true, because I've heard of these kinds of attempts at communication too often to discount them as fantasies. Sometimes the dead, or those who we think are dead—I often wonder who is really dead—sometimes they will come in a dream to tell us they are well and happy. That they are, in fact, deliriously happy. Often people ignore their dreams or can't remember them, so these souls go to more drastic, or should I say dramatic, attempts to communicate. Do you ever remember your dreams?"

"No, I don't," admitted Franz. He didn't want to say that he was usually too drunk even to dream, let alone remember anything.

Another thought came to Pasterwicz. "Yes, of course! You are 'not alone' because Wolfgang is with you when you work on the mass!" Pasterwicz suddenly slipped into Italian.

"He was anxious, before he died, that it be finished. You told me that yourself. And he said you would finish it together, no? Well! It looks to me like you are both still working on it. Together!"

In the midst of Pasterwicz's arm-waving, floor-pacing exposition, Franz's eyes began to well up as he remembered Wolfgang's dying words: "I will come to you in a dream...I will never leave you." They were words he had never repeated to anyone, even Pasterwicz.

Yes, Franz realized, I have been too intoxicated to dream, or to remember what I dream. But is Father right? Has Wolfgang been trying to make me see? All those times I felt as though I were not alone in the room, in the night. That time something—or someone—squeezed my hand as I began work on the mass for the first time? Could that have been him? And the way my thoughts come so quickly when I compose. It must be him! How could I be so blind? So stupid! So wrapped up in myself! But...even if it is....

So involved was Pasterwicz that he did not see Franz lean forward as his shoulders shook with tearful sobs. Franz covered his face with his hands.

"Why do you cry, my son?" asked Pasterwicz as he leaned over Franz. "This is a miracle. You should be joyous."

"I miss him too much! It's not enough! It's not enough!"

Pasterwicz drew his chair closer to Franz and sat down. Soberly, gently, he took Franz's hands from his face and told him, "It will have to be enough. But at least now you know. You *know.* Most people never realize that they are loved so much by those who have gone before. Loved so much that he will come back to this dreary world to comfort you, to be near you. Franz, you are one of the lucky ones to have had such a close, loving friendship. You still have it, and it's stronger. It endures even death! You and Wolfgang are closer now than you were when he was alive. I know that sounds impossible, but think about it. Think it over carefully. He is closer to you now, for he knows your thoughts and needs. And he loves you so much he will leave God's presence to be with you here. It can't be easy. But he does it. *For you.* Do you see what I mean?"

Franz nodded mutely as he looked at Pasterwicz. It was starting to make some sense. But the hard knot of grief and loneliness that had settled in his heart when Wolfgang died would not go away. He sat back and sighed.

"Thank you, Father. What you say is...beginning to make sense. I must think on it, however. Give me time."

It's all too much for him, thought Pasterwicz as he looked around the room, rubbing his hands against the cold. He spotted the wine on the stove and set about pouring out two glasses.

"Here, Franz, drink some of this. It will help you feel better," he said, handing him a glass. He paused and then saluted Franz with his glass, saying quietly, "To Wolfgang."

Franz clutched his glass as he glanced at Pasterwicz. "Yes," he said at last. "To Wolfgang."

ALBUQUERQUE, 1987.

Dear —,

I know who Willy is. The one in my sleep. The one who nudges my hand now and then, like he said he would. The one who is ancient and familiar. Do I sound bizarre? Again? Why aren't you used to it yet?

Let me explain. Elda is a kind and gentle friend, and a sleeping medium. Her entities are known collectively as Lo Tsi, whose accent I have yet to place. The accent is a mix of maybe Balkan and Oriental. Very wise person(s). Once, when Elda led the study group's meditation, it was Lo Tsi's voice speaking. Elda had stepped aside, and we were led by Lo Tsi, as if it were the most natural thing to happen. And it was. He's a friend, after all.

Lo Tsi has told me that Willy and Mozart are the same. Lo Tsi is also pleased about the book. Says it is necessary that it be written. Then he told me Willy's last name. As soon as I could after that, I looked it up in the Fine Arts Library and found a photo on the back of an old record cover. It took my breath away. I had seen that face so many times. Of course, not on anyone I actually knew here and now. Only in dreams. It was *my* Willy. The maker of little miracles.

Shall I tell you about his visits to jog my hand? The first time it happened I was on the bed with one arm propped on a pillow so that my hand hung over my face. With one nudge, my thumb touched the tip of my nose. It was so subtle and unexpected. Quiet as a breath. Over before I noticed it. I had been thinking cloudy thoughts and the nudge said, in essence, "Lighten up." Little miracle #1. Then again, on a long,

195

dull car trip (Opera in the Red was performing Opera in the Sticks again), I sat with my hands together in my lap so that my left thumb rested lightly on top of my right thumb. Quite unobtrusively—I believe he waits until my attention is elsewhere in order to work the muscle freely—my right thumb moved up to form an inverted V with my left thumb, almost as if we were to play "this is the church, this is the steeple" with my hands. I don't have to tell you I wasn't bored after that. Little miracle #2.

On another occasion, I was sick in bed with a terrible cold and had been dozing off and on all day. I wasn't entirely awake or asleep when I felt what I can describe only as the "breeze" of his presence as his energy entered my left hand. The thumb was especially strong and that's what moved—my thumb. It moved against the sheet, making a sound. This time, I wasn't taken unawares. He let me feel the process. I know what you must be thinking. It wasn't eerie at all. It was—how can I describe it?—very loving, and playful. Always. And reassuring.

During a particularly trying time of writing the story of Mozart and Sussmayr, I will feel a brief squeeze of my entire hand. You can't imagine how comforting it is to have that kind of encouragement. It can't be easy for him to do that, either. This is a dense planet with more than its share of negative energies whirling higher and higher. It can't be easy for him, and I'm grateful. And so impressed. What an extraordinary soul!

I have attempted to collect Willy's music wherever I find it. Fortunately, he recorded about seven and a half hours of music in his life. Unfortunately, most of it is unreleased (but is kept at the University of Maryland at College Park along with all his diaries and photos and other memorabilia). And what is in release is profoundly poetic and brilliant. I've never heard anyone play Prokofiev's Piano Concerto No. 3 quite like he does. The boundless energy he displays in those relentless runs in the first movement is unbelievable. I'll show you when you visit next.

I've also begun asking people if they've ever heard him perform. I met someone at one of those hopelessly interminable meetings of the opera's fundraising committee. Fred Stoessel is an engaging gentleman who recently moved to Albuquerque from Manhattan, where he grew up. His father,

Albert Stoessel, was a well-known conductor in his time, and Fred still has all his valuable conducting notes and transcriptions, which he tends and rents from his home in Rio Rancho.

We were leaving after the meeting broke up when something prompted me to ask him if he ever knew a pianist by the name of William Kapell. "Oh, yeah. He was a friend of the family," said Fred. I immediately asked more questions.

Willy not only knew the Stoessels, but often visited them at home. He performed with the elder Stoessel on a few occasions. Albert Stoessel founded the conducting and opera departments at Juilliard, according to Fred. And although Fred was "only a kid" at the time (he was seven years younger than Willy), he remembered Willy often played boogie woogie on their piano, saying it strengthened the left hand. He couldn't stay away from the piano ("like Gershwin"). Fred also remembered how "exceedingly thin" he was, and that his face seemed flushed ("like Bernstein"). He had a prominent, aristocratic, yet "wild" face.

"He had this intense energy," Fred told me. "He couldn't relax." That figures. Mozart couldn't relax either.

L.

That night, Lina and Willy sat on a huge granite boulder observing the stars. Far below to the west, Albuquerque's twinkling lights lit the night sky for miles around. Willy gestured animatedly as he explained.

Of course I couldn't relax! I had so much to do! Who could relax under all that pressure? Could you? No, don't answer that, you're never relaxed either.

Oh, yes I am!

Really? Just look at you, then. You work on the book all night long, and run a household and a career all day long. You hardly get any sleep.

No! I work at night because it's the only time I get the solitude to meditate and think and remember. I didn't work tonight because I'm trying to rest up....

Your nights are the least of it. You're overworking yourself. What about your five-part "to do" lists? You think we haven't noticed?

They're in five parts because it's easier to keep track....

They're in five parts because you've divided your atten-

tion into five major arenas of life, my dear. The sooner you stop doing that, the sooner you can slow down and smell the roses.

Lina laughed. Look who's lecturing whom! My list should be down to four parts soon. Really. One list will be gone soon. The opera company's folding any day now.

No, it isn't. Don't be so hasty, cautioned Willy sagely.

Hasty? It's been on the verge of folding for years. Nobody cares if it lives or dies. This isn't Europe, you know, it's the West, and it's still wild in many more ways than I'd care to think about. And this isn't the 18th century, either. It's the trenches of the 20th, and regional opera is dead.

Trust me. It's got a few more years left in it.

Lina turned away to watch the first rosy light of dawn steal across the eastern sky.

Rats! she whispered.

Rats? Willy repeated, amused.

Yes, rats. Rats, rats, rats! I was hoping to move on. The opera is wearing me out. And the zarzuela company is hard work, too. Trying to do it with only a handful of us—the fundraising, the scheduling, the rehearsing, the schmoozing, the paperwork, the publicity, the traveling—it's all uphill.

Don't be stupid. Opera is always uphill. But it's much more exciting than working in a bank, or for the government. It's not as wearing as boredom would be. Besides, you only perceive that you're tired of it. You seem to have forgotten how happy you are when you see troops of children at a dress rehearsal, or the faces of an enchanted audience.

You know, in my next life, I'm going to sing onstage....

That's a worthy goal.

...or I'm not coming back.

Oh, you'll come back, all right.

Going to talk me into another one?

Maybe. In the meantime, you can begin practicing now. Sing this! In a rich tenor voice, Willy began singing Pedrillo's lyrics:

"In Moorish land a lovely maid
Was bound by lock and key."

Sing with me! called Willy, taking her hand. It's about you!

Lina joined him:
"White was her skin
And black her hair,

198

Long did she weep in deep despair.
Would no one set her free?
Then from a foreign land there came
A young and daring knight. (A pun, Lina!)
And when he heard the maiden's plea,
'I'll risk my head and heart,' quoth he,
'To help you in your plight.'"

Even after she awoke, Lina's head still rang with the tune of the midnight aria from Mozart's *Die Entfuhrung aus dem Serail.*

VIENNA, February, 1792.

Dear Father Pasterwicz,

As you requested, I am writing, now, to you for the purpose of setting your mind at ease as to my state of mind, and, of course, this project that currently consumes my waking hours. I believe that after reading this letter you will be considerably less anxious for me.

In the few weeks since your visit, I have worked steadily and without fear. I only briefly wonder about the new calm that has settled about me. I am simply grateful that it allows me to reach the end of this project that much sooner. I am beginning, also, to recognize Wolfgang's stronger influence throughout the most recently written sections which render the work, in places, more his than my own. Yet I do not much attempt to understand how this is possible. To me, I must admit, this similarity of style is as much a fortunate result of his effectiveness as a composition teacher as it is a result of my months and years of copying his music. Still, I am aware of many flaws in the work that would have caused him to frown, and cause me to pray for the end of this ordeal.

Although the music has begun to flow easily, I cannot entirely subscribe to your kind theory that Wolfgang is somehow helping me write the mass, certain manifestations notwithstanding. Yet I do not startle or resist when my hand occasionally moves almost on its own. To be sure, my heart beats faster, yet I must and do attribute my lively hand to too much wine. Still, you will be happy to know that, on the best days, I hear more Mozart than Sussmayr in these passages still wet on the sheet.

You also will be happy to know that I no longer hide in my apartment. Indeed, I have begun to seek out a few friends— Eybler, for one, and Vogl, Wetzlar and some musicians of the theatre orchestra mostly. They have all rejoiced in seeing me, relieved, I suspect, to know that I am again out and about and that I can still smile. (Vogl told me I must improve my smile, because my eyes have no trace of a smile's joy. I told him a bottle of wine would fix that soon enough.)

My friends were anxious to tell me that *Die Zauberflote* has continued to be a magnificent success even after Wolfgang's death. The theatre has been packed at every performance with lower, and, surprisingly, even upper class patrons. Tunes from the opera are sung and whistled everywhere—you already knew that, I think. Emmanual Schikaneder, the theatre manager-actor who sings Papageno, is apparently making a lot of money, with Wolfgang's share, no doubt, going to Constanze.

Unfortunately, I have paid no attention at all to the go-ings-on at the theatre. But you should know of my chance meeting with Schikaneder. It was only a brief conversation— we were both hurrying on our separate ways—during which this rather self-important impresario said nothing to me of the opera's sustained success. However, he wasted no time in of-fering me a commission for a similar work. "It must be similar to *Die Zauberflote,* you understand," he told me. "Can you manage the same variety of music?"

Indeed! Another opera for his infested barn of a the-atre! Needless to say, I will certainly think that one over very carefully. Although Schikaneder is a genial and even enter-taining acquaintance, I have never trusted him. He has been known to pass off someone else's work as his own without so much as a twitch of remorse. His name, if you didn't know, was the only one listed as librettist of *Zauberflote* despite the many people who had worked on it. And his composers never get more than passing reference in all his playbills.

Well! Here I am condemning Schikaneder for something I am, right now, doing myself. What is that? you may ask. It's Wolfgang's mass, of course. Constanze's attorney, a certain Herr Hammerschmidt, has informed me she must pass it off as entirely Wolfgang's work or risk forfeiting the deposit, as well as the final payment. I am to keep my work a secret.

This curious conspiracy of circumstance! I wonder now if this is any less dishonest than what Schikaneder does. You know, normally I would say that this doesn't matter—that discerning ears will know if this is truly a Mozart work or not. But then when I play certain passages that have just flowed from my pen, and I hear so much of his very soul in it, so that not even I know what to make of those finer touches...those exquisite passages written in places that he never even started while he was alive; well, then, I don't know what to think!

But enough! I am so close to finishing now, I must make this letter short and get back to work. Please take care of your health, and write as soon as you can to your

Humble Servant
and Grateful Friend:
F: X: Sussmayr

ONE WEEK LATER.

On a moonlit evening by the light of a candle stub, Franz slowly, and with wistful ceremony, tied the string over the portfolio that held the finished *Requiem.* Standing at the worktable, he laid his hands on the leather cover and briefly closed his eyes.

He turned and donned his greatcoat. He stopped to snuff the candle and see that the pale orange embers in the stove would last until his return. At last he took the portfolio and slipped noiselessly out the door.

A light snow was gradually covering an already snowbound city as he strode purposefully down the dark, narrow street. An occasional streetlamp shone down on clusters of Viennese rushing home to warmth and families. Franz studiously ignored them, avoiding eye contact, as he made his way to the home of Herr Hammerschmidt.

It was a long walk, but Franz could not afford a carriage, and his elation over completing the work was carrying him along almost as though he were flying. At length he found the house, its windows giving off the inviting soft glow of several candelabra. Franz knocked, and the elation melted into mild anxiety, for he had lately been in the company of friends and sympathetic acquaintances. He had yet to confront strangers in business. Hammerschmidt was, after all, Constanze's attorney. He realized he was not entirely prepared for any uncomfortable, or even hostile, encounters.

A kindly woman opened the door and ushered him into a warm, well-lit library. He found himself standing before a massive desk at which Hammerschmidt sat. He was a much older man, with a hard, unchanging gaze. Franz placed the portfolio on his desk.

"The *Requiem,*" he announced neutrally. "It's done."

"Let us see what you have, then," said Hammerschmidt. His voice betrayed a shadow of cordiality that surprised Franz. He watched the man untie the string and lay the leather cover aside. As the old man studied the sheets, Franz approached the big hearth where a fire crackled heat and light. From there, he watched Hammerschmidt, wondering how seriously he intended to examine the music. At length, the attorney looked up and met Franz's eyes.

"I'm sure Frau Mozart will be pleased," he said with a bland smile. "I cannot tell where Herr Mozart's music stops and where yours begins."

Franz pursed his lips to mask a sardonic smile.

What a fool! But let this idiot think what he will. I have done what I can.

Hammerschmidt continued, "I'm afraid Frau Mozart left no instructions for payment for your services. I would ad—"

"Please, sir," interrupted Franz, arching his brow. "I seek no payment."

Can't you see? *I did it for Wolfgang.*

Minutes later, and after proper and meaningless pleasantries, Franz was again out in the cold night.

It was all over. It was done.

Franz went directly to a tavern after leaving Hammerschmidt's. He considered it a kind of perverse progress that, rather than buying several bottles of wine and going home, he sat down and drank in the tavern instead. Fortunately, no one recognized him and he was left alone.

Franz poured a second glass and gazed out the window, indifferently watching the snow fall.

It might be a good idea to leave Vienna for a while, he mused. Go to Baden, maybe. Stay with Stoll, maybe. Where in the world will I get the money to go anywhere? It's time to find work again. It's time to find a commission. Something simple. But substantial. But I don't want to think about that now.... When will I think about it, then? Tomorrow? The next day? Never?

"Franz?" whispered a low-toned voice. Franz broke out of his reverie and looked up into the homely, kind face of Michael Puchberg. "What a surprise to see you! May I join you? How are you faring these days?"

"Michael," breathed Franz, perplexed to see a familiar face so far out of his own neighborhood. "How good to see you...yes, please, sit down."

"I see you are no longer ill," ventured Michael, settling into the chair opposite Franz. "I heard you were gravely ill, in fact. It's good to know you are well."

"Thank you, you're very kind," responded Franz automatically.

What does he want from me? he wondered. Money? Wolfgang still owed him quite a bit before he died. What will I tell him? It's obvious! I'll have to promise to pay him later.

Franz watched Michael carefully as he ordered another beer. He had always liked Michael. He was agreeable and friendly, with an open, happy demeanor. Small wonder Wolfgang had asked him for money instead of so many of his wealthy acquaintances. Wolfgang had told him Michael had enough tact to keep their dealings a secret.

"You look pleased, Franz." Michael smiled. He remembered Franz as somewhat soft-spoken, but since Wolfgang died, he seemed to have withdrawn entirely. Certainly few persons had seen him since before Wolfgang's death.

"Are you working on any commissions?" Michael inquired.

Franz guessed he would never ask outright for his money. He was too courteous. "None at the moment, but I hope to find work soon. Then, if you can wait—with your kind indulgence—I will...then...repay you. All of it...." Franz cleared his throat and continued, "How much did Wolfgang still owe you?"

A puzzled expression crossed Michael's face as he considered.

"Franz, what are you talking about? Do you wish to pay the widow Mozart's debts?" Then an expression of sudden comprehension lit Michael's face. He suddenly realized. Impulsively, he reached across the table and grasped Franz's hand. But of course! he thought.

"I'm sorry! You were like brothers! You certainly must be suffering the most for his passing."

"Well, I...."

"You have been through much with him, haven't you? You deserve as much respectful condolence as Constanze, if not more, for I happen to know of her shameful behavior of the last few years.... You're still deep in mourning. I can see by your eyes...."

"We all miss him," Franz said distantly.

"If there is anything I can do!"

"Yes, there is something. Have you talked with Constanze?"

"Oh, yes, we helped with the children, as her mother is not well this winter."

"Does she realize there is still no grave marker in place? What does she intend to do about that? Does she ever mention it?"

Michael stopped to remember. "If I recall...she told me she expects the church to provide one. She says she has no money."

"Do you believe her?"

"I believe she has expenses, but I don't think she's destitute. She has, after all, several gentlemen friends and her mother, all of whom are comfortably well off." Michael lowered his voice. "I don't like saying this, but between you and me, Franz, I don't think she cares if a marker goes up or not."

Franz searched Michael's face and confirmed what he had suspected. As they sat in silent contemplation, Franz remembered Wolfgang once telling Constanze how happy he would be if she loved him only half as much as he loved her.

"It won't be the first Viennese grave without a marker, Franz," offered Michael. "Don't let it bother you. Wolfgang won't be forgotten, not for centuries."

"You're right. But it would be comforting to know he was valued enough by his contemporaries to have the most minor of tributes at his death," replied Franz. "It's the least she can do...." His voice trailed off. "Michael, if Wolfgang were here now...he would embrace you a thousand times for the brother you are and always have been...." Franz paused. Meeting old friends was not as easy as he had hoped it would be. "You are right when you say Wolfgang was my brother, and so by logic, you are my brother too. I hope some day to be of service to you in his memory...for your generosity, for your support when he needed it. For now, I can offer only my deepest gratitude."

Franz stood up and embraced Michael. Then he was gone.

Michael watched Franz disappear into the night. How long would it be before Franz would finish grieving? he wondered. How long, in fact, would it take us all to get over it?

Maybe never.

VII.

The path to love is found
By experiencing what it is like without love.
Just as the path to Light
Is to be aware of darkness.

—Emmanuel, 1985

ALBUQUERQUE, 1988.

Lina lay exhausted and breathless on the bed, speaking intermittently into a tape recorder's microphone attached to the front of her pullover. It was her second experiment in self-regression, and she spoke slowly and carefully, anxious to preserve every sight, sound and feeling.

Her head swam with impressions of many weeks of illness. "They found him in a dark, dirty basement apartment. He was...unable to call for help. Had been there many days. They took him away, somewhere safe and clean. Sunny. Very sunny. Hurts the eyes." Lina winced again and again; her hands clenched and unclenched as she continued her solitary narrative.

"Head aching. Lungs aching...feeling so...heavy. Determined to see his death all the way through. So warm in here. For a long, long time, weeks maybe, his chest has burned and ached...no feeling on his left side...I can hear his heart pounding in his ears...and every breath is an agony...getting worse. A young woman is taking care of him. Sister, maybe? I'm moving ahead in time, if I can...."

Moments passed.

"On an empty stage...something happened. He suddenly felt light and now he's here, on a stage of all places, looking around calmly. The pain is forgotten. Wonder what happened. Seeing Wolfgang sitting at...a harpsichord near the wings."

Do you remember Die Zauberflote, *Franz?*

How can I forget it? I tried to recreate it in so many of my own operas.

I was the surprised one to learn that we had both begun writing that music before we were born.

Franz smiled. This was an enchanting conversation in an enchanting place. The theatre. He loved its smells and aura. They had embraced the theatre, he and Wolfgang. It was the home of all hopes and glories.

Before we were born? he asked.

Do you have any idea of the amount of preparation one life takes? Wolfgang was saying. *Do you know how many lives I experienced to prepare for this one?*

Franz heard people in the wings preparing for a rehearsal. He glanced offstage.

They are unaware of us, said Wolfgang. He began playing the harpsichord.

A searing cough pulled Franz back to his bed. He was suddenly aware of the white curly hair of his friend Pasterwicz where he sat in Maria's chair, watching him. Franz blinked. The old priest had died the previous winter. It had been the beginning of the end of Franz's own shaky health when he heard of the old man's death, for he knew his last real friend was gone.

Father! he cried from his bed, unable to move.

Franz, my son, whispered Pasterwicz.

Where is Wolfgang? We were just talking.

All will be right. Be patient. He is waiting for you.

But you're so serious. What's wrong? The priest had always worried for Franz, even at a time when Franz did not care enough to worry about himself. Now he looked concerned again.

You must be strong, Franz. Do not let unhappy thoughts cloud your mind. Wolfgang has been waiting a long time. Twelve years by Earth reckoning. Take care, Franz. Hear me. Don't allow dark memories to break your new bond.

What do you mean? I don't understand....

But Pasterwicz was gone.

A loving warmth surrounded him as a roaring sound engulfed the room. His arms finally lifted, lighter than air, toward two outstretched hands.

He held on through a brief moment of disorientation and blinding light. The roaring subsided and he was looking again into the light of Wolfgang's serene smile. The light encircled them both and those who surrounded them—Mama, a smiling Pasterwicz, Franz's sister, Theresa. An overwhelming love, joy and peace enveloped him. The pain was gone. He gulped in great breaths with ease.

Lina gasped as she continued to record her sensations. "That peculiar warmth he felt when he was alone was Mozart's love! A love so strong it penetrated the veil of death. Now he's surrounded again by that love. It's indescribable...a feeling of 'beingness' with the love that is his own essence as well."

209

The pull of his physical body caused him to look back, and he saw down a long tunnel to a far-away room where Maria had nursed him in his illness. The sight continued to shrink, so far away and so small, so fleeting an image as Franz grew brighter and stronger in the love and light around him.

Don't look back, said Mama gently. *Maria is loved and guided.*

It was at once a voice and a thought, for Franz realized with the same feeling of familiarity that he could communicate in a wordless thought transference that conveyed the precise essence of expression. Thus did Wolfgang and Franz know their mutual joy and profound relief at the end of their trial. They floated upward over a gleaming blue lake so bright that it made Franz squint.

Where are we going? he asked.

To the most extraordinary places, feelings and expressions you have ever experienced, Wolfgang answered. And, to Franz's astonished delight, Wolfgang immediately transformed his own brilliant light and sound into a dancing sunbeam of harmony and color.

Hold your breath! he called.

As Franz held his breath, he watched the light and sound disperse into thousands of tiny sparkling particles speeding around him. Franz's senses burst with transcendent joy and love.

Now exhale!

And the particles of light merged with Franz's own light in an explosion of brilliant yellow crystalline rays. Their beings were in perfect unison. Their shared light gained momentum and strength as together they sped round and round in a radiant kaleidoscope of color bands and rhythms. A multi-harmonic luminosity caressed his soul—and Franz realized it was more than music. He realized he had *become* music. As it reverberated and rejoiced within him, he was ecstatic.

Can you hear the colors? Can you see the music?

Yes!

Franz opened his mind's eye and beheld colors unknown to him before now, flying about before him like a million fiery diamonds. The indescribable love grew stronger and stronger until Franz balked, afraid that his heart would burst. At that moment, the love subsided and Franz found himself at the crest of a high mountain range. The view was breathtaking as it, too, seemed to sparkle with the very essence of life.

When you have fully rested, Franz, I will show you so much! We have much to do, you and I and the others! So much, and your share is waiting.

My share? asked Franz, suddenly remembering. *How can I help? I surely can't. Not after letting everyone down. If it hadn't been for me....*

No, Franz! Don't!

Slowly, a gray misty veil descended around Franz. Immediately Wolfgang concentrated his energies and directed them toward dispelling the veil. Frustrated in the attempt, he called out.

It's a cloud of your own mind, Franz, and only you can disperse your dark thoughts. Concentrate! Help me help you!

Franz sighed unhappily as he faded from sight.

But I don't deserve it. I know that. What's happening? Don't let me go!

Franz!

Where did he go? asked Wolfgang of his Teacher.

He has migrated to a lower plane. Be assured, he is loved and guided there. And comfortable.

Why is he there?

You know that thoughts are things here. Franz will work out the feelings of self-reproach and undeservedness which he has turned into tangible barriers to growth. If necessary, he eventually may choose to excise these barriers in yet another life. We will monitor his progress with love and hope.

Then I will see him again?

You may visit him from time to time. But the frequency there is of a slow vibration and you will find it nearly as difficult as visiting the Earth plane.

When will he return here?

"Oh, God," Lina exhaled. "When I learn to forgive myself!"

VIENNA, March, 1792.

It was an unseasonably warm day for March.

As Franz walked briskly along the wide avenue toward

211

the home of Antonio Salieri, he noticed the crystalline quality of the air in the quieter quarter of Vienna, where the noise and dust of the inner city seemed almost another town entirely. So charmed by the unusual surroundings was he that he almost forgot his impending meeting with the court composer. He realized the contradiction of not really wanting to study composition with Salieri, but knowing, too, that he had promised Wolfgang to continue his studies with him. And now he would need a teacher, because Schikaneder had made good on his idle talk and had actually commissioned an opera from Franz. For his part, Franz wanted the assurance of a master who would look over his work before he committed it—and his reputation—to the stage.

Schikaneder and Franz had had surprisingly little trouble agreeing on a subject. It would be on Moses and the Exodus. Perhaps, Franz had suggested, it was a bit too much material for one opera. Nonsense, said Schikaneder, we'll take only the highlights. As you wish, Franz had said, not really caring, although knowing that ultimately he would have to care if his name was to go on it.

In an unusually provident moment, almost immediately after accepting the commission, he had written a note to Salieri asking for an appointment. Salieri had replied immediately, agreeing to see him.

Franz walked now along the cobblestone drive as he neared Salieri's imposing residence. He glanced up apprehensively. The tall, graceful trees that surrounded these larger, impressive homes imparted a serene pastoral atmosphere. The only other time Franz noticed trees, it seemed to him, was in Baden, or on the long rides to that remote country resort, and on walks in the Prater, Vienna's only public park worth visiting. Here, in this wealthy suburb, one had the best of both worlds. The contact with the city and all it had to offer, and the quiet richness of the country and its equally important solitude.

A liveried servant showed Franz into a cold, marble room dominated by a round white marble table, a fireplace with no fire and long, high windows draped in heavy green brocade. Franz laid his portfolio on the table and rubbed his hands nervously as he waited.

"Herr Sussmayr? Welcome."

Salieri appeared at the double doors and strode forward with his hand outstretched in cordial greeting. He was a short, compact man whose serious gaze met Franz's briefly. His small eyes would not hold onto another's for very long. Franz had always judged the man to be less impressive at close range than at a distance.

"Thank you, sir, for agreeing to meet with me," Franz began formally.

"Nonsense, I am pleased to see you again," said the older man coolly as he motioned for him to sit. "About Herr Mozart, please accept my sincerest condolences at his passing. He was a great musician and composer."

"Yes, he was." Franz studied Salieri guilelessly, surprised that he would care enough to offer his sympathies. Might he really care? he wondered. It was difficult to read those distant eyes.

Suddenly uncomfortable at the silence, Salieri shifted and cleared his throat. He would not have a young upstart like Mozart's copyist watching him so carefully. It was bad enough that all of Vienna was accusing him of having poisoned Mozart, without this kind of unwarranted examination.

Salieri was a fearful Catholic who had long since decided that if nothing else, there *was* a heaven and hell. Yet only recently had he begun to fathom the consequences of his ruthless climb to the top of Vienna's music world, and his equally ruthless struggle to stay there. He had recently begun to wonder if his actions were not creating for him a path directly to hell, and whether he should start making amends before it was too late. No, he was not interested in being a good Christian. He just didn't want to go to hell. It was not part of his plans. Nor would these prattling Viennese be so convinced he was a murderer if he aided Mozart's family in whatever way he could. Would a murderer help his victim's family in this manner? And was not this Sussmayr fellow practically family, from what he'd heard? Thus he had agreed to see him, and, if need be, to take him as a student. For as determinedly as he had blocked Mozart's success in Vienna, he was as intent now to help his survivors. It would not hurt him to do it, and it might help him avoid God's wrath.

"I understand from your note that you are anxious to study composition," he said, smiling only with his mouth.

"Yes, that is why I am here," replied Franz quickly. He hesitated, wondering whether to speak, then added, "Before he died, Herr Mozart recommended that I study with you. He said you were the only other master in Vienna."

"I see," Salieri responded slowly. Though moved, he betrayed no emotion as he silently took the portfolio, and with slow, deliberate movements, began examining portions of Franz's music.

Sensing that Salieri could not tolerate being watched, Franz turned his gaze on the dark fireplace for what seemed too long a time. A cold emptiness crept into his heart, as he had nothing more to think about than his need for a new teacher.

He blinked and turned to look briefly at Salieri, who was taking several sheets to the window to study them in the light.

Coming here had been difficult, Franz recalled, and then again it wasn't. He really had no personal respect for Salieri, for this man had almost single-handedly ruined Wolfgang's career through unending and apparently shameless intrigue. If it hadn't been for Salieri, maybe, just maybe, Wolfgang might have had an income. And enough money to eat properly, and keep himself warm. And, most importantly, he might have had more opportunities to perform and to feel that his work was accepted, and was finding its way into the hearts of others.

But what good is this kind of speculation now?

"Would you like to begin next week? My Tuesday mornings are free," said Salieri, still avoiding Franz's eyes. "I will take whatever you can afford to pay me, so please do not concern yourself about that." Franz noticed that, after all these years in Vienna, Salieri still spoke German with a pronounced Italian accent.

"You are most generous, Herr Salieri," replied Franz quietly. "Tuesday morning, then." He reached for the portfolio.

"I hear you are to write an opera on Moses for the Theatre an der Wien," said Salieri. "If you have not already started, we can work on that. Bring what text you have now, and whatever music you have begun to sketch."

Franz was aghast but attempted to look nonchalant. *How did Salieri know?* Schikaneder had only settled with him last week.

"Yes, sir," he said evenly, trying to mask his surprise.

"Have you a Bible? Even with a libretto already prepared, you should look to the original version for inspiration," suggested Salieri as he stood up. Franz remembered his Bible had been carried off by Hammerschmidt when he had come for Wolfgang's music.

"I'm afraid my copy is missing."

"Come. I'll lend you mine," said Salieri, surprised at his own generosity. He ushered the young man out of the room, and together they proceeded down a long hall and into the library. Franz's eyes opened wide. He had not seen so many books in one place outside of Van Swieten's library. And he hadn't seen that in a long time.

"It is just the Old Testament." Salieri was reaching for a book with a blue broadcloth cover. He handed it to Franz, who held it carefully in both hands. He looked across the rows of shelving and began scanning titles, ignoring the older man.

Salieri smiled faintly at the pale, thin young man with the light-colored hair and frail smile.

He looks like a starved ghost, Salieri observed. Not long out of the countryside either. Judging from his guileless manner, this young man has a long way to go before he learns to hide his thoughts properly. Or falls prey to certain misfortune. Mozart, the poor wretch, had been the same way. Couldn't keep his thoughts to himself, even with his mouth shut. One could almost always read his face like these books. Well, I suppose it wouldn't hurt to let this one take another book.

"Would you like to borrow another one?" he asked in his most magnanimous manner. Franz turned and looked at him with unguarded delight. "Go ahead, then, choose another," said Salieri, feeling somewhat like a grandfather.

Franz chose *The Iliad* in Italian and turned to face his new benefactor. "Thank you, sir, you are most kind. I will return them Tuesday."

"No need. Take your time with them. Just remember whose they are."

Franz decided to walk home from Salieri's. It was a fine day and the books had made it a better day yet. He wanted to walk and enjoy the sunshine, to listen to the fortepiano music drifting occasionally from the homes he passed. Tomorrow he would be moving into new quarters nearer the theatre, at Schikaneder's suggestion. He had not realized, until Maria had so carefully pointed it out to him, that he was living in the past in that apartment. If he was to begin living again, she continued, it

215

would be better to move. Then she had told him that Schikaneder had been by to see him on the day he had gone to the cathedral.

Schikaneder originally had wanted the opera for Lent, but Pasterwicz had discouraged him from approaching Franz earlier than he had. Now he would have to make quick work of the project.

No matter, thought Franz. It will be good to work, and it's not as if I haven't rushed through operas before. We made short work of *Die Zauberflote,* and Wolfgang was sick much of the time. He was feeling much worse when we finished *La Clemenza* in even less time.

I will manage. With the help of my friends, I will manage.

VIENNA, April, 1792.

Franz felt conspicuous as he waited for the musicians to begin. Why was he sitting so far up front? Why did he feel so many eyes on him? Why was he even here tonight? Hadn't Puchberg and Wetzlar insisted he join their musical evening? He had accepted reluctantly, and only because it was part of his attempt—his campaign—to return to life. He had begun to notice that among the less superstitious Viennese, Wolfgang's reputation was re-establishing itself now that he was dead, and that despite his own reclusive habits, Franz was increasingly recognized as one of Wolfgang's last and closest friends. Thus, he was approached more often than he cared to be by casual acquaintances who had previously ignored Wolfgang as inconsequential.

He had been touched, on arriving at Wetzlar's, to find that he was not only remembered, but warmly welcomed by the twenty or more people gathered there. So many familiar, smiling faces moving suddenly before him in swift succession, so many pairs of warm hands taking his, so many genial voices asking after his health. One or two of the men—friends and musicians close to Wolfgang—clasped Franz in a sympathetic embrace and offered consolences on "our mutual loss." Franz blinked back his feelings and accepted a glass of wine as voices buzzed around him.

Now he sat, still and self-conscious, as the musicians

tuned their instruments. He was to sit here, in front of everyone in the first row of chairs. A place of honor, they said. It was an unlikely place for him, near the musicians, even when Wolfgang was alive and performing. In those not so distant days, Franz stationed himself alongside a wall or near the back where he might concentrate on the music, unobserved—undisturbed. Now the lovely ladies and their gracious gentlemen were taking their seats all around him.

The crowd grew silent. Franz watched in detachment as the quartet of musicians suddenly sat still, backs straight, instruments and bows poised, waiting for the first violinist's cue. A woman's hand reached out and squeezed Franz's arm reassuringly. The gesture puzzled him. The first violinist signaled the cue with a quick downbeat movement.

The first measures took Franz by surprise, as his heart and head were suddenly filled with Wolfgang's music. He inhaled deeply. It had been so long since he had heard this piece. He closed his eyes and tilted his head slightly backwards as his sensibilities gradually awakened to myriad luminous colors, sparkling like sunlight on water. It swept through him, carrying him to realms he had almost forgotten existed.

A melody of meltingly sweet beauty caressed his senses. It was Love itself, drawn from higher planes and distilled for human ears. He reveled.

Yes, *this* is why I am a musician. This is why I persist! I want to live in unending pursuit of exquisite musical expression. I want to soar through time on streams of beauty....

How could I have forgotten?

A new warmth enfolded him. He sighed and savored his vitality.

Has it been that long that I have been so overwhelmed by the mundane business of living, that I have been completely lost to music?

Not so long as you think.

This music! Wolfgang's incredible, extraordinary, unutterably expressive music....

It is your music, too.

No, it is Wolfgang's.

You were there to love him. He could not have written this music without that Love. In loving him, you nurtured his art.

But many people loved him.

Yes, many people loved him, but you accepted the suffer-

217

ing others declined.

ALBUQUERQUE, Winter, 1988.

Lina squinted lazily at the falling snow outside her window. Her eyelids grew heavier with the white glare of the winter's first storm. Snow fascinated her, and she strained against the sleep that gently descended on her as she sat crouched in the wide, cushioned wicker chair. The music of a Mozart quartet sounded lightly in her head.

You never did believe that, did you?

Believe what?

That Franz's love helped make possible Wolfgang's music.

I thought I was hallucinating whenever I heard that voice.

What do you think now? I'm only a voice in your head right now.

Lina quickly opened her eyes to see Willy leaning on the window sill, the bright, diffused light of the snowfall effecting a halo around his slight form.

That's better, isn't it? So you don't like voices in your head.

Not really. It's spooky.

Even if it's your own voice?

But it's not my voice, Willy, it's yours.

No, it's your own voice, too.

You're talking in riddles.

Am I? We all continue, in each lifetime, to exist and develop as individuals, do you agree?

Yes, but what does that have to do with it?

I'll tell you. The vast power and extraordinary energy of an Old Soul would overwhelm one physical body. It's simply too much. It would be like trying to hold a lake in a glass. Instead, the soul fragments into individual personalities—as many as several hundred, although it is a finite number.

Are you saying Franz and Wolfgang are soul fragments?

Yes, and as such they are closer than brothers, and though their facades may change from lifetime to lifetime, they are forever part of the same oversoul which simply IS and will always BE. They resonate to one another's presence.

Do oversouls have specialties? Like, possibly, music?

Yes. But nothing is static. We will eventually find other favorite expressions.

Do all fragments meet like this, the way we do?

Willy smiled and paused.

Like this? No, only when one of the fragments is in a body.

What if both fragments are trapped in a body and want to meet?

Fellow fragments meet astrally. If they want to meet on the physical level, they often find one another through recognition of themselves, behind the facades of temporary personalities. The current excitement of finding a "soulmate" is actually a mundane application of connecting with a fellow fragment. The idea is right, but the goal should be more sublime and lasting than what most earthbound soulmate explorers expect to gain in one marriage in one lifetime.

You sound so scholarly, Willy. How do you know all this?

Willy laughed.

You know all this, too, only being trapped in the physical, and growing older in the physical, has caused you to forget, temporarily. When you're in the spirit, you're usually a fountain of information. A virtual geyser! Quite unbearable, actually.

He laughed again, and Lina found herself smiling, unable to resist his infectious good humor even as she struggled to absorb the information and make sense of it. She also had noticed, as they spoke, that neither of them actually were speaking out loud, but seemed only to exchange thoughts.

Willy spoke. *If you didn't know you were so loved and protected right now, you'd probably decide to worry about that, too.*

About what?

About our not speaking out loud.

Now you're reading my thoughts!

How else can we communicate? Don't forget, my dear, you are part of me and I am part of you.

I can't keep up with you!

Yes, you can! You're unnerved because you're not taking your endless notes, which you do because you don't think you can remember anything. I know you can. Now tell me, what do you think is happening when you feel that tingling warm feeling you so often experience?

Happening? What's happening? Someone's visiting me!

219

Making the air electric—I don't know....

Did it ever occur to you that it might be me? Or another of our fellow fragments?

But how?

I thought you'd never ask! In the last decades of the 20th century, the Earth's vibrations have been steadily rising as the planet begins its evolution from the third dimension into the fourth dimension. This vibrational shift has many effects, including an increased facility to communicate with those of us on the non-physical planes, and vice versa. So certain things are possible, including making your air electric. I'll show you, but you must give me your absolute trust and your clearest, most positive thoughts. Otherwise it may not work, now that you're almost conscious and expecting it.

I trust you, I trust you. Show me how you do it! It is you, then, who visits me?

Willy smiled enigmatically, reminding Lina of the faces on the Sistine Chapel walls. He faded from the window sill and suddenly she was filled with the warmth she so often felt in moments of solitude and quiet, usually on first waking in the morning. It was as if the air around her had been charged with energy, and it shot through her like a ray of light. As usual, she couldn't help but smile and sigh. His voice sounded in her head:

I have more to say about Wolfgang. It's important and should go in the book. He expressed his soul's energy in music with the supporting love and complimentary vibratory presence of Franz, without whom he would have died much sooner, of exhaustion. This exhaustion was alleviated by the life energy from Franz, transmitted astrally at night and in their embraces, an exchange that is not easily achieved by non-related fragments. The Wolfgang/Franz association was a convergence of lives arranged at the eleventh hour, if you will, by their spirit guides and teachers. It was their wish that the life of the Wolfgang entity be prolonged to allow for several more musical masterpieces, particularly the Requiem. *Hence, Franz was called into his sphere of influence, having agreed to act as protector and assistant, but most primarily as transmitter of life force to sustain the body and spirit. It was a life of magnificent endeavor, assisted by other fellow fragments who contributed from the astral plane, like so many lines of light shining on one center, and from that center, brilliant rays continue to beam out to the world, and cover the weary planet with shimmering ribbons of Mozartean light and sound. It was all done for Love, of course, and Compassion.*

Lina blinked and sat up in the chair, serene, hearing again the strains of a Mozart quartet that had blossomed suddenly in her mind as she dozed. She glanced out the window. The snow was beginning to drift against the house and in frozen crests along the fence.

Shimmering white snow, she thought.

She turned to the typewriter and swiftly typed what she had just heard. She ripped the page out of the machine and dropped it into her "book box." She pulled out another, half-typed page and continued her three-day letter:

"I remember my stroll through St. Marx Cemetery in Vienna. Kathy was sick and I was depressed, but we were determined to be tourists. I did a little research after we got back. If I had known then what I know now—that, as we walked through that cemetery, we walked on Mozart's very bones, crushed and spaded back into the earth.

"I discovered that the custom in his day was to bury the poor four at a toss in communal graves and then wait a respectable length of time before digging up the bones, crushing them up and returning the dust and bits to the soil. Row after row of these pits were rotated like this for years and decades. So it goes, I suppose. In the meantime, 20th century Austrians set up a false gravesite on which pilgrims innocently center their attentions. Someone had to do it. Constanze never bothered with a marker. In fact, it took her seventeen years even to visit the grave, according to historians. And then only at the insistence of someone else.

"Well, it doesn't matter anymore. I don't think it ever did. Mozart isn't remembered by a chunk of marble in a grimy little Viennese garden of crushed bones. I know now that his sad funeral and lost remains profoundly underscore the fact that his life and art thoroughly transcend Earth life and death."

Lina fell back in her chair as she thought over what more to write. She stared absently at the flower on her desk as she turned it over in her mind.

"Just the same, how much do you want to bet it was Franz Xaver Wolfgang, the second son, who dragged his mother to the cemetery to find the grave? He would have been seventeen years old by then—old enough to come to his own conclusions about certain things."

Stretching her arms above her head, Lina carelessly scanned the wall behind the desk. A calendar of floral displays...a picture of her sisters, arm in arm at a picnic twenty years prior...a photocopied picture of Willy taken from the *Time Magazine* announcement of his death—the intense, arrogant stare, the necktie askew...a penciled poem attached with a map pin...a dry cleaning claim check...a watercolor mandala....

Her eyes wandered to the desk. A box of chalk...a blue and green paperweight...a facetious letterhead she'd typed for the opera staff: "We the unwilling, led by the unqualified"...a bottle of dried liquid paper...a stack of typing paper...one carnation in a clear glass vase...beautiful, luminous white carnation....

Didn't I buy three carnations several weeks a go? Yes, a red, a pink and a white. The red wilted first, then the pink—I threw it out last week, and...it's been so long now, why hasn't the white one wilted yet?

Puzzled, she reached over and pulled the white flower out of the vase, dripping water across her desk. She examined it in silence.

It's as fresh as the day I first brought it home!

She loved its exquisite fragrance. She swirled its stem between thumb and forefinger. Not one petal had even begun to turn brown. Each was still shimmering and pure and iridescent. Slowly she sat up in her chair, wide-eyed in new wonder and awe, as she suddenly remembered the single white carnation she'd left at Wolfgang's "grave" in Vienna.

"Thank you for the flower," she said, preferring to speak out loud. "And may I add, you do take my breath away!"

KREMSMUNSTER, June, 1793.

"And that's when I decided to concentrate my attentions entirely on music, no matter what," said Franz. "I knew that I needed to do something. I had forgotten that music was like an elixir to me. And that it *would* be my livelihood as I had always intended it to be."

Pasterwicz smiled broadly as he listened. This was the answer to his prayers. Franz was coming around at last. And it was all thanks to a simple concert at Wetzlar's less than a year ago. God works in mysterious ways indeed.

Today they sat outdoors enjoying the warmth of a brilliant June sun.

"It's just that I had forgotten, you see, I had forgotten that music is my life. That it reinforces me," Franz concluded. He looked intensely at his old friend. He had come to Kremsmunster on his old mentor's invitation, to visit, rest and perform again at his school's anniversary ceremonies.

"And what is your next move?" asked the old man.

Franz took another swallow of wine and spoke slowly. "Salieri is impressed with my work. It was he who got me the position of acting Kapellmeister and harpsichordist at the National Theatre. It's a good step toward a better position later if my work continues to please. I work hard, very hard, Father. For what else can I do?"

"What do you mean?"

"I don't exactly have a family, except for Maria, and she's not in Vienna right now," he replied. "So I don't have much of a personal life. But I will have a good career. And it will be my life, from now on."

Pasterwicz didn't like the sound of that idea, but he remained silent. Why, it was enough that he had come to grips with at least one part of his life. In time, he might find the wherewithal to establish a private life. Maybe even marry. In time. Patience.

"Salieri liked my ballet, Father, and he wants me to do another opera," Franz was saying. "And I will. It will be a fantasy, like *Zauberflote,* with magic and whatnot. That's what the public seems to like, so that is what I will give them. And then another, and another. Until...."

"Until?"

Franz looked pained. He leaned back in his chair. "Until I can forget...."

"Forget?"

"When I'm not on a project...how can I say it? I start thinking again and...."

Pasterwicz could no longer hold his tongue. "So you think by working yourself into the grave the way he did you will soon forget him? Franz, do you think this is such a good plan?"

"It's the best plan I've got. It will work because I will make it work, for as long as it needs to work. What else can I do? I don't want to go back to Schwanenstadt, for surely there

I will be bored, and the memories and the regrets will return. No, I will stay in Vienna and work."

Pasterwicz studied the young man closely. He was determined. And desperate. But at least he was trying.

"You are determined, and I think you will succeed, Franz. You have my blessing, of course."

"Thank you, Father."

"Did you happen to hear your *Requiem* last month at the benefit concert? I didn't have a chance to attend; I wondered if you might have."

"Yes, I was there. Vogl insisted that I go with him. He thought I should hear it at least once in my life."

"How did it sound? Did they play it well?"

"It was a fair performance. I don't think they had enough time to rehearse it properly, as usual. But it was...." Franz scratched his ear pensively as he searched for the right words. Pasterwicz sat up in anticipation, for he remembered well the circumstances of its creation.

"Yes?"

"Actually, you know, I fully expected to hear more of my clumsy style and less of Wolfgang's brilliant voice there, but I must admit I was impressed."

"Your clumsy style? How can you say that?"

"Father, come now. Anyone's style is clumsy in comparison to Wolfgang's most trifling piece."

"No, of course, I realize that," said Pasterwicz impatiently. "I was only referring to...well, never mind."

"And, do you know, I felt the strangest sensations during the performance. I felt a kind of unusual...lightness about me. Yes, a lightness. But don't misunderstand. It was a trial to be there. I didn't really want to hear it. And Vogl was such a nuisance, always watching me, never leaving my side. I was on pins and needles throughout. The music, I discovered, is as fearful as it is beautiful." Franz pondered for a moment. "Can you understand that? I often wonder if I make sense to you, or anyone."

A robin chirped from a nearby fence as the two men sat in silence. An errant breeze ruffled Franz's hair. Pasterwicz frowned and studied his glass of watered wine. "I understand it is still a painful piece of work for you."

"I suppose it always will be...." Franz threw his head back and sighed. "She was there. Constance. With the children."

Pasterwicz looked up and snorted. "And?"

"And I tried to arrange a meeting with her. I wanted to see the children. I wanted...I suppose I wanted to say hello and see if all was forgiven between us. I sent a note to her box asking her leave to visit briefly with me after the performance. It came back unopened."

"I'm sorry, Franz."

"It's quite all right. I really didn't expect.... But I would dearly have liked visiting with little Franz Xaver Wolfgang. He would be about a year and a half now...." Franz mumbled. "I sometimes wonder what kind of men Wolfgang's boys will become, and if I will ever know them. When they are old enough to visit with me on their own, I mean."

"Time will tell. I think perseverance is in order."

"I must somehow arrange to have you hear my *Ave Verum*, Father. I wrote it a year ago May for Herr Stoll at Baden."

"Stoll? The choirmaster? Didn't Wolfgang write for him, too?"

"Yes, he did," said Franz, amazed at the old man's memory. "Also an *Ave Verum*, in May, the year before. Well, I went to Baden last year just to get out of Vienna, and Stoll asked me to write something for his choir. I must admit, I wrote it more for Wolfgang than for anyone else. I am quite proud of it and I do want you to hear it."

"A prayer for Wolfgang?" Pasterwicz was pleased. "Who has it now?"

"Stoll kept it. It's his now. But I have a copy."

"Hold on to it. It's probably a masterpiece, if I know you," Pasterwicz laughed. "I'm sorry, Franz, I just can't hide my delight at your apparent recovery from the trials of last year. You are happy and relatively healthy looking. How do you feel?"

"Certainly better than last year, but I must ask, don't stop praying for me. There are times when I feel the only way to get through the day is to become somehow unconscious. And then...I drink," he admitted quietly, then hastened to add, "But that's only when I have no composition to occupy my thoughts!"

"You must guard against too much drink. It has ruined stronger men than you. Tell me, have you dreamed of Wolfgang?"

Franz sighed and looked away. "Almost never. When I do, he is standing alone, silently, to one side while I go about my dream business, whatever it may be. He watches. But that's only happened once or twice in the past year. Some mornings I wake up with a strong feeling of having been with him. As if I had spent the entire night in conversation with him. Those are rare feelings, indeed. Have you dreamed him?" he asked hopefully, for now he believed in dreams and voices.

"I'm afraid not. He's not about in my dreams. He's too busy with you, I think." Pasterwicz ventured a small laugh.

Franz's smile faded as quickly as it had appeared. Pasterwicz studied the young man as he prepared to speak.

"You have been more than a friend to me," he said quietly as he reached for Pasterwicz's hand. "You have been like a real father to me. You alone know what I think and feel. You alone care. Wolfgang once said I was an orphan. He was wrong. I had him, and I have you. There alone is more love and support than anyone could hope for in one lifetime. Thank you, Father."

Franz bent over and kissed the priest's hand. Pasterwicz placed his free hand on the young man's head, and blessed him.

VIENNA, Ten Years Later.

Maria put down her pen and stared pensively at her sleeping brother. He was dying. He had been unconscious, and unaware, for several hours. He would wake up and the pain would resume, until he could stand it no longer. Then he would become unaware again. He was pale and waxen, and exhausted from the effort of breathing, which came in small, tired gasps now. The lung disease, the doctor had said. She had written to Papa once. He could not come, he wrote back, but do keep him informed. Maria was puzzled. Was it because the lung disease had taken Mama too, and their sister Theresa? And now that it was taking Franz....

He had suffered for months, and now he was bedridden, unable to move from weakness and constantly coughing up blood. Not that he seemed to care. Franz had never seemed happy, not in years. Even when he was fairly well off in the world, having done so well for himself at the National Theatre.

226

Yet, even then, he had stopped feeling something, inside, long ago. Yes, he smiled and was conversant in the proper way, but he was distant in a way he never had been before. He would never let anyone know what he really thought. And he never laughed out loud.

This illness was the final distancing from an already distant family. She had tried to make the best of a bad situation. Many years ago, when Franz refused to return home after finishing his schooling, Papa had virtually disowned him. Why, Papa had shouted, had he spent so much money on Franz? To waste himself in Vienna among the lower elements? No. Of course not! As the oldest son, Franz was meant only to inherit his father's position with no questions asked.

Maria sighed and continued her letter.

"Herr Deiner found Franz in his apartment, which, as you may remember, is situated in a rather dark basement. He had been there for days, Papa, in the worst of conditions, unable to call for help or take care of himself...."

The tragedy was that he didn't seem to care, mused Maria. He wanted to die, he had told Herr Deiner. How could he say that? How? A good Catholic must endure pain and privations, and accept them as penance.

His drinking had not helped. She had pleaded with him often to eat more and drink less, but he didn't listen. Not that he drank constantly. He didn't. He drank when he wasn't working on a project, she had noticed. One day she had come by to bring him a basket of food, and found him hard at work on another score. A solemn high mass. He was as cheerful as she had ever seen him and when she sat for a visit, he had offered her watered wine. It puzzled her.

"I take as little wine as possible when I compose," he had told her. "It keeps my head clear. And when I perform, too."

So it had surprised her to realize he could drink heavily. While being the oldest of their family of four children, he had turned out to be the most vulnerable to life's extremes. Not that he hadn't worked hard. He was probably the hardest working of all of them. So many operas, what was it, about twenty or so all told? And that beautiful mass, the *Missa Solemnis* in D. But he was not happy. Not the least bit happy.

She wiped a tear from her cheek so that it wouldn't fall on her letter.

"So maybe it is best, my brother, that you are about to return to God."

She got down on her knees by the bed again, crossed herself, and bowed her head.

The sensation that came suddenly to him was quite warm. It took his mind off the pain. For so long, his chest had burned and ached. He had no feeling in his left side, yet he could hear his heart pounding in his ears, and every breath was an agony to draw.

This new warmth surrounded all of him. And it seemed to him, as he lay there unable to move, that his body was expanding like sunlight diffusing in a mist. His body felt like millions of sparks moving on their own.

Is this how it begins? he wondered. If so, then dying isn't so terribly bad. It is only different. It is subtle. *Am I finally dying?*

Almost, came the reply.

What was that?

I am here, Franz, waiting with you, said the familiar voice.

Franz felt his body expand even more, and he waited in hopeful expectation.

Who is it? Who is addressing me? Please tell me your name.

It is your brother and friend, Wolfgang.

The voice filled his head as Franz opened his eyes and looked wildly around the room. He saw only Maria's bowed head not far from his hand. She was praying for his salvation again. He closed his eyes as another coughing spell burned through his chest and head.

It...hurts....

Franz winced as the residual waves of pain subsided. He lay gasping.

It will begin to hurt less.

What do you mean? Wolfgang! Don't leave me!

I have never left you. That is impossible.

Tears began to well as Franz tried to raise his arms. They were too heavy.

I want to see you. Where are you?

I am with you, here.

Where? I don't see anything!

I-am-you-are-me. We are one. I am a part of you. You

are coming into awareness now. Come, let's go for a walk.

Franz felt the intense tingling warmth again, and his head felt light. A buzzing in his ears grew louder and louder.

Suddenly he was standing in the Prater under a brilliant blue sky. The trees were brighter in color than he had ever remembered seeing them. Wolfgang stood beside him, smiling as though he owned the world, or at least the park. Franz blinked. Wolfgang looked absolutely robust. Healthier than he had ever known him to be before.

Of course! exclaimed Wolfgang, reading Franz's thoughts. *You knew me only when I was sick. Not that I was ever really well...there, Snai!* Even as he spoke in his swift, smooth German, Franz had thrown his arms around him, shouting with relief.

At last! Oh, God, at last!

And look at you, Wolfgang continued as he laughed and alternately held Franz close and at arm's length. *You look* much *better in this light.*

Franz searched his face, wondering how they came to be here. He wiped his tears with his free hand as he glanced self-consciously at those promenading the park.

Don't mind them, they can't see us, said Wolfgang, pulling a handkerchief from his pocket and handing it to Franz. Their eyes met and Wolfgang became silent. They pulled into another embrace. Energy swirled around and through them for several minutes.

Franz felt light and serene. Understanding came easily.

You have always been with me, he stated simply.

I was as close to you as I am now, Wolfgang explained. *Separation is impossible for us, even by death.*

Franz contemplated. He looked up and smiled.

We are here to love and experience, he said. *I know this now, standing here, in this light, with you. It's something I've always known, isn't it?* He hesitated, then asked, *Why don't we know all this while we are there?*

Many do. But most refuse to open themselves up to their true reality. They're too caught up in their safe circles of perception.

Franz looked down at his body. *Am I dead?*

No, not yet. You're only visiting.

Then...I must go back? No, don't make me go back!

You will be finished here soon. Wolfgang turned and led Franz along a quiet path with the warmth of the late afternoon sun caressing their backs.

Franz frowned as he began to contemplate the past twelve years of alternating hard work and self-imposed isolation.

I needed your friendship and presence, he said. *Why didn't you show yourself to me? Why didn't we visit like this?*

I was there, Franz. I was within you, helping you to hold on. It was more important for you to hold on than to see me. Believe me, I never left you, because I knew how disconsolate you were. I felt your despair. I knew you might have destroyed yourself.

When I wasn't wrapped up in my work, the fear and loneliness came. So I tried always to keep busy.

I know, Snai. Wolfgang's compassionate eyes again turned to Franz. *Don't you see? For all those years, your anguish and my anguish were what we had in common. I knew I could assist you only in a limited way while you were in the physical realm. We were both limited by your physical existence. But you see, you survived! You endured. You did not destroy yourself, and there was a strong possibility that you might. It was a hard test. You are the new initiate now!*

Franz's thoughts tumbled through his mind. He suddenly exclaimed, *You helped me finish the Mass!*

Which one? laughed Wolfgang.

Which one? How many did you help me with?

Two. Mine and yours. And some of your operas. But of the masses, twelve years ago we finished the Requiem. *I have to admit, it wasn't easy. You were giving me trouble, as usual, and I found it very frustrating that you would take a few extra swallows of that terrible cheap wine and then I'd find it so much harder to get through. Do you remember that.*

You squeezed my hand, remembered Franz pensively as he turned and stopped.

I was trying to get your attention. It wasn't easy, but then it never was easy to get your attention, even when I was alive. Suddenly he grew serious. Franz had taken him by the shoulders and looked again as if he might break down.

Do you know how much that meant to me? I would remember that moment and, hoping against reason, I tried to tell myself that it had been you. That it was a sign from you. He paused. *Mostly because I remembered before you died your telling me you would come back and tell me about God.*

That, said Wolfgang, *was in the music I gave you.*

You mean after you died?

Yes. After. Everything I wrote in the Requiem *before I died was mostly inspired by fear.*

How diligently we worked on that Mass while you were dying. Why did you push yourself so hard?

I was half out of my mind with fear. Fear of leaving this life. Then I realized I had to let go.

How could you think I could finish it?

Wolfgang smiled. *Now think a moment. Think! How do you imagine posterity will explain this* Requiem Mass? *That you, who were at the time essentially a student of composition, could write masterful passages that I obviously didn't write while I lived? There is only one way to explain it—the explanation is that I helped you! But in order to believe that, posterity will have to consider life after death, don't you see? It's the only explanation. And it's deliberate.*

Wolfgang took Franz's hand and squeezed it again. Franz grinned conspiratorially as they continued their stroll. *The second mass we wrote together was your* Missa Solemnis *in D. The key of D seems to be our key, doesn't it? It is the key of joy, Franz. Remember that little air you gave me as a birthday present? The one with the poem you wrote for me? And I worked it into an aria for tenor and orchestra? That was in D. What was that aria again?*

Musst ich auch....

Ah, yes!...durch tausend Drachen, yes, now I remember. That was for the opera we tried to finish.

You were too ill.

And this mass in D. It is good, Franz. I think you learned a lot from me and Salieri, didn't you? But you were always an excellent student.

How did you get through to me for my Mass?

The same way I did for the other one. And also in your dreams. You weren't remembering too many dreams when we wrote the first one, but for this one, it was much easier to sing to you in your dreams.

And I would remember it in the morning.

And you would remember it in the morning.

231

A coughing spell brought Franz back into his bed. He opened his eyes to pain and the panic-stricken face of Maria leaning over him.

"Oh, my God, Franz, I thought you were...you stopped breathing!" she cried in fearful agitation. "I must run and find someone to get the doctor. I will be back as soon as I can."

"Maria! Wait!" gasped Franz.

She turned and hesitated. "Yes?"

"Maria...I love you."

Impulsively, she kissed her brother's forehead, turned, and ran out the door fighting back her tears.

It's too late, Maria.

But the words never came out. He had no breath, and no strength to move breath.

Franz stared at the all-too-familiar ceiling as his mouth began to move in prayer. "Please, dear God, let me die now. I want to go back...home. I want to go home. Take me home."

He closed his eyes, and it was over.

ALBUQUERQUE, May, 1994.

Is it true? Is it true, Willy? Lina's voice rang out in the night. It was another lucid dream brought about by sheer will. She had to have an answer. *I need to know if she's right! Come and tell me if it's true!*

At first, and for what seemed so long, there was no answer, no stirring. Lina could barely contain herself. It had been so long since she'd called for him in a dream, she almost didn't know what to expect.

The book had languished for years after several attempts to interest an agent. Then her life took a turn into what Dorothy carefully called "times of testing." There seemed to be no respite for the next four years, as Lina grappled with Life on Earth in several of its infinite and treacherous variations, including divorce, illness and separation. Throughout the struggles, her reticence about sharing the story of Franz and Wolfgang, like her loneliness, had prevailed. "I'm not ready for this," she had told herself. "And, besides, who would believe it?" Still, throughout these times of trouble, she had continued to sense his presence and, occasionally, felt the reassuring squeeze of his unseen hand.

Lina, for heaven's sake, you're waking the dead. His laughter rippled through her consciousness. She turned toward the voice that she knew and loved.

Where are you? Why can't I see you? Then she saw his light and breathed a sigh of relief.

Come with me, he said. *I have a delight for you.*

In a heartbeat, they were strolling, hand in hand, through an extraordinary art exhibit. Lina's urgency was diluted by her fascination with the irresistably brilliant and bold works of art that constantly changed before her. Even as she gazed on one piece, its colors evolved before her, at once charming and calming her. Willy stood by, waiting for the moment her heart stopped racing.

So, what's the crisis? he asked, finally. He knew she had been through troubling times, but he also knew she was well-guided and protected.

She blinked and turned to face him. *Is it true?*

Is what true? he teased.

Mary, my psychic friend, had a sudden revelation in the middle of another conversation! We were talking about something else entirely, and she suddenly said, 'Oh, I have some news for you!' She told me you're coming here, to Earth, to be with me!

He remained silent as his smile widened. He wanted to draw out the surprise as long as he could. Lina grabbed his shoulders. *Don't tease me! Is it true?*

It's true. It's true, he whispered gently. *Your test times are behind you, for now, and we want you to concentrate on getting this book published. So I'm coming to help, and to be near you. Mostly to be near you. Are those tears? Well, maybe I shouldn't come if you're going to cry the whole time.*

It's true...I can't believe it. How can it be? How?

You know those flowers you love so much, the ones that push up through the cracks in the road? We can do anything, you and I. We're like those flowers.

You've got to know that this is the best news I've heard in a long time. I've been so...alone. I feel like such an outsider here, like Franz did. I'm sorry, I can't help the tears. I should be stronger.

At least they're tears of joy.

I'm so grateful...that you would make such a journey, such an effort...for me.

His arms encircled her as she clung to him and wept

quietly. She could not remember a time when she hadn't felt alone in the world—an outsider among friends. It had taken its toll—in the last four years, her heart more often than not alternated between a dim longing and a mild anxiety. No end seemed in sight. Nor had she quite forgiven Franz for lapsing on his watch.

Lina, how could you have known it was Constanze, and that you couldn't have stopped her? Nobody knew that! There are reasons for not knowing—it would have killed us to know that kind of betrayal. Stop terrorizing yourself with guilt, Willy had long ago counseled. *It has crippled your spirit. The moment you stop assuming the responsibility for that death, that is the moment you will no longer be isolated in this life. You will have forgiven yourself and allowed yourself to be worthy to be a part of humanity again. Why? Because you feel you also let down all of humanity. Lina, Lina, it's time to cast off the guilt and join the dance of life again. When you listen to the* Requiem, *don't visualize a dying man—visualize triumph over darkness through love.*

She had once read a passage written about Mozart that he was "not of this world"—that he was "by race, an angel." He was only a visitor here, the writer continued, at once naive and overly trusting about the world, while detached and divine in its interpretation.

The art exhibit was gone, and they stood in the university's fine arts library next to a tall shelf of several hundred books on Mozart. Books whose facts were drawn from his own letters and artifacts, and from descriptive letters of friends, as well as from undeclared foes whose unflattering comments were taken as truth. All this knowledge was then analyzed and re-analyzed until his essence had nearly, or completely, faded. Thank God for the music, Lina mused, the music where his essence is fresh and whole and unfettered by lies. Lina and Willy watched as students leaned over their books, cramming for final exams. *It's now or never for them,* Lina realized.

And it's now or never for us, Willy interrupted her thoughts. *The message of our book is important and must have its moment, too. You've been promising for two hundred years to write this book, and you've done the hardest part. Now it's time to push the bird out of the nest and let it fly. Let it sing its bittersweet song in the world.*

I know. Lina's hand slid across two hundred years of

234

scholarship on Mozart's life and work. She felt humbled, wondering how she could know more than these scholars.

We know more because we are their subject matter. It is they who should be humbled. And Mary is right—you should stop slamming doors in your own face. He squeezed her hand reassuringly, concerned at her distractability.

I need to know, how are you going to do it? Visit me, I mean. Are you going to start from scratch?

No, there's no time for being born, and I don't want to be tied down like that anyway.

You don't really need to any more, do you? Lina scanned the room for music teachers she had known. Would they understand this book?

Actually, no, I don't, and yes, they might understand the book. Look at me, Lina. Remember how I told you about the earth's planetary vibrations increasing more each year?

Yes, everyone I know has insomnia or a permanent case of nerves. It seems like we've all gone into hyperdrive....

Yes, but it's also providing ideal conditions for what I can only describe now as "merging." It's happening quite frequently all over the planet.

Merging? He had her complete attention.

Yes, a spirit like me merges with a willing individual on a temporary basis, to influence change. The change can be as sweeping as a major shift in government, as in Russia or South Africa, or the falling of the Berlin Wall, or as subtle as a change of heart about...publishing a book.

You'll take over someone's body? She was fascinated.

It's more of a sharing with a willing participant. And I want to point out that the body's owner actually feels quite good as a result, because only the highest entities are allowed to merge. It's never done without everyone's consent.

Have you done it before?

No. It will be a new experience for me. Even when we wrote the Requiem, *I was only manipulating your hand or giving you thoughts, but I never really "joined" you in your body. It wasn't possible then because the planet was at a lower vibrational level. Now, I will be able to do much more.*

Will you be merging with me?

Yes and no. This will be different. I will exist apart from you, and through you. We have a job to do. Two heads are better than one. Like Wolfgang and Franz.

Willy's presence was again beginning, gradually and profoundly, to affect Lina's thoughts and mood. She had almost forgotten how serenity felt. But she still had one more question.

Why are you doing this, here and now?

He gazed at her with his singular mix of humor, love, and compassion.

You prayed for help. Help is here.

Oh...God! Lina whispered, recognizing the words Franz had spoken to the destitute Wolfgang many winters ago.

She remembered sitting up in bed at midnight two weeks before and begging for relief from the relentless business of life. *I had forgotten. I did pray for help. I was so alone.*

You have never been alone, Lina. You have been right here. He pointed to his heart. *For eons. Just as I have been here.* He pointed to her heart. *When you are happy, I am happy. When you are pleased, I am pleased. Love me with all your heart and depth, and I will continue to love you twice as much. Believe it. Believe it with all your strength, because in believing this, you are mine once again in a way that you have not been since we were last together beyond earth. This is why I'm here. It's happening all over the world. No one is unloved. Tell your readers that. Tell them they are loved beyond measure.*

Appendix

Note: Passages in italics give information drawn from psychic research. All other information is drawn from traditional history.

Wolfgang Amadé *(he preferred this version over Amadeus)* Mozart was born in Salzburg, Austria, on January 27, 1756, to Leopold Mozart and his wife, Anna Maria Pertl Mozart. Leopold had left his family of architects and bookbinders in Augsburg, Germany, to pursue a career as musician, composer and music scholar at the court of the prince-archbishop of Salzburg. In Salzburg, he married and settled into a life as deputy Kapellmeister. The Pertl family had, for years, pursued administrative work in Salzburg. Wolfgang was the last of seven children, only two of whom survived, including Maria Anna.

Leopold provided his children with all their musical and academic education. Wolfgang's talent grew more quickly than he did. At age three, he was picking out chords at the harpsichord; at age four, he was performing short pieces; and at age five, he was composing. Just before his sixth birthday, Wolfgang and his family traveled to Vienna and Munich to perform before nobility. His sister was also musically talented and the two were presented as child wonders. When he was seven, the family undertook a three-year tour of the musical centers of Europe, including Paris, London, Mannheim, Brussels and Frankfurt. At age thirteen, his father took him to Italy for the first of three visits crisscrossing that nation as Wolfgang performed, composed and amazed. As on a previous visit to Vienna, however, honors and applause were not enough to win the Mozarts any permanent position or financial gain. On a subsequent and prolonged visit to Paris, Wolfgang's mother died. Throughout his life, Wolfgang's travels ultimately took him from points as far afield as London, Rome, Paris, Dresden, and Berlin. As before, he was generally appreciated, but not employed.

At twenty-five, Mozart moved permanently to Vienna to establish a career, having refused to follow in Leopold's footsteps in court service in Salzburg, a town he had always professed to hate. He had, in fact, left the service of the prince-archibishop where he had served as a violinist and later as an organist. Not long after these breaks, he again defied his father by marrying Constanze Weber, third of four daughters of a music copyist known to the Mozarts. Wolfgang had lived with the family when he first moved to Vienna. His real love was Constanze's older sister, Aloysia, who had disappointed him by marrying someone else. Wolfgang and Constanze had two children who survived: Karl Thomas (1784-1858) and Franz Xaver Wolfgang (1791-1844). The latter became a professional pianist and died childless in 1844. Karl became a government official.

Wolfgang's career had begun well enough in Vienna in the early years, when he was popular among the concert- and opera-going public. In his short life, he wrote over six hundred works in virtually every genre ranging from clock tunes to grand opera. (He was the only composer of his time to excel in all genres.) In 1787, he was appointed Kammermusicus of the royal court, which paid very little, and required only that he provide dance music for royal balls. *It was always his wish that musicians and composers receive more respect and consideration than they did. His knowing his own worth was often misunderstood as arrogance by his peers. His search as an artist for such respect in the hierarchy of society presaged similar, and more successful, efforts by musicians and artists of the following century.*

Despite his prodigious and extraordinary output, he eventually fell into poverty and ill health. He died in 1791 at age thirty-five. Doctors initially listed miliary disease as the cause of death, and later indicated rheumatic inflammatory fever. He was buried in a communal grave. No marker was erected until the 20th century.

Father Pasterwicz died in February, 1803, eight months before Sussmayr's death.

History records that, in 1831, Josef Eybler, one of Mozart's most loyal friends, suffered a paralyzing stroke while conducting the *Requiem,* forcing him to retire.

Constanze Mozart outlived her husband by fifty years and Sussmayr by thirty-nine years. During part of that time, she and her second husband, Georg von Nissen, edited Mozart's letters, destroying selected letters from Leopold Mozart, *and destroying or marking through most references to Sussmayr.* Prior to writing the first Mozart biography, von Nissen worked as a government censor for ten years.

"Lina" is the author. She is a writer on music and the

arts, and an arts advocate and administrator, living in New Mexico. Still devoted to national opera, she catalogued and researched a large collection of handwritten 19th century zarzuela (Spanish comic opera) manuscripts discovered in Arizona in 1952; then helped found, fund and operate a professional zarzuela company to perform in schools in rural New Mexico and at an international zarzuela festival in El Paso.

Willy Kapell's letters and notes show that, at the time of his death in 1953, he had planned for the 1954 season two concerts devoted entirely to American piano music. In addition, he was planning to record the works of several American composers including Copland, Thompson, Sessions and Ruggles.

Through Salieri's influence, Sussmayr was promoted to Kapellmeister of the German Opera, a post he held until his death in September, 1803. During these years he wrote twenty-two operas and ballets, and enjoyed a moderate success in both Vienna and Prague, where he traveled to oversee productions of his works.

Like Mozart, Sussmayr died in poverty and received a pauper's burial at St. Marx Cemetery. Two years after her brother's death, Maria Sussmayr sold most of his music to Prince Esterhazy of Eisenstadt. Salieri bought his *Missa Solemnis* in D for the royal library, a work that was still being performed annually at St. Stephen's Cathedral well into the middle of the 19th century.

The Esterhazy collection of Sussmayr's music was transferred in 1949 (the year of the author's birth) to the national library in Budapest. *Letters between Mozart and Sussmayr exist, but are not known for what they are, and can be found in private collections in Russia, Japan, and Iran, and in collections of the Hohenzollerns.*